Sylvie
And Bruno
Concluded

LEWIS CARROLL

Sylvie and Bruno Concluded, L. Carroll
Jazzybee Verlag Jürgen Beck
86450 Altenmünster, Loschberg 9
Germany

ISBN: 9783849699505

www.jazzybee-verlag.de
www.facebook.com/jazzybeeverlag
admin@jazzybee-verlag.de

CONTENTS:

Dreams, that elude the Maker's frenzied grasp—
Hands, stark and still, on a dead Mother's breast,
Which nevermore shall render clasp for clasp,
Or deftly soothe a weeping Child to rest—
In suchlike forms me listeth to portray
My Tale, here ended. Thou delicious Fay—
The guardian of a Sprite that lives to tease thee—
Loving in earnest, chiding but in play
The merry mocking Bruno! Who, that sees thee,
Can fail to love thee, Darling, even as I?—
My sweetest Sylvie, we must say "Good-bye!"

BRUNO'S LESSONS

During the next month or two my solitary town-life seemed, by contrast, unusually dull and tedious. I missed the pleasant friends I had left behind at Elveston—the genial interchange of thought—the sympathy which gave to one's ideas a new and vivid reality: but, perhaps more than all, I missed the companionship of the two Fairies—or Dream-Children, for I had not yet solved the problem as to who or what they were whose sweet playfulness had shed a magic radiance over my life.

In office-hours—which I suppose reduce most men to the mental condition of a coffee-mill or a mangle—time sped along much as usual: it was in the pauses of life, the desolate hours when books and newspapers palled on the sated appetite, and when, thrown back upon one's own dreary musings, one strove—all in vain—to people the vacant air with the dear faces of absent friends, that the real bitterness of solitude made itself felt.

One evening, feeling my life a little more wearisome than usual, I strolled down to my Club, not so much with the hope of meeting any friend there, for London was now "out of town", as with the feeling that here, at least, I should hear "sweet words of human speech", and come into contact with human thought.

However, almost the first face I saw there was that of a friend. Eric Lindon was lounging, with rather a "bored" expression of face, over a newspaper; and we fell into conversation with a mutual satisfaction which neither of us tried to conceal.

After a while I ventured to introduce what was just then the main subject of my thoughts. "And so the Doctor" (a name we had adopted by a tacit agreement, as a convenient compromise between the formality of "Doctor Forester" and the intimacy—to which Eric Lindon hardly seemed entitled—of "Arthur") "has gone abroad by this time, I suppose? Can you give me his present address?"

"He is still at Elveston—I believe," was the reply. "But I have not been there since I last met you."

I did not know which part of this intelligence to wonder at most. "And might I ask—if it isn't taking too much of a liberty—when your wedding-bells are to—or perhaps they have rung, already?"

"No," said Eric, in a steady voice, which betrayed scarcely a trace of emotion: "that engagement is at an end. I am still 'Benedick the unmarried man'."

After this, the thick-coming fancies—all radiant with new possibilities of happiness for Arthur—were far too bewildering to admit of any further conversation, and I was only too glad to avail myself of the first decent excuse, that offered itself, for retiring into silence

The next day I wrote to Arthur, with as much of a reprimand for his long silence as I could bring myself to put into words, begging him to tell me how the world went with him.

Needs must that three or four days—possibly more— should elapse before I could receive his reply; and never had I known days drag their slow length along with a more tedious indolence.

To while away the time, I strolled, one afternoon, into Kensington Gardens, and, wandering aimlessly along any path that presented itself, I soon became aware that I had somehow strayed into one that was wholly new to me. Still, my elfish experiences seemed to have so completely faded out of my life that nothing was further from my thoughts than the idea of again meeting my fairyfriends, when I chanced to notice a small creature, moving among the grass that fringed the path, that did not seem to be an insect, or a frog, or any other living thing that I could think of. Cautiously kneeling down, and making an ex tempore cage of my two hands, I imprisoned the little wanderer, and felt a sudden thrill of surprise and delight on discovering that my prisoner was no other than Bruno himself!

Bruno took the matter very coolly, and, when I had replaced him on the ground, where he would be within easy conversational distance, he began talking, just as if it were only a few minutes since last we had met.

"Doos oo know what the Rule is", he enquired, "when oo catches a Fairy, withouten its having tolded oo where it was?" (Bruno's notions of English Grammar had certainly not improved since our last meeting.)

"No," I said. "I didn't know there was any Rule about it."

"I think oo've got a right to eat me," said the little fellow, looking up into my face with a winning smile. "But I'm not pruffickly sure. Oo'd better not do it wizout asking."

It did indeed seem reasonable not to take so irrevocable a step as that,, without due enquiry. "I'll certainly ask about it, first," I said. "Besides, I don't know yet whether you would be worth eating!"

"I guess I'm deliciously good to eat," Bruno remarked in a satisfied tone, as if it were something to be rather proud of.

"And what are you doing here, Bruno?"

"That's not my name!" said my cunning little friend. "Don't oo know my name's 'Oh Bruno!'? That's what Sylvie always calls me, when I says mine lessons."

"Well then, what are you doing here, oh Bruno?"

"Doing mine lessons, a-course!" With that roguish twinkle in his eye, that always came when he knew he was talking nonsense.

"Oh, that's the way you do your lessons, is it? And do you remember them well?"

"Always can 'member mine lessons," said Bruno. "It's Sylvie's lessons that's so drefully hard to 'member!" He frowned, as if in agonies of thought, and tapped his forehead with his knuckles. "I ca'n't think enough to understand them!" he said despairingly.' It wants double thinking, I believe!"

"But where's Sylvie gone?"

"That's just what I want to know!" said Bruno disconsolately. "What ever's the good of setting me lessons when she isn't here to 'sprain the hard bits?"

"I'll find her for you!" I volunteered; and, getting up I wandered round the tree under whose shade I had been reclining, looking on all sides for Sylvie. In another minute I again noticed some strange thing moving among the grass, and, kneeling down, was immediately confronted with Sylvie's innocent face, lighted up with a joyful surprise at seeing me, and was accosted, in the sweet voice I knew so well, with what seemed to be the end of a sentence whose beginning I had failed to catch.

"and I think he ought to have finished them by this time. So I'm going back to him. Will you come too? It's only just round at the other side of this tree."

It was but a few steps for me; but it was a great many for Sylvie; and I had to be very careful to walk slowly, in order not to leave the little creature so far behind as to lose sight of her.

To find Bruno's lessons was easy enough: they appeared to be neatly written out on large smooth ivy-leaves, which were scattered in some confusion over a little patch of ground where the grass had been worn away; but the pale student, who ought by rights to have been bending over them, was nowhere to be seen: we looked in all directions, for some time in vain; but at last Sylvie's sharp eyes detected him, swinging on a tendril of ivy, and Sylvie's stern voice commanded his instant return to terra firma and to the business of Life.

"Pleasure first and business afterwards" seemed to be the motto of these tiny folk, so many hugs and kisses had to be interchanged before anything else could be done.

"Now, Bruno," Sylvie said reproachfully, "didn't I tell you you were to go on with your lessons, unless you heard to the contrary?"

"But I did heard to the contrary!" Bruno insisted, with a mischievous twinkle in his eye.

"What did you hear, you wicked boy?"

"It were a sort of noise in the air," said Bruno: "a sort of a scrambling noise. Didn't oo hear it, Mister Sir?"

"Well, anyhow, you needn't go to sleep over them, you lazy-lazy!" For Bruno had curled himself up, on the largest "lesson", and was arranging another as a pillow.

"I wasn't asleep!" said Bruno, in a deeply-injured tone. "When I shuts mine eyes, it's to show that I'm awake!"

"Well, how much have you learned, then?"

"I've learned a little tiny bit," said Bruno, modestly, being evidently afraid of overstating his achievement. "Ca'n't learn no more!"

"Oh Bruno! You know you can, if you like."

"Course I can, if I like," the pale student replied; "but I ca'n't if I don't like!"

Sylvie had a way—which I could not too highly admire —of evading Bruno's logical perplexities by suddenly striking into a new line of thought; and this masterly stratagem she now adopted.

"Well, I must say one thing

"Did oo know, Mister Sir," Bruno thoughtfully remarked, "that Sylvie ca'n't count? Whenever she says 'I must say one thing', I know quite well she'll say two things! And she always doos."

"Two heads are better than one, Bruno," I said, but with no very distinct idea as to what I meant by it.

"I shouldn't mind having two heads," Bruno said softly to himself: "one head to eat mine dinner, and one head to argue wiz Sylvie—doos oo think oo'd look prettier if oo'd got two heads, Mister Sir?"

The case did not, I assured him, admit of a doubt.

"The reason why Sylvie's so cross—' Bruno went on very seriously, almost sadly.

Sylvie's eyes grew large and round with surprise at this new line of enquiry—her rosy face being perfectly radiant with good humour. But she said nothing.

"Wouldn't it be better to tell me after the lessons are over?" I suggested.

"Very well," Bruno said with a resigned air: "only she wo'n't be cross then."

"There's only three lessons to do," said Sylvie. "Spelling, and Geography, and Singing."

"Not Arithmetic?" I said.

"No, he hasn't a head for Arithmetic—"

"Course I haven't!" said Bruno. "Mine head's for hair. I haven't got a lot of heads!"

"—and he ca'n't learn his Multiplication-table—"

11

"I like History ever so much better," Bruno remarked. "Oo has to repeat that Muddlecome table—"

"Well, and you have to repeat—"

"No, oo hasn't!" Bruno interrupted. "History repeats itself. The Professor said so!"

Sylvie was arranging some letters on a board—E-V-I-L. "Now, Bruno," she said, "what does that spell?"

Bruno looked at it, in solemn silence, for a minute. "I know what it doesn't spell!" he said at last.

"That's no good," said Sylvie. "What does it spell?"

Bruno took another look at the mysterious letters. "Why, it's 'LIVE', backwards!" he exclaimed. (I thought it was, indeed.)

"How did you manage to see that?" said Sylvie.

"I just twiddled my eyes," said Bruno, "and then I saw it directly. Now may I sing the King-fisher Song?"

"Geography next," said Sylvie. "Don't you know the Rules?"

"I think there oughtn't to be such a lot of Rules, Sylvie! I thinks—"

"Yes, there ought to be such a lot of Rules, you wicked, wicked boy! And how dare you think at all about it? And shut up that mouth directly!"

So, as "that mouth" didn't seem inclined to shut up of itself, Sylvie shut it for him—with both hands—and sealed it with a kiss, just as you would fasten up a letter.

"Now that Bruno is fastened up from talking," she went on, turning to me, "I'll show you the Map he does his lessons on."

And there it was, a large Map of the World, spread out on the ground. It was so large that Bruno had to crawl about on it, to point out the places named in the "Kingfisher Lesson".

"When a King-fisher sees a Lady-bird flying away, he says 'Ceylon, if you Candia!' And when he catches it, he says 'Come to Media! And if you're Hungary or thirsty, I'll give you some Nubia!' When he takes it in his claws, he says 'Europe!' When he puts it into his beak, he says 'India!' When he's swallowed it, he says 'Eton!' That's all."

"That's quite perfect," said Sylvie. "Now, you may sing the King-fisher Song."

"Will oo sing the chorus?" Bruno said to me.

I was just beginning to say "I'm afraid I don't know the words", when Sylvie silently turned the map over, and I found the words were all written on the back. In one respect it was a very peculiar song: the chorus to each verse came in the middle, instead of at the end of it. However, the tune was so easy that I soon picked it up, and managed the chorus as well, perhaps, as it is possible for one person to manage such a thing. It was in vain that I signed to Sylvie to help me: she only smiled sweetly and shook her head.

"King Fisher courted Lady Bird—
Sing Beans, sing Bones, sing Butterflies!
'Find me my match,' he said,
'With such a noble head—
With such a beard, as white as curd—
With such expressive eyes!'
"'Yet pins have heads,' said Lady Bird—
Sing Prunes, sing Prawns, sing Primrose-Hill!
'And, where you stick them in,
They stay, and thus a pin
Is very much to be preferred
To one that's never still!'
"'Oysters have beards,' said Lady Bird—
Sing Flies, sing Frogs, sing Fiddle-strings!
'I love them, for I know
They never chatter so:

They would not say one single word—
Not if you crowned them Kings!'
"'Needles have Eyes,' said Lady Bird—
Sing Cats, sing Corks, sing Cowslip-tea!
'And they are sharp—just what
Your Majesty is not:
So get you gone—'tis too absurd
To come a-courting me!'"

"So he went away," Bruno added as a kind of postscript, when the last note of the song had died away "Just like he always did."

"Oh' my dear Bruno!" Sylvie exclaimed, with her hands over her ears. "You shouldn't say 'like': you should say 'what'.

To which Bruno replied, doggedly, "I only says 'what!' when oo doosn't speak loud, so as I can hear oo."

"Where did he go to?" I asked, hoping to prevent an argument.

"He went more far than he'd never been before," said Bruno.

"You should never say 'more far'," Sylvie corrected him: "you should say 'farther'."

"Then oo shouldn't say 'more broth', when we're at dinner," Bruno retorted: "oo should say 'brother'!"

This time Sylvie evaded an argument by turning away, and beginning to roll up the Map. "Lessons are over!" she proclaimed in her sweetest tones.

"And has there been no crying over them?" I enquired. "Little boys always cry over their lessons, don't they?"

"I never cries after twelve o'clock," said Bruno: "'cause then it's getting so near to dinner-time."

"Sometimes, in the morning," Sylvie said in a low voice; "when it's Geography-day, and when he's been disrobe—"

"What a fellow you are to talk, Sylvie!" Bruno hastily interposed. "Doos oo think the world was made for oo to talk in?"

"Why, where would you have me talk, then?" Sylvie said, evidently quite ready for an argument.

But Bruno answered resolutely. "I'm not going to argue about it, 'cause it's getting late, and there wo'n't be time—but oo's as 'ong as ever oo can be!" And he rubbed the back of his hand across his eyes, in which tears were beginning to glitter.

Sylvie's eyes filled with tears in a moment. "I didn't mean it, Bruno, darling!" she whispered; and the rest of the argument was lost "amid the tangles of Neæra's hair", while the two disputants hugged and kissed each other.

But this new form of argument was brought to a sudden end by a flash of lightning, which was closely followed by a peal of thunder, and by a torrent of raindrops, which came hissing and spitting, almost like live creatures, through the leaves of the tree that sheltered us. "Why, it's raining cats and dogs!" I said.

"And all the dogs has come down first," said Bruno: "there's nothing but cats coming down now!"

In another minute the pattering ceased, as suddenly as it had begun. I stepped out from under the tree, and found that the storm was over; but I looked in vain, on my return, for my tiny companions. They had vanished with the storm, and there was nothing for it but to make the best of my way home.

On the table lay, awaiting my return, an envelope of that peculiar yellow tint which always announces a telegram, and which must be, in the memories of so many of us, inseparably linked with some great and sudden sorrow—something that has cast a shadow, never in this world to be wholly lifted off, on the brightness of Life. No doubt it has also heralded—for many of us—some sudden news of joy; but this, I think, is less common: human life seems, on the whole, to contain more of sorrow than of joy. And yet the world goes on. Who knows why?

This time, however, there was no shock of sorrow to be faced: in fact, the few words it contained ("Could not bring myself to write. Come soon. Always welcome. A letter follows this. Arthur.") seemed so like Arthur himself speaking, that it gave me quite a thrill of pleasure and I at once began the preparations needed for the journey.

LOVE'S CURFEW

"Fayfield Junction! Change for Elveston!"

What subtle memory could there be, linked to these commonplace words, that caused such a flood of happy thoughts to fill my brain? I dismounted from the carriage in a state of joyful excitement for which I could not at first account. True, I had taken this very journey, and at the same hour of the day, six months ago; but many things had happened since then, and an old man's memory has but a slender hold on recent events: I sought "the missing link" in vain. Suddenly I caught sight of a bench—the only one provided on the cheerless platform—with a lady seated on it, and the whole forgotten scene flashed upon me as vividly as if it were happening over again.

"Yes," I thought. "This bare platform is, for me, rich with the memory of a dear friend! She was sitting on that very bench, and invited me to share it, with some quotation from Shakespeare—I forget what. I'll try the Earl's plan for the Dramatization of Life, and fancy that figure to be Lady Muriel; and I wo'n't undeceive myself too soon!"

So I strolled along the platform, resolutely "making believe" (as children say) that the casual passenger, seated on that bench, was the Lady Muriel I remembered so well. She was facing away from me, which aided the elaborate cheatery I was practicing on myself: but, though I was careful, in passing the spot, to look the other way, in order to prolong the pleasant illusion, it was inevitable that, when I turned to walk back again, I should see who it was. It was Lady Muriel herself!

The whole scene now returned vividly to my memory; and, to make this repetition of it stranger still, there was the same old man, whom I remembered seeing so roughly ordered off, by the Station-Master, to make room for his titled passenger. The same, but "with a difference": no longer tottering feebly along the platform, but actually seated at Lady Muriel's side, and in conversation with her! "Yes, put it in your purse," she was saying, "and remember you're to spend it all for Minnie. And mind you bring her something nice, that'll do her real good! And give her my love!" So intent was she on saying these words, that, although the sound of my footstep had made her lift her head and look at me, she did not at first recognize me.

I raised my hat as I approached, and then there flashed across her face a genuine look of joy, which so exactly recalled the sweet face of Sylvie, when last we met in Kensington Gardens, that I felt quite bewildered.

Rather than disturb the poor old man at her side, she rose from her seat, and joined me in my walk up and down the platform, and for a minute or two our conversation was as utterly trivial and commonplace as if we were merely two casual guests in a London drawing-room. Each of us seemed to shrink, just at first, from touching on the deeper interests which linked our lives together.

The Elveston train had drawn up at the platform, while we talked; and, in obedience to the Station Master's obsequious hint of "This way, my

Lady! Time's up!", we were making the best of our way towards the end which contained the sole first-class carriage, and were just passing the now-empty bench, when Lady Muriel noticed, lying on it, the purse in which her gift had just been so carefully bestowed, the owner of which, all unconscious of his loss, was being helped into a carriage at the other end of the train. She pounced on it instantly. "Poor old man!" she cried. "He mustn't go off, and think he's lost it!"

"Let me run with it! I can go quicker than you!" I said. But she was already half-way down the platform flying ("running" is much too mundane a word for such fairy-like motion) at a pace that left all possible efforts of mine hopelessly in the rear.

She was back again before I had well completed my audacious boast of speed in running, and was saying, quite demurely, as we entered our carriage, "and you really think you could have done it quicker?"

"No, indeed!" I replied. "I plead 'Guilty' of gross exaggeration, and throw myself on the mercy of the Court!"

"The Court will overlook it—for this once!" Then her manner suddenly changed from playfulness to an anxious gravity.

"You are not looking your best!" she said with an anxious glance. "In fact, I think you look more of an invalid than when you left us. I very much doubt if London agrees with you?"

"It may be the London air," I said, "or it may be the hard work—or my rather lonely life: anyhow, I've not been feeling very well, lately. But Elveston will soon set me up again. Arthur's prescription—he's my doctor, you know, and I heard from him this morning—is 'plenty of ozone, and new milk, and pleasant society'!"

"Pleasant society?" said Lady Muriel, with a pretty make-believe of considering the question. "Well, really I don't know where we can find that for you! We have so few neighbours. But new milk we can manage. Do get it of my old friend Mrs. Hunter, up there, on the hill-side. You may rely upon the quality. And her little Bessie comes to school every day, and passes your lodgings. So it would be very easy to send it."

"I'll follow your advice with pleasure," I said; "and I'll go and arrange about it to-morrow. I know Arthur will want a walk."

"You'll find it quite an easy walk—under three miles, I think."

"Well, now that we've settled that point, let me retort your own remark upon yourself. I don't think you're looking quite your best!"

"I daresay not," she replied in a low voice; and a sudden shadow seemed to overspread her face. "I've had some troubles lately. It's a matter about which I've been long wishing to consult you, but I couldn't easily write about it. I'm so glad to have this opportunity!"

"Do you think", she began again, after a minute's silence, and with a visible embarrassment of manner most unusual in her, "that a promise, deliberately and solemnly given, is always binding except, of course, where its fulfillment would involve some actual sin?"

"I ca'n't think of any other exception at this moment," I said. "That branch of casuistry is usually, I believe, treated as a question of truth and untruth—"

"Surely that is the principle?" she eagerly interrupted. "I always thought the Bible-teaching about it consisted of such texts 'lie not one to another'?"

"I have thought about that point," I replied; "and it seems to me that the essence of lying is the intention of deceiving. If you give a promise, fully intending to fulfil it, you are certainly acting truthfully then; and, if you afterwards break it, that does not involve any deception I cannot call it untruthful."

Another pause of silence ensued. Lady Muriel's face was hard to read: she looked pleased, I thought, but also puzzled; and I felt curious to know whether her question had, as I began to suspect, some bearing on the breaking off of her engagement with Captain (now Major) Lindon.

"You have relieved me from a great fear," she said "but the thing is of course wrong, somehow. What texts would you quote, to prove it wrong?"

"Any that enforce the payment of debts. If A promises something to B, B has a claim upon A. And A's sin, if he breaks his promise, seems to me more analogous to stealing than to lying."

"It's a new way of looking at it—to me," she said; "but it seems a true way, also. However, I wo'n't deal in generalities, with an old friend like you! For we are old friends somehow. Do you know, I think we began as old friends?' she said with a playfulness of tone that ill accorded with the tears that glistened in her eyes.

"Thank you very much for saying so," I replied. "I like to think of you as an old friend," ('—though you don't look it!" would have been the almost necessary sequence, with any other lady; but she and I seemed to have long passed out of the time when compliments, or any such trivialities, were possible).

Here the train paused at a station, where two or three passengers entered the carriage; so no more was said till we had reached our journey's end.

On our arrival at Elveston, she readily adopted my suggestion that we should walk up together; so, as soon as our luggage had been duly taken charge of—hers by the servant who met her at the station, and mine by one of the porters—we set out together along the familiar lanes, now linked in my memory with so many delightful associations. Lady Muriel at once recommended the conversation at the point where it had been interrupted.

"You knew of my engagement to my cousin Eric. Did you also hear—"

"Yes," I interrupted, anxious to spare her the pain of giving any details. "I heard it had all come to an end."

"I would like to tell you how it happened," she said; "as that is the very point I want your advice about. I had long realized that we were not in sympathy in religious belief. His ideas of Christianity are very shadowy; and even as to the existence of a God he lives in a sort of dreamland. But it has not affected his life! I feel sure, now, that the most absolute Atheist may be leading, though walking blindfold, a pure and noble life. And if you knew half the good deeds—" she broke off suddenly, and turned away her head.

"I entirely agree with you," I said. "And have we not our Saviour's own promise that such a life shall surely lead to the light?"

"Yes, I know it," she said in a broken voice, still keeping her head turned away. "And so I told him. He said he would believe, for my sake, if he could. And he wished for my sake, he could see things as I did. But that is all wrong!" she went on passionately. "God cannot approve such low motives as that! Still it was not I that broke it off. I knew he loved me; and I had promised; and—'

"Then it was he that broke it off?"

"He released me unconditionally." She faced me again now, having quite recovered her usual calmness of manner.

"Then what difficulty remains?"

"It is this, that I don't believe he did it of his own free will. Now, supposing he hid it against his will, merely to satisfy my scruples, would not his claim on me remain just as strong as ever? And would not my promise be as binding as ever? My father says 'no'; but I ca'n't help fearing he is biased by his love for me. And I've asked no one else. I have many friends—friends for the bright sunny weather; not friends for the clouds and storms of life; not old friends like you!"

"Let me think a little," I said: and for some. minutes we walked on in silence, while, pained to the heart at seeing the bitter trial that had come upon this pure and gentle soul, I strove in vain to see my way through the tangled skein of conflicting motives.

"If she loves him truly", (I seemed at last to grasp the clue to the problem) "is not that, for her the voice of God? May she not hope that she is sent to him, even as Ananias was sent to Saul in his blindness, that he may receive his sight?" Once more I seemed to hear Arthur whispering "What knowest thou, O wife, whether thou shalt save thy husband?" and I broke the silence with the words "If you still love him truly—"

"I do not!" she hastily interrupted. "At least—not in that way. I believe I loved him when I promised, but I was very young: it is hard to know. But, whatever the feeling was, it is dead now. The motive on his side is Love: on mine it is—Duty!"

Again there was a long silence. The whole skein of thought was tangled worse than ever. This time she broke the silence. "Don't misunderstand me!" she said. "When I said my heart was not his, I did not mean it was any one else's! At present I feel bound to him; and, till I know I am absolutely free, in the sight of God, to love any other than him, I'll never even think of any one else—in that way, I mean. I would die sooner!" I had never imagined my gentle friend capable of such passionate utterances.

I ventured on no further remark until we had nearly arrived at the Hall-gate; but, the longer I reflected, the clearer it became to me that no call of Duty demanded the sacrifice—possibly of the happiness of a life—which she seemed ready to make. I tried to make this clear to her also, adding some warnings on the dangers that surely awaited a union in which mutual love was wanting. "The only argument for it, worth considering," I said in conclusion, "seems to be his supposed reluctance in releasing you from your promise. I have tried to give to that argument its full weight, and my conclusion is that it does not affect the rights of the case, or invalidate the release he has given you. My belief is that you are entirely free to act as now seems right."

"I am very grateful to you," she said earnestly. "Believe it, please! I ca'n't put it into proper words!" and the subject was dropped by mutual consent and I only learned, long afterwards, that our discussion had really served to dispel the doubts that had harassed her so long.

We parted at the Hall-gate, and I found Arthur eagerly awaiting my arrival; and, before we parted for the night, I had heard the whole story— how he had put off his journey from day to day, feeling that he could not go away from the place till his fate had been irrevocably settled by the wedding taking place: how the preparations for the wedding, and the excitement in the neighbourhood, had suddenly come to an end, and he had learned (from Major Lindon, who called to wish him good-bye) that the engagement had been broken off by mutual consent: how he had instantly abandoned all his plans for going abroad, and had decided to stay on at Elveston, for a year or two at any rate, till his newly-awakened hopes should prove true or false; and how, since that memorable day, he had avoided all meetings with Lady Muriel, fearing to betray his feelings before he had had any sufficient evidence as to how she regarded him. "But it is nearly six weeks since all that happened," he said in conclusion, "and we can meet in the ordinary way, now, with no need for any painful allusions. I would have written to tell you all this: only I kept hoping from day to day that—that there would be more to tell!"

"And how should there be more, you foolish fellow," I fondly urged, "if you never even go near her? Do you expect the offer to come from her?"

Arthur was betrayed into a smile. "No," he said, "I hardly expect that. But I'm a desperate coward. There's no doubt about it!"

"And what reasons have you heard of for breaking off the engagement?"

"A good many," Arthur replied, and proceeded to count them on his fingers. "First, it was found that she was dying of—something; so he broke it off. Then it was found that he was dying of—some other thing; so she broke it off. Then the Major turned out to be a confirmed gamester; so the Earl broke it off. Then the Earl insulted him; so the Major broke it off. It got a good deal broken off, all things considered!"

"You have all this on the very best authority, of course?"

"Oh, certainly! And communicated in the strictest confidence! Whatever defects Elveston society suffers from want of information isn't one of them!"

"Nor reticence, either, it seems. But, seriously, do you know the real reason?"

"No, I'm quite in the dark."

I did not feel that I had any right to enlighten him; so I changed the subject, to the less engrossing one of "new milk", and we agreed that I should walk over, next day to Hunter's farm, Arthur undertaking to set me part of the way, after which he had to return to keep a business engagement.

STREAKS OF DAWN

Next day proved warm and sunny, and we started early, to enjoy the luxury of a good long chat before he would be obliged to leave me.

"This neighbourhood has more than its due proportion of the very poor," I remarked, as we passed a group of hovels, too dilapidated to deserve the name of "cottages".

"But the few rich", Arthur replied, "give more than their due proportion of help in charity. So the balance is kept."

"I suppose the Earl does a good deal?"

"He gives liberally; but he has not the health or strength to do more. Lady Muriel does more in the way of school-teaching and cottage-visiting than she would like me to reveal."

"Then she, at least, is not one of the 'idle mouths' one so often meets with among the upper classes. I have sometimes thought they would have a hard time of it, if suddenly called on to give their raison d'être, and to show cause why they should be allowed to live any longer!"

"The whole subject", said Arthur, "of what we may call 'idle mouths' (I mean persons who absorb some of the material wealth of a community—in the form of food, clothes, and so on—without contributing its equivalent in the form of productive labour) is a complicated one, no doubt. I've tried to think it out. And it seemed to me that the simplest form of the problem, to start with, is a community without money, who buy and sell by barter only; and it makes it yet simpler to suppose the food and other things to be capable of keeping for many years without spoiling."

"Yours is an excellent plan," I said. "What is your solution of the problem?"

"The commonest type of 'idle mouths'", said Arthur, "is no doubt due to money being left by parents to their own children. So I imagined a man either exceptionally clever, or exceptionally strong and industrious—who had contributed so much valuable labour to the needs of the community that its equivalent, in clothes, etc., was (say) five times as much as he needed for himself. We cannot deny his absolute right to give the superfluous wealth as he chooses. So, if he [eaves four children behind him (say two sons and two daughters), with enough of all the necessaries of life to last them a life-time, I cannot see that the community is in any way wronged if they choose to do nothing in life but to 'eat, drink, and be merry'. Most certainly, the community could not fairly say, in reference to them, 'if a man will not work, neither let him eat.' Their reply would be crushing. 'The labour has already been done, which is a fair equivalent for the food we are eating; and you have had the benefit of it. On what principle of justice can you demand two quotas of work for one quota of food?"'

"Yet surely", I said, "there is something wrong somewhere, if these four people are well able to do useful work and if that work is actually needed by the community and they elect to sit idle?"

"I think there is," said Arthur: "but it seems to me to arise from a Law of God—that every one shall do as much as he can to help others—and not from any rights on the part of the community, to exact labour as an equivalent for food that has already been fairly earned."

"I suppose the second form of the problem is where the idle mouths possess money instead of material wealth?"

"Yes, replied Arthur: "and I think the simplest case is that of paper-money. Gold is itself a form of material wealth; but a bank-note is merely a promise to hand over so much material wealth when called upon to do so. The father of these four 'idle mouths', had done (let us say) five thousand pounds' worth of useful work for the community. In return for this, the community had given him what amounted to a written promise to hand over, whenever called upon to do so, five thousand pounds' worth of food, etc. Then, if he only uses one thousand pounds' worth himself, and leaves the rest of the notes to his children, surely they have a full right to present these written promises, and to say 'hand over the food, for which the equivalent labour has been already done'. Now I think this case well worth stating, publicly and clearly. I should like to drive it into the heads of those Socialists who are priming our ignorant paupers with such sentiments as 'Look at them bloated haristocrats! Doing not a stroke o' work for theirselves, and living on the sweat of our brows!' I should like to force them to see that the money, which those 'haristocrats' are spending, represents so much labour already done for the community, and whose equivalent, in material wealth, is due from the community."

"Might not the Socialists reply 'Much of this money does not represent honest labour at all. If you could trace it back, from owner to owner, though you might begin with several legitimate steps, such as gifts, or bequeathing by will, or 'value received', you would soon reach an owner who had no moral right to it but had got it by fraud or other crimes; and of course his successors in the line would have no better right to it than he had."

"No doubt, no doubt," Arthur replied. "But surely that involves the logical fallacy of proving too much? It is quite as applicable to material wealth, as it is to money. If we once begin to go back beyond the fact that the present owner of certain property came by it honestly, and to ask whether any previous owner, in past ages, got it by fraud would any property be secure?

After a minute's thought, I felt obliged to admit the truth of this.

"My general conclusion," Arthur continued, "from the mere standpoint of human rights, man against man, was this—that if some wealthy 'idle mouth', who has come by his money in a lawful way, even though not one atom of the labour it represents has been his own doing, chooses to spend it on his own needs, without contributing any labour to the community from whom he buys his food and clothes, that community has no right to interfere with him. But it's quite another thing, when we come to consider the divine law. Measured by that standard, such a man is undoubtedly doing wrong, if he fails to use, for the good of those in need, the strength or the skill, that God has given him. That strength and skill do not belong to the community, to be paid to them as a debt: they do not belong to the man himself, to be used for his own enjoyment: they do belong to God, to be used according to His will; and we are not left in doubt as to what this will is. 'Do good, and lend, hoping for nothing again.' "

"Anyhow," I said, "an 'idle mouth' very often gives away a great deal in charity."

"In so-called 'charity'," he corrected me. "Excuse me if I seem to speak uncharitably. I would not dream of applying the term to any individual. But I would say, generally, that a man who gratifies every fancy that occurs to him— denying himself in nothing—and merely gives to the poor some part, or even all, of his superfluous wealth, is only deceiving himself if he calls it charity."

"But, even in giving away superfluous wealth, he may be denying himself the miser's pleasure in hoarding?"

"I grant you that, gladly," said Arthur. "Given that he has that morbid craving, he is doing a good deed in restraining it."

"But, even in spending on himself", I persisted, "our typical rich man often does good, by employing people who would otherwise be out of work: and that is often better than pauperizing them by giving the money."

"I'm glad you've said that!" said Arthur. "I would not like to quit the subject without exposing the two fallacies of that statement—which have gone so long uncontradicted that Society now accepts it as an axiom!"

"What are they?" I said. "I don't even see one, myself."

"One is merely the fallacy of ambiguity—the assumption that 'doing good' (that is, benefiting somebody) is necessarily a good thing to do (that is, a right thing). The other is the assumption that, if one of two specified acts is better than another, it is necessarily a good act in itself. I should like to call this the fallacy of comparison—meaning that it assumes that what is comparatively good is therefore positively good."

"Then what is your test of a good act?"

"That it shall be our best," Arthur confidently replied. "And even then 'we are 'unprofitable servants'. But let me illustrate the two fallacies.

Nothing illustrates a fallacy so well as an extreme case, which fairly comes under it. Suppose I find two children drowning in a pond. I rush in, and save one of the children, and then walk away, leaving the other to drown. Clearly I have 'done good', in saving a child's life? But—Again, supposing I meet an inoffensive stranger, and knock him down and walk on. Clearly that is 'better' than if I had proceeded to jump upon him and break his ribs? But—"

"Those 'buts' are quite unanswerable," I said. "But I should like an instance from real life."

"Well, let us take one of those abominations of modern Society, a Charity-Bazaar. It's an interesting question to think out—how much of the money, that reaches the object in view, is genuine charity; and whether even that is spent in the best way. But the subject needs regular classification, and analysis, to understand it properly."

"I should be glad to have it analysed," I said: "it has often puzzled me."

"Well, if I am really not boring you. Let us suppose our Charity-Bazaar to have been organized to aid the funds of some Hospital: and that A, B, C give their services in making articles to sell, and in acting as salesmen, while X, Y, Z buy the articles, and the money so paid goes to the Hospital.

"There are two distinct species of such Bazaars: one, where the payment exacted is merely the market-value of the goods supplied, that is, exactly what you would have to pay at a shop: the other, where fancy-prices are asked. We must take these separately.

"First, the 'market-value' case. Here A, B, C are exactly in the same position as ordinary shopkeepers; the only difference being that they give the proceeds to the Hospital. Practically, they are giving their skilled labour for the benefit of the Hospital. This seems to me to be genuine charity. And I don't see how they could use it better. But X, Y, Z are exactly in the same position as any ordinary purchasers of goods. To talk of 'charity' in connection with their share of the business, is sheer nonsense. Yet they are very likely to do so.

"Secondly, the case of 'fancy-prices'. Here I think the simplest plan is to divide the payment into two parts, the 'market-value' and the excess over that. The 'market-value' part is on the same footing as in the first case: the excess is all we have to consider. Well, A, B, C do not earn it; so we may put them out of the question: it is a gift, from X, Y, Z, to the Hospital. And my opinion is that it is not given in the best way: far better buy what they choose to buy, and give what they choose to give, as two separate transactions: then there is some chance that their motive in giving may be real charity, instead of a mixed motive—half charity, half self-pleasing. 'The trail of the serpent is over it all.' And therefore it is that I hold all such spurious 'Charities' in utter abomination!" He ended with unusual energy, and savagely beheaded, with his stick, a tall thistle at the road-side, behind which I was startled to see Sylvie and Bruno standing. I caught at his arm, but too late to stop him. Whether the stick reached them, or not, I could not feel sure: at any rate they took not the smallest notice of it, but smiled gaily, and nodded to me: and I saw at once that they were only visible to me: the "eerie" influence had not reached to Arthur.

"Why did you try to save it?" he said. "That's not the wheedling Secretary of a Charity-Bazaar! I only wish it were!" he added grimly.

"Does oo know, that stick went right froo my head!" said Bruno. (They had run round to me by this time, and each had secured a hand.) "Just under my chin! I are glad I aren't a thistle!"

"Well, we've threshed that subject out, anyhow!" Arthur resumed. "I'm afraid I've been talking too much, for your patience and for my strength. I must be turning soon. This is about the end of my tether."

"Take, O boatman, thrice thy fee;

Take, I give it willingly;

For, invisible to thee,

Spirits twain have crossed with me!"

I quoted, involuntarily.

"For utterly inappropriate and irrelevant quotations," laughed Arthur, "you are 'ekalled by few, and excelled by none'!" And we strolled on.

As we passed the head of the lane that led down to the beach, I noticed a single figure moving slowly along it, seawards. She was a good way off, and had her back to us: but it was Lady Muriel, unmistakably. Knowing that Arthur had not seen her, as he had been looking, in the other direction, at a gathering rain-cloud, I made no remark, but tried to think of some plausible pretext for sending him back by the sea.

The opportunity instantly presented itself. "I'm getting tired," he said. "I don't think it would be prudent to go further. I had better turn here."

I turned with him, for a few steps, and as we again approached the head of the lane, I said, as carelessly as I could, "Don't go back by the road. It's too hot and dusty. Down this lane, and along the beach, is nearly as short; and you'll get a breeze off the sea."

"Yes, I think I will," Arthur began; but at that moment we came into sight of Lady Muriel, and he checked himself. "No, it's too far round. Yet it certainly would be cooler—" He stood, hesitating, looking first one way and then the other—a melancholy picture of utter infirmity of purpose!

How long this humiliating scene would have continued, if I had been the only external influence, it is impossible to say; for at this moment Sylvie, with a swift decision worthy of Napoleon himself, took the matter into her own hands "You go and drive her, up this way," she said to Bruno. "I'll get him along!" And she took hold of the stick that Arthur was carrying, and gently pulled him down the lane.

He was totally unconscious that any will but his own was acting on the stick, and appeared to think it had taken a horizontal position simply because he was pointing with it. "Are not those orchises under the hedge there?" he said. "I think that decides me. I'll gather some as I go along."

Meanwhile Bruno had run on behind Lady Muriel, and, with much jumping about and shouting (shouts audible to no one but Sylvie and myself), much as if he were driving sheep, he managed to turn her round and make her walk, with eyes demurely cast upon the ground, in our direction.

The victory was ours! And, since it was evident that the lovers, thus urged together, must meet in another minute, I turned and walked on, hoping that Sylvie and Bruno would follow my example, as I felt sure that the fewer the spectators the better it would be for Arthur and his good angel.

"And what sort of meeting was it?" I wondered, as I paced dreamily on.

THE DOG-KING

"They shooked hands," said Bruno, who was trotting at my side, in answer to the unspoken question.

"And they looked ever so pleased!" Sylvie added from the other side.

"Well, we must get on, now, as quick as we can," I said. "If only I knew the best way to Hunter's farm!"

"They'll be sure to know in this cottage," said Sylvie.

"Yes, I suppose they will. Bruno, would you run in and ask?"

Sylvie stopped him, laughingly, as he ran off. "Wait a minute," she said. "I must make you visible first, you know."

"And audible too, I suppose?" I said, as she took the jewel, that hung round her neck, and waved it over his head, and touched his eyes and lips with it.

"Yes," said Sylvie: "and once, do you know, I made him audible, and forgot to make him visible! And he went to buy some sweeties in a shop. And the man was so frightened! A voice seemed to come out of the air, 'Please, I want two ounces of barley-sugar drops!' And a shilling came bang down upon the counter! And the man said 'I ca'n't see you!' And Bruno said 'It doosn't sinnify seeing me, so long as oo can see the shilling!' But the man said he never sold barley-sugar drops to people he couldn't see. So we had to—Now, Bruno, you're ready!" And away he trotted.

Sylvie spent the time, while we were waiting for him, in making herself visible also. "It's rather awkward, you know," she explained to me, "when we meet people, and they can see one of us, and ca'n't see the other!"

In a minute or two Bruno returned, looking rather disconsolate. "He'd got friends with him, and he were cross!" he said. "He asked me who I were. And I said 'I'm Bruno: who is these peoples?' And he said 'One's my half-brother, and 'other's my half-sister: and I don't want no more company! Go along with yer!' And I said 'I ca'n't go along wizout mine self!' And I said 'Oo shouldn't have bits of peoples lying about like that! It's welly untidy!' And he said 'Oh, don't talk to me!' And he pushted me outside! And he shutted the door!"

"And you never asked where Hunter's farm was?" queried Sylvie.

"Hadn't room for any questions," said Bruno. "The room were so crowded."

"Three people couldn't crowd a room," said Sylvie.

"They did, though," Bruno persisted. "He crowded it most. He's such a welly thick man—so as oo couldn't knock him down."

I failed to see the drift of Bruno's argument. "Surely anybody could be knocked down," I said: "thick or thin wouldn't matter."

"Oo couldn't knock him down," said Bruno. "He's more wide than he's high: so, when he's lying down he's more higher than when he's standing: so a-course oo couldn't knock him down!"

"Here's another cottage," I said: "I'll ask the way, this time."

There was no need to go in, this time, as the woman was standing in the doorway, with a baby in her arms talking to a respectably dressed man—a farmer, as I guessed—who seemed to be on his way to the town.

"—and when there's drink to be had," he was saying, "he's just the worst o' the lot, is your Willie. So they tell me. He gets fairly mad wi' it!"

"I'd have given 'em the lie to their faces, a twelve-month back!" the woman said in a broken voice. "But a' canna noo! A' canna noo!" She checked herself on catching sight of us, and hastily retreated into the house shutting the door after her.

"Perhaps you can tell me where Hunter's farm is?" I said to the man, as he turned away from the house.

"I can that, Sir!" he replied with a smile. "I'm John Hunter hissel, at your service. It's nobbut half a mile further—the only house in sight, when you get round bend o' the road yonder. You'll find my good woman within, if so be you've business wi' her. Or mebbe I'll do as well?"

"Thanks," I said. "I want to order some milk. Perhaps I had better arrange it with your wife?"

"Aye," said the man. "She minds all that. Good day t'ye, Master—and to your bonnie childer, as well!" And he trudged on.

"He should have said 'child', not 'childer'," said Bruno. "Sylvie's not a childer!"

"He meant both of us," said Sylvie.

"No, he didn't!" Bruno persisted. "'cause he said 'bonnie', oo know!"

"Well, at any rate he looked at us both," Sylvie maintained.

"Well, then he must have seen we're not both bonnie!" Bruno retorted. "A-course I'm much uglier than oo! Didn't he mean Sylvie, Mister Sir?" he shouted over his shoulder, as he ran off.

But there was no use in replying, as he had already vanished round the bend of the road. When we overtook him he was climbing a gate, and was gazing earnestly into the field, where a horse, a cow, and a kid were browsing amicably together. "For its father, a Horse," he murmured to himself. "For its mother, a Cow. For their dear little child, a little Goat, is the most curiousest thing I ever seen in my world!"

"Bruno's World!" I pondered. "Yes, I suppose every child has a world of his own—and every man, too, for the matter of that. I wonder if that's the cause for all the misunderstanding there is in Life?"

"That must be Hunter's farm!" said Sylvie, pointing to a house on the brow of the hill, led up to by a cart-road. "There's no other farm in sight, this way; and you said we must be nearly there by this time."

I had thought it, while Bruno was climbing the gate, but I couldn't remember having said it. However, Sylvie was evidently in the right. "Get down, Bruno," I said, "and open the gate for us."

"It's a good thing we's with oo, isn't it, Mister Sir?" said Bruno, as we entered the field. "That big dog might have bited oo, if oo'd been alone! Oo needn't be frightened of it!" he whispered, clinging tight to my hand to encourage me. "It aren't fierce!"

"Fierce!" Sylvie scornfully echoed, as the dog—a magnificent Newfoundland—that had come galloping down the field to meet us, began curveting round us, in gambols full of graceful beauty, and welcoming us with short joyful barks. "Fierce! Why, it's as gentle as a lamb! It's—why, Bruno, don't you know? It's—"

"So it are!" cried Bruno, rushing forwards and throwing his arms round its neck. "Oh, you dear dog!" And it seemed as if the two children would never have done hugging and stroking it.

"And how ever did he get here?" said Bruno. "Ask him, Sylvie. I doosn't know how."

And then began an eager talk in Doggee, which of course was lost upon me; and I could only guess, when the beautiful creature, with a sly glance at me, whispered something in Sylvie's ear, that I was now the subject of conversation. Sylvie looked round laughingly.

"He asked me who you are," she explained. "And I said 'He's our friend'. And he said 'What's his name?' And I said 'It's Mister Sir'. And he said 'Bosh!'"

"What is 'Bosh!' in Doggee," I enquired.

"It's the same as in English," said Sylvie. "Only, when a dog says it, it's a sort of whisper, that's half a cough and half a bark. Nero, say 'Bosh!' "

And Nero, who had now begun gamboling round us again, said "Bosh!" several times; and I found that Sylvie's description of the sound was perfectly accurate.

"I wonder what's behind this long wall?" I said, as we walked on.

"It's the Orchard," Sylvie replied, after a consultation with Nero. "See, there's a boy getting down off the wall, at that far corner. And now he's running away across the field. I do believe he's been stealing the apples!"

Bruno set off after him, but returned to us in a few moments, as he had evidently no chance of overtaking the young rascal.

"I couldn't catch him!" he said. "I wiss I'd started a little sooner. His pockets was full of apples!"

The Dog-King looked up at Sylvie, and said something in Doggee.

"Why, of course you can!" Sylvie exclaimed. "How stupid not to think of it! Nero'll hold him for us, Bruno! But I'd better make him invisible, first." And she hastily got out the Magic Jewel, and began waving it over Nero's head, and down along his back.

"That'll do!" cried Bruno, impatiently. "After him, good Doggie!"

"Oh, Bruno!" Sylvie exclaimed reproachfully. "You shouldn't have sent him off so quick! I hadn't done the tail!"

Meanwhile Nero was coursing like a greyhound down the field: so at least I concluded from all I could see of him—the long feathery tail, which floated like a meteor through the air—and in a very few seconds he had come up with the little thief.

"He's got him safe, by one foot!" cried Sylvie, who was eagerly watching the chase. "Now there's no hurry, Bruno!"

So we walked, quite leisurely, down the field, to where the frightened lad stood. A more curious sight I had seldom seen, in all my "eerie" experiences. Every bit of him was in violent action, except the left foot, which was apparently glued to the ground—there being nothing visibly holding it: while, at some little distance, the long feathery tail was waving gracefully from side to side, showing that Nero, at least, regarded the whole affair as nothing but a magnificent game of play.

"What's the matter with you?" I said, as gravely as I could.

"Got the crahmp in me ahnkle!" the thief groaned in reply. "An' me fut's gone to sleep!" And he began to blubber aloud.

"Now, look here!" Bruno said in a commanding tone, getting in front of him. "Oo've got to give up those apples!

33

The lad glanced at me, but didn't seem to reckon my interference as worth anything. Then he glanced at Sylvie: she clearly didn't count for very much, either. Then he took courage. "It'll take a better man than any of yer to get 'em!" he retorted defiantly.

Sylvie stooped and patted the invisible Nero. "A little tighter!" she whispered. And a sharp yell from the ragged boy showed how promptly the Dog-King had taken the hint.

"What's the matter now?" I said. "Is your ankle worse?"

"And it'll get worse, and worse, and worse," Bruno solemnly assured him, "till oo gives up those apples!"

Apparently the thief was convinced of this at last, and he sulkily began emptying his pockets of the apples. The children watched from a little distance, Bruno dancing with delight at every fresh yell extracted from Nero's terrified prisoner.

"That's all," the boy said at last.

"It isn't all!" cried Bruno. "There's three more in that pocket!"

Another hint from Sylvie to the Dog-King—another sharp yell from the thief, now convicted of lying also— and the remaining three apples were surrendered.

"Let him go, please," Sylvie said in Doggee, and the lad limped away at a great pace, stooping now and then to rub the ailing ankle in fear, seemingly, that the "crahmp" might attack it again.

Bruno ran back, with his booty, to the orchard wall, and pitched the apples over it one by one. "I's welly afraid some of them's gone under the wrong trees!" he panted, on overtaking us again.

"The wrong trees!" laughed Sylvie. "Trees ca'n't do wrong! There's no such things as wrong trees!"

"Then there's no such things as right trees, neither!" cried Bruno. And Sylvie gave up the point.

"Wait a minute, please!" she said to me. "I must make Nero visible, you know!"

"No, please don't!" cried Bruno, who had by this time mounted on the Royal back, and was twisting the Royal hair into a bridle. "It'll be such fun to have him like this!"

"Well, it does look funny," Sylvie admitted, and led the way to the farm-house, where the farmer's wife stood, evidently much perplexed at the weird procession now approaching her. "It's summat gone wrong wi' my spectacles, I doubt!" she murmured, as she took them off, and began diligently rubbing them with a corner of her apron.

Meanwhile Sylvie had hastily pulled Bruno down from his steed, and had just time to make His Majesty, wholly visible before the spectacles were resumed.

All was natural, now; but the good woman still looked a little uneasy about it. "My eyesight's getting bad," she said, "but I see you now, my darlings! You'll give me a kiss, won't you?"

Bruno got behind me, in a moment: however Sylvie put up her face, to be kissed, as representative of both, and we all went in together.

MATILDA JANE

"Come to me, my little gentleman," said our hostess, lifting Bruno into her lap," and tell me everything."

"I ca'n't," said Bruno. "There wouldn't be time. Besides, I don't know everything."

The good woman looked a little puzzled, and turned to Sylvie for help. "Does he like riding?" she asked.

"Yes, I think so," Sylvie gently replied. "He's just had a ride on Nero."

"Ah, Nero's a grand dog, isn't he? Were you ever outside a horse, my little man?"

"Always!" Bruno said with great decision. "Never was inside one. Was oo?"

Here I thought it well to interpose, and to mention the business on which we had come, and so relieved her, for a few minutes, from Bruno's perplexing questions.

"And those dear children will like a bit of cake, I'll warrant!" said the farmer's hospitable wife, when the business was concluded, as she opened her cupboard, and brought out a cake. "And don't you waste the crust, little gentleman!" she added, as she handed a good slice of it to Bruno. "You know what the poetry-book says about wilful waste?"

"No, I don't," said Bruno. "What doos he say about it,"

"Tell him, Bessie!" And the mother looked down, proudly and lovingly, on a rosy little maiden, who had just crept shyly into the room, and was leaning against her knee. "What's that your poetry-book says about wilful waste?"

"For wilful waste makes woeful want," Bessie recited, in an almost inaudible whisper: "and you may live to say 'How much I wish I had the crust that then I threw away!' "

"Now try if you can say it, my dear! For wilful—"

"For wifful—sumfinoruvver—" Bruno began, readily enough; and then there came a dead pause. "Ca'n't remember no more!"

"Well, what do you learn from it, then? You can tell us that, at any rate?"

Bruno ate a little more cake, and considered: but the moral did not seem to him to be a very obvious one.

"Always to—" Sylvie prompted him in a whisper.

"Always to—" Bruno softly repeated: and then, with sudden inspiration, "always to look where it goes to!"

"Where what goes to, darling?"

"Why the crust, a course!" said Bruno. "Then, if I lived to say 'How much I wiss I had the crust—' (and all that), I'd know where I frew it to!"

This new interpretation quite puzzled the good woman. She returned to the subject of "Bessie". "Wouldn't you like to see Bessie's doll, my dears! Bessie, take the little lady and gentleman to see Matilda Jane!"

Bessie's shyness thawed away in a moment. "Matilda Jane has just woke up," she stated, confidentially, to Sylvie. "Won't you help me on with her frock? Them strings is such a bother to tie!"

"I can tie strings," we heard, in Sylvie's gentle voice, as the two little girls left the room together. Bruno ignored the whole proceeding, and strolled to the window, quite with the air of a fashionable gentleman. Little girls, and dolls, were not at all in his line.

And forthwith the fond mother proceeded to tell me (as what mother is not ready to do?) of all Bessie's virtues (and vices too, for the matter of that) and of the many fearful maladies which, notwithstanding those ruddy cheeks and that plump little figure, had nearly, time and again, swept her from the face of the earth.

When the full stream of loving memories had nearly run itself out, I began to question her about the working men of that neighbourhood, and specially the "Willie"whom we had heard of at his cottage. "He was a good fellow once," said my kind hostess: "but it's the drink has ruined him! Not that I'd rob them of the drink—it's good for the most of them—but there's some as is too weak to stand agin' temptations: it's a thousand pities, for them, as they ever built the Golden Lion at the corner there!"

"The Golden Lion?" I repeated.

"It's the new Public," my hostess explained. "And it stands right in the way, and handy for the workmen, as they come back from the brickfields, as it might be to-day, with their week's wages. A deal of money gets wasted that way. And some of 'em gets drunk."

"If only they could have it in their own houses—" I mused, hardly knowing I had said the words out loud.

"That's it!" she eagerly exclaimed. It was evidently a solution, of the problem, that she had already thought out. "If only you could manage, so's each man to have his own little barrel in his own house—there'd hardly be a drunken man in the length and breadth of the land!"

And then I told her the old story—about a certain cottager who bought himself a little barrel of beer, and installed his wife as bar-keeper: and how, every time he wanted his mug of beer, he regularly paid her over the counter for it: and how she never would let him go on "tick", and was a perfectly inflexible bar-keeper in never letting him have more than his proper allowance: and how, every time the barrel needed refilling, she had plenty to do it with, and something over for her money-box: and how, at the end of the year, he not only found himself in first-rate health and spirits, with that undefinable but quite unmistakable air which always distinguishes the sober man from the one who takes "a drop too much", but had quite a box full of money, all saved out of his own pence!

"If only they'd all do like that!" said the good woman, wiping her eyes, which were overflowing with kindly sympathy. "Drink hadn't need to be the curse it is to some—"

"Only a curse", I said, "when it is used wrongly. Any of God's gifts may be turned into a curse, unless we use it wisely. But we must be getting home. Would you call the little girls? Matilda Jane has seen enough of company, for one day, I'm sure!"

"I'll find 'em in a minute," said my hostess, as she rose to leave the room. "Maybe that young gentleman saw which way they went?"

"Where are they, Bruno?" I said.

"They ain't in the field," was Bruno's rather evasive reply, "'cause there's nothing but pigs there, and Sylvie isn't a pig. Now don't interrupt me any more, 'cause I'm telling a story to this fly; and it wo'n't attend!"

"They're among the apples, I'll warrant 'em!" said the Farmer's wife. So we left Bruno to finish his story, and went out into the orchard, where we soon came upon the children, walking sedately side by side, Sylvie carrying the doll, while little Bess carefully shaded its face, with a large cabbage-leaf for a parasol.

As soon as they caught sight of us, little Bess dropped her cabbage-leaf and came running to meet us, Sylvie following more slowly, as her precious charge evidently needed great care and attention.

"I'm its Mamma, and Sylvie's the Head-Nurse," Bessie explained: "and Sylvie's taught me ever such a pretty song, for me to sing to Matilda Jane!"

"Let's hear it once more, Sylvie," I said, delighted at getting the chance I had long wished for, of hearing her sing. But Sylvie turned shy and frightened in a moment.

"No, please not!" she said, in an earnest "aside" to me. "Bessie knows it quite perfect now. Bessie can sing it!"

"Aye, aye! Let Bessie sing it!" said the proud mother. "Bessie has a bonny voice of her own," (this again was an "aside" to me) "though I say it as shouldn't!"

Bessie was only too happy to accept the "encore". So the plump little Mamma sat down at our feet, with her hideous daughter reclining stiffly across her lap (it was one of a kind that wo'n't sit down, under any amount of persuasion), and, with a face simply beaming with delight, began the lullaby, in a shout that ought to have frightened the poor baby into fits. The Head-Nurse crouched down behind her, keeping herself respectfully in the background, with her hands on the shoulders of her little mistress, so as to be ready to act as Prompter, if required, and to supply "each gap in faithless memory void".

The shout, with which she began, proved to be only a momentary effort. After a very few notes, Bessie toned down, and sang on in a small but very sweet voice. At first her great black eyes were fixed on her mother, but soon her gaze wandered upwards, among the apples, and she seemed to have quite forgotten that she had any other audience than her Baby, and her Head-Nurse, who once or twice supplied, almost inaudibly, the right note, when the singer was getting a little "flat".

> "Matilda Jane, you never look
> At any toy or picture-book:
> I show you pretty things in vain—
> You must be blind, Matilda Jane
> "I ask you riddles, tell you tales,
> But all our conversation fails:
> You never answer me again—
> I fear you're dumb, Matilda Jane!
> "Matilda, darling, when I call,
> You never seem to hear at all:
> I shout with all my might and main—
> but you're so deaf, Matilda Jane!
> "Matilda Jane, you needn't mind:
> For, though you're deaf, and dumb, and blind,
> There's some one loves you, it is plain—
> And that is me, Matilda Jane!"

She sang three of the verses in a rather perfunctory style, but the last stanza evidently excited the little maiden. Her voice rose, ever clearer and louder: she had a rapt look on her face, as if suddenly inspired, and, as she sang the last few words, she clasped to her heart the inattentive Matilda Jane.

"Kiss it now!" prompted the Head-Nurse. And in a moment the simpering meaningless face of the Baby was covered with a shower of passionate kisses.

"What a bonny song!" cried the Farmer's wife. "Who made the words, dearie?"

"I—I think I'll look for Bruno," Sylvie said demurely, and left us hastily. The curious child seemed always afraid of being praised, or even noticed.

"Sylvie planned the words," Bessie informed us, proud of her superior information: "and Bruno planned the music—and I sang it!" (this last circumstance, by the way, we did not need to be told).

So we followed Sylvie, and all entered the parlour together. Bruno was still standing at the window, with his elbows on the sill. He had, apparently, finished the story that he was telling to the fly, and had found a new occupation. "Don't imperrupt!" he said as we came in. "I'm counting the Pigs in the field!"

"How many are there?" I enquired.

"About a thousand and four," said Bruno.

"You mean 'about a thousand'," Sylvie corrected him. "There's no good saying 'and four': you ca'n't be sure about the four!"

"And you're as wrong as ever!" Bruno exclaimed triumphantly. "It's just the four I can be sure about; 'cause they're here, grubbling under the window! It's the thousand I isn't pruffickly sure about!"

"But some of them have gone into the sty," Sylvie said, leaning over him to look out of the window.

"Yes," said Bruno; "but they went so slowly and so fewly, I didn't care to count them."

"We must be going, children," I said. "Wish Bessie good-bye." Sylvie flung her arms round the little maiden's neck, and kissed her: but Bruno stood aloof, looking unusually shy. ("I never kiss nobody but Sylvie!" he explained to me afterwards.) The Farmer's wife showed us out: and we were soon on our way back to Elveston.

"And that's the new public-house that we were talking about, I suppose?" I said, as we came in sight of a long low building, with the words "THE GOLDEN LION" over the door.

"Yes, that's it," said Sylvie. "I wonder if her Willie's inside? Run in, Bruno, and see if he's there."

I interposed, feeling that Bruno was, in a sort of way, in my care. "That's not a place to send a child into." For already the revellers were getting noisy: and a wild discord of singing, shouting, and meaningless laughter came to us through the open windows.

"They wo'n't see him, you know," Sylvie explained. "Wait a minute, Bruno!" She clasped the jewel, that always hung round her neck, between the palms of her hands, and muttered a few words to herself. What they were I could not at all make out, but some mysterious change seemed instantly to pass over us. My feet seemed to me no longer to press the ground, and the dream-like feeling came upon me, that I was suddenly endowed with the power of floating in the air. I could still just see the children: but their forms were shadowy and unsubstantial, and their voices sounded as if they came from some distant place and time, they were so unreal. However, I offered no further opposition to Bruno's going into the house. He was back again in a few moments. "No, he isn't come yet," he said. "They're talking about him inside, and saying how drunk he was last week."

While he was speaking, one of the men lounged out through the door, a pipe in one hand and a mug of beer in the other, and crossed to where we were standing, so as to get a better view along the road. Two or three others leaned out through the open window, each holding his mug of beer, with red faces and sleepy eyes. "Canst see him, lad?" one of them asked.

"I dunnot know," the man said, taking a step forwards, which brought us nearly face to face. Sylvie hastily pulled me out of his way. "Thanks, child," I said. "I had forgotten he couldn't see us. What would have happened if I had stayed in his way?"

"I don't know," Sylvie said gravely. "It wouldn't matter to us; but you may be different." She said this in her usual voice, but the man took no sort of notice, though she was standing close in front of him, and looking up into his face as she spoke.

"He's coming now!" cried Bruno, pointing down the road.

"He be a-coomin noo!" echoed the man, stretching out his arm exactly over Bruno's head, and pointing with his pipe.

"Then chorus agin!" was shouted out by one of the red-faced men in the window: and forthwith a dozen voices yelled, to a harsh discordant melody, the refrain:

"There's him, an' yo', an' me,
Roarin' laddies!
We loves a bit o' spree,
Roarin' laddies we,
Roarin' laddies
Roarin' laddies!"

The man lounged back again to the house, joining lustily in the chorus as he went: so that only the children and I were in the road when "Willie" came   up.

WILLIE'S WIFE

He made for the door of the public-house, but the children intercepted him. Sylvie clung to one arm; while Bruno, on the opposite side, was pushing him with all his strength, and many inarticulate cries of "Gee-up! Gee-back! Woah then!" which he had picked up from the waggoners.

"Willie" took not the least notice of them: he was simply conscious that something had checked him: and, for want of any other way of accounting for it, he seemed to regard it as his own act.

"I wunnut coom in," he said: "not to-day."

"A mug o' beer wunnut hurt 'ee!" his friends shouted in chorus. "Two mugs wunnut hurt 'ee! Nor a dozen mugs!"

"Nay," said Willie. "I'm agoan whoam."

"What, withouten thy drink, Willie man?" shouted the others. But "Willie man" would have no more discussion, and turned doggedly away, the children keeping one on each side of him, to guard him against any change in his sudden resolution.

For a while he walked on stoutly enough, keeping his hands in his pockets, and softly whistling a tune, in time to his heavy tread: his success, in appearing entirely at his ease, was almost complete; but a careful observer would have noted that he had forgotten the second part of the air, and that, when it broke down, he instantly began it again, being too nervous to think of another, and too restless to endure silence.

It was not the old fear that possessed him now—the old fear that had been his dreary companion every Saturday night he could remember as he had reeled along, steadying himself against gates and garden-palings, and when the thrill reproaches of his wife had seemed to his dazed brain only the echo of a yet more piercing voice within, the intolerable wail of a hopeless remorse: it was a wholly new fear that had come to him now: life had taken on itself a new set of colours, and was lighted up with a new and dazzling radiance, and he did not see, as yet, how his home-life, and his wife and child, would fit into the new order of things: the very novelty of it all was, to his simple mind, a perplexity and an overwhelming terror.

And now the tune died into sudden silence on the trembling lips, as he turned a sharp corner, and came in sight of his own cottage, where his wife stood, leaning with folded arms on the wicket-gate, and looking up the road with a pale face, that had in it no glimmer of the light of hope—only the heavy shadow of a deep stony despair.

"Fine an' early, lad! Fine an' early!" the words might have been words of welcoming, but oh, the bitterness of the tone in which she said it! "What brings thee from thy merry mates, and all the fiddling and the jigging? Pockets empty, I doubt? Or thou'st come, mebbe, for to see thy little one die? The bairnie's clemmed, and I've nor bite nor sup to gie her. But what does thou care?" She flung the gate open, and met him with blazing eyes of fury.

The man said no word. Slowly, and with downcast eyes, he passed into the house, while she, half terrified at his strange silence, followed him in without another word; and it was not till he had sunk into a chair, with his arms crossed on the table and with drooping head, that she found her voice again.

It seemed entirely natural for us to go in with them: at another time one would have asked leave for this, but I felt, I knew not why, that we were in some mysterious way invisible, and as free to come and to go as disembodied spirits.

The child in the cradle woke up, and raised a piteous cry, which in a moment brought the children to its side: Bruno rocked the cradle, while Sylvie tenderly replaced the little head on the pillow from which it had slipped. But the mother took no heed of the cry, nor yet of the satisfied "coo" that it set up when Sylvie had made it happy again: she only stood gazing at her husband, and vainly trying, with white quivering lips (I believe she thought he was mad), to speak in the old tones of shrill upbraiding that he knew so well.

"And thou'st spent all thy wages—I'll swear thou hast —on the devil's own drink—and thou'st been and made thysen a beast again—as thou allus dost—"

"Hasna!" the man muttered, his voice hardly rising above a whisper, as he slowly emptied his pockets on the table. "There's th' wage, Missus, every penny on't."

The woman gasped and put one hand to her heart, as if under some great shock of surprise. "Then how's thee gotten th' drink?"

"Hasna gotten it," he answered her, in a tone more sad than sullen. "I hanna touched a drop this blessed day. No!" he cried aloud, bringing his clenched fist heavily down upon the table, and looking up at her with gleaming eyes, "nor I'll never touch another drop o' the cursed drink—till I die—so help me God my Maker!" His voice, which had suddenly risen to a hoarse shout, dropped again as suddenly: and once more he bowed his head, and buried his face in his folded arms.

The woman had dropped upon her knees by the cradle, while he was speaking. She neither looked at him nor seemed to hear him. With hands clasped above her head, she rocked herself wildly to and fro. "Oh my God! Oh my God!" was all she said, over and over again.

Sylvie and Bruno gently unclasped her hands and drew them down—till she had an arm round each of them, though she took no notice of them, but knelt on with eyes gazing upwards, and lips that moved as if in silent thanksgiving. The man kept his face hidden, and uttered no sound: but one could see the sobs that shook him from head to foot.

After a while he raised his head—his face all wet with tears. "folly!" he said softly; and then, louder, "Old Poll!"

Then she rose from her knees and came to him, with a dazed look, as if she were walking in her sleep. "Who was it called me old Poll?" she asked: her voice took on it a tender playfulness: her eyes sparkled; and the rosy light of Youth flushed her pale cheeks, till she looked more like a happy girl of seventeen than a worn woman of forty. "Was that my own lad, my Willie, a-waiting for me at the stile?"

His face too was transformed, in the same magic light, to the likeness of a bashful boy: and boy and girl they seemed, as he wound an arm about her, and drew her to his side, while with the other hand he thrust from him the heap of money, as though it were something hateful to the touch. "Tak it, lass," he said, "tak it all! An' fetch us summat to eat: but get a sup o' milk, first, for t'bairn.

"My little bairn!" she murmured as she gathered up the coins. "My own little lassie!" Then she moved to the door, and was passing out, but a sudden thought seemed to arrest her: she hastily returned—first to kneel down and kiss the sleeping child, and then to throw herself into her husband's arms and be strained to his heart. The next moment she was on her way, taking with her a jug that hung on a peg near the door: we followed close behind.

We had not gone far before we came in sight of a swinging sign-board bearing the word "DAIRY" on it, and here she went in, welcomed by a little curly white dog, who, not being under the "eerie" influence, saw the children, and received them with the most effusive affection. When I got inside, the dairyman was in the act of taking the money. "Is's for thysen, Missus, or for t' bairn?" he asked, when he had filled the jug, pausing with it in his hand.

"For t' bairn!" she said, almost reproachfully. "Think'st tha I'd touch a drop mysen, while as she hadna got her fill?"

"All right, Missus," the man replied, turning away with the jug in his hand. "Let's just mak sure it's good measure." He went back among his shelves of milk-bowls, carefully keeping his back towards her while he emptied a little measure of cream into the jug, muttering to himself "mebbe it'll hearten her up a bit, the little lassie!"

The woman never noticed the kind deed, but took back the jug with a simple "Good evening, Master," and went her way: but the children had been more observant, and, as we followed her out, Bruno remarked "That were welly kind: and I loves that man: and if I was welly rich I'd give him a hundred pounds—and a bun. That little grummeling dog doosn't know its business!" He referred to the dairyman's little dog, who had apparently quite forgotten the affectionate welcome he had given us on our arrival, and was now following at a respectful distance, doing his best to "speed the parting guest" with a shower of little shrill barks, that seemed to tread on one another's heels.

"What is a dog's business?" laughed Sylvie. "Dogs ca'n't keep shops and give change!"

"Sisters' businesses isn't to laugh at their brothers," Bruno replied with perfect gravity. "And dogs' businesses is to bark—not like that: it should finish one bark before it begins another: and it should—Oh Sylvie, there's some dindledums!"

And in another moment the happy children were flying across the common, racing for the patch of dandelions.

While I stood watching them, a strange dreamy feeling came upon me: a railway-platform seemed to take the place of the green sward, and, instead of the light figure of Sylvie bounding along, I seemed to see the flying form of Lady Muriel; but whether Bruno had also undergone a transformation, and had become the old man whom she was running to overtake, I was unable to judge, so instantaneously did the feeling come and go.

When I re-entered the little sitting-room which I shared with Arthur, he was standing with his back to me, looking out of the open window, and evidently had not heard me enter. A cup of tea, apparently just tasted and pushed aside, stood on the table, on the opposite side of which was a letter, just begun, with the pen lying across it: an open book lay on the sofa: the London paper occupied the easy chair; and on the little table which stood by it, I noticed an unlighted cigar and an open box of cigar-lights: all things betokened that the Doctor, usually so methodical and so self-contained, had been trying every form of occupation, and could settle to none!

"This is very unlike you, Doctor!" I was beginning, but checked myself, as he turned at the sound of my voice, in sheer amazement at the wonderful change that had taken place in his appearance. Never had I seen a face so radiant with happiness, or eyes that sparkled with such unearthly light! "Even thus", I thought, "must the herald-angel have looked, who brought to the shepherds, watching over their flocks by night, that sweet message of 'peace on earth, good-will to men'!"

"Yes, dear friend!" he said, as if in answer to the question that I suppose he read in my face. "It is true! It is true!"

No need to ask what was true. "God bless you both!" I said, as I felt the happy tears brimming to my eyes. "You were made for each other!"

"Yes," he said, simply, "I believe we were. And what a change it makes in one's Life! This isn't the same world! That isn't the sky I saw yesterday! Those clouds— I never saw such clouds in all my life before! They look like troops of hovering angels!"

To me they looked very ordinary clouds indeed: but then I had not fed "on honeydew, And drunk the milk of Paradise"!

"She wants to see you—at once," he continued, descending suddenly to the things of earth. "She says that is the one drop yet wanting in her cup of happiness!"

"I'll go at once," I said, as I turned to leave the room. "Wo'n't you come with me?"

"No, Sir!" said the Doctor, with a sudden effort— which proved an utter failure—to resume his professional manner. "Do I look like coming with you? Have you never heard that two is company, and—"

"Yes," I said, "I have heard it: and I'm painfully aware that I am Number Three! But, when shall we three meet again?"

"When the hurly-burly's done!" he answered with a happy laugh, such as I had not heard from him for many a year.

MEIN HERR

So I went on my lonely way, and, on reaching the Hall, I found Lady Muriel standing at the garden-gate waiting for me.

"No need to give you joy, or to wish you joy?" I began.

"None whatever!" she replied, with the joyous laugh of a child. "We give people what they haven't got: we wish for something that is yet to come. For me, it's all here! It's all mine! Dear friend," she suddenly broke off, "do you think Heaven ever begins on Earth, for any of us?"

"For some," I said. "For some, perhaps, who are simple and childlike. You know he said 'of such is the Kingdom of Heaven'."

Lady Muriel clasped her hands, and gazed up into the cloudless sky, with a look I had often seen in Sylvie's eyes. "I feel as if it had begun for me," she almost whispered. "I feel as if I were one of the happy children, whom He bid them bring near to Him, though the people would have kept them back. Yes, He has seen me in the throng. He has read the wistful longing in my eyes. He has beckoned me to Him. They have had to make way for me. He has taken me up in His arms. He has put His hands upon me and blessed me!" She paused, breathless in her perfect happiness.

"Yes," I said, "I think He has!"

"You must come and speak to my father,'" she went on, as we stood side by side at the gate, looking down the shady lane. But, even as she said the words, the "eerie" sensation came over me like a flood: I saw the dear old Professor approaching us, and also saw, what was stranger still, that he was visible to Lady Muriel!

What was to be done? Had the fairy-life been merged in the real life? Or was Lady Muriel "eerie" also, and thus able to enter into the fairy-world along with me? The words were on my lips (''I see an old friend of mine in the lane: if you don't know him, may I introduce him to you?'') when the strangest thing of all happened: Lady Muriel spoke:

"I see an old friend of mine in the lane," she said: "if you don't know him, may I introduce him to you?"

I seemed to wake out of a dream: for the "eerie" feeling was still strong upon me, and the figure outside seemed to be changing at every moment, like one of the shapes in a kaleidoscope: now he was the Professor, and now he was somebody else! By the time he had reached the gate, he certainly was somebody else: and I felt that the proper course was for Lady Muriel, not for me, to introduce him. She greeted him kindly, and, opening the gate, admitted the venerable old man—a German, obviously—who looked about him with dazed eyes, as if he, too, had but just awaked from a dream!

No, it was certainly not the Professor! My old friend could not have grown that magnificent beard since last we met: moreover, he would have recognised me, for I was certain that I had not changed much in the time.

As it was, he simply looked at me vaguely, and took off his hat in response to Lady Muriel's words "Let me introduce Mein Herr to you"; while in the words, spoken in a strong German accent, "proud to make your acquaintance, Sir!" I could detect no trace of an idea that we had ever met before.

Lady Muriel led us to the well-known shady nook where preparations for afternoon-tea had already been made, and, while she went in to look for the Earl, we seated ourselves in two easy-chairs, and "Mein Herr" took up Lady Muriel's work, and examined it through his large spectacles (one of the adjuncts that made him so provokingly like the Professor). "Hemming pocket-handkerchiefs?" he said, musingly. "So that is what the English miladies occupy themselves with, is it?"

"It is the one accomplishment", I said, "in which Man has never yet rivalled Woman!"

Here Lady Muriel returned with her father; and, after he had exchanged some friendly words with "Mein Herr", and we had all been supplied with the needful "creature-comforts", the newcomer returned to the suggestive subject of Pocket-handkerchiefs.

"You have heard of Fortunatus's Purse, Miladi? Ah, so! Would you be surprised to hear that, with three of these leetle handkerchiefs, you shall make the Purse of Fortunatus, quite soon, quite easily?"

"Shall I indeed?" Lady Muriel eagerly replied, as she took a heap of them into her lap, and threaded her needle. "Please tell me how, Mein Herr! I'll make one before I touch another drop of tea!"

"You shall first," said Mein Herr, possessing himself of two of the handkerchiefs, spreading one upon the other, and holding them up by two corners, "you shall first join together these upper corners, the right to the right, the left to the left; and the opening between them shall be the mouth of the Purse."

A very few stitches sufficed to carry out this direction. "Now, if I sew the other three edges together", she suggested, "the bag is complete?"

"Not so, Miladi: the lower edges shall first be joined— ah, not so!" (as she was beginning to sew them together). "Turn one of them over, and join the right lower corner of the one to the left lower corner of the other, and sew the lower edges together in what you would call the wrong way."

"I see!" said Lady Muriel, as she deftly executed the order. "And a very twisted, uncomfortable, uncanny-looking bag it makes! But the moral is a lovely one. Unlimited wealth can only be attained by doing things in the wrong way! And how are we to join up these mysterious—no, I mean this mysterious opening?" (twisting the thing round and round with a puzzled air). "Yes, it is one opening. I thought it was two, at first."

"You have seen the puzzle of the Paper Ring?" Mein Herr said, addressing the Earl. "Where you take a slip of paper, and join its ends together, first twisting one, so as to join the upper corner of one end to the lower corner of the other?"

"I saw one made, only yesterday," the Earl replied. "Muriel, my child, were you not making one, to amuse the children you had to tea?"

"Yes, I know that Puzzle," said Lady Muriel. "The Ring has only one surface, and only one edge, It's very mysterious!"

"The bag is just like that, isn't it?" I suggested. "Is not the outer surface of one side of it continuous with the inner surface of the other side?"

"So it is!" she exclaimed. "Only it isn't a bag, just yet. How shall we fill up this opening, Mein Herr?"

"Thus!" said the old man impressively, taking the bag from her, and rising to his feet in the excitement of the explanation. "The edge of the opening consists of four handkerchief edges, and you can trace it continuously, round and round the opening: down the right edge of one handkerchief, up the left edge of the other, and then down the left edge of the one, and up the right edge of the other!"

"So you can!" Lady Muriel murmured thoughtfully, leaning her head on her hand, and earnestly watching the old man. "And that proves it to be only one opening!"

She looked so strangely like a child, puzzling over a difficult lesson, and Mein Herr had become, for the moment, so strangely like the old Professor, that I felt utterly bewildered: the "eerie" feeling was on me in its full force, and I felt almost impelled to say "Do you understand it, Sylvie?" However I checked myself by a great effort, and let the dream (if indeed it was a dream) go on to its end.

"Now, this third handkerchief", Mein Herr proceeded "has also four edges, which you can trace continuously round and round: all you need do is to join its four edges to the four edges of the opening. The Purse is then complete, and its outer surface—"

"I see!" Lady Muriel eagerly interrupted. "Its outer surface will be continuous with its inner surface! But it will take time. I'll sew it up after tea." She laid aside the bag, and resumed her cup of tea. "But why do you call it Fortunatus's Purse, Mein Herr?"

The dear old man beamed upon her, with a jolly smile, looking more exactly like the Professor than ever. "Don't you see, my child—I should say Miladi? Whatever is inside that Purse, is outside it; and whatever is outside it, is inside it. So you have all the wealth of the world in that leetle Purse!"

His pupil clapped her hands, in unrestrained delight. "I'll certainly sew the third handkerchief in—some time," she said: "but I wo'n't take up your time by trying it now. Tell us some more wonderful things, please!" And her face and her voice so exactly recalled Sylvie, that I could not help glancing round, half-expecting to see Bruno also!

Mein Herr began thoughtfully balancing his spoon on the edge of his teacup, while he pondered over this request. "Something wonderful—like Fortunatus's Purse? That will give you—when it is made—wealth beyond your wildest dreams: but it will not give you Time!"

A pause of silence ensued—utilized by Lady Muriel for the very practical purpose of refilling the teacups.

"In your country", Mein Herr began with a startling abruptness, "what becomes of all the wasted Time?"

Lady Muriel looked grave. "Who can tell?" she half whispered to herself. "All one knows is that it is gone—past recall!"

"Well, in my—I mean in a country I have visited", said the old man, "they store it up: and it comes in very useful, years afterwards! For example, suppose you have a long tedious evening before you: nobody to talk to: nothing you care to do: and yet hours too soon to go to bed. How do you behave then?"

"I get very cross," she frankly admitted: "and I want to throw things about the room!"

"When that happens to—to the people I have visited, they never act so. By a short and simple process—which I cannot explain to you—they store up the useless hours: and, on some other occasion, when they happen to need extra time, they get them out again."

The Earl was listening with a slightly incredulous smile. "Why cannot you explain the process?" he enquired.

Mein Herr was ready with a quite unanswerable reason. "Because you have no words, in your language, to convey the ideas which are needed. I could explain it in—in— but you would not understand it!"

"No indeed!" said Lady Muriel, graciously dispensing with the name of the unknown language. "I never learnt it—at least, not to speak it fluently, you know. Please tell us some more wonderful things!"

"They run their railway-trains without any engines—nothing is needed but machinery to stop them with. Is that wonderful enough, Miladi?"

"But where does the force come from?" I ventured to ask.

Mein Herr turned quickly round, to look at the new speaker. Then he took off his spectacles, and polished, them, and looked at me again, in evident bewilderment. I could see he was thinking—as indeed I was also—that we must have met before.

"They use the force of gravity," he said. "It is a force known also in your country, I believe?"

"But that would need a railway going down-hill," the Earl remarked. "You ca'n't have all your railways going down-hill?"

"They all do", said Mein Herr.

"Not from both ends?"

"From both ends."

"Then I give it up!" said the Earl.

"Can you explain the process?" said Lady Muriel. "Without using that language, that I ca'n't speak fluently?"

"Easily," said Mein Herr. "Each railway is in a long tunnel, perfectly straight: so of course the middle of it is nearer the centre of the globe than the two ends: so every train runs half-way down-hill, and that gives it force enough to run the other half up-hill."

"Thank you. I understand that perfectly," said Lady Muriel. "But the velocity, in the middle of the tunnel, must be something fearful!"

Mein Herr was evidently much gratified at the intelligent interest Lady Muriel took in his remarks. At every moment the old man seemed to grow more chatty and more fluent. "You would like to know our methods of driving?" he smilingly enquired. "To us, a run-away horse is of no import at all!"

Lady Muriel slightly shuddered. "To us it is a very real danger," she said.

"That is because your carriage is wholly behind your horse. Your horse runs. Your carriage follows. Perhaps your horse has the bit in his teeth. Who shall stop him? You fly, ever faster and faster! Finally comes the inevitable upset!"

"But suppose your horse manages to get the bit in his teeth?"

"No matter! We would not concern ourselves. Our horse is harnessed in the very centre of our carriage. Two wheels are in front of him, and two behind. To the roof is attached one end of a broad belt. This goes under the horse's body, and the other end is attached to a leetle—what you call a 'windlass', I think. The horse takes the bit in his teeth. He runs away. We are flying at ten miles an hour! We turn our little windlass, five turns, six turns, seven turns, and—poof! Our horse is off the ground! Now let him gallop in the air as much as he pleases: our carriage stands still. We sit round him, and watch him till he is tired. Then we let him down. Our horse is glad, very much glad, when his feet once more touch the ground!"

"Capital!" said the Earl, who had been listening attentively. "Are there any other peculiarities in your carriages?"

"In the wheels, sometimes, my Lord. For your health, you go to sea: to be pitched, to be rolled, occasionally to be drowned. We do all that on land: we are pitched, as you; we are rolled, as you; but drowned, no! There is no water!"

"What are the wheels like, then?"

"They are oval, my Lord. Therefore the carriages rise and fall."

"Yes, and pitch the carriage backwards and forwards: but how do they make it roll?"

"They do not match, my Lord. The end of one wheel answers to the side of the opposite wheel. So first one side of the carriage rises, then the other. And it pitches all the while. Ah, you must be a good sailor, to drive in our boat-carriages!"

"I can easily believe it," said the Earl.

Mein Herr rose to his feet. "I must leave you now, Miladi," he said, consulting his watch. "I have another engagement."

"I only wish we had stored up some extra time!" Lady Muriel said, as she shook hands with him. "Then we could have kept you a little longer!"

"In that case I would gladly stay," replied Mein Herr. "As it is—I fear I must say goodbye!"

"Where did you first meet him?" I asked Lady Muriel, when Mein Herr had left us. "And where does he live? And what is his real name?"

"We first—met—him—" she musingly replied, "really, I ca'n't remember where! And I've no idea where he lives! And I never heard any other name! It's very curious. It never occurred to me before to consider what a mystery he is!"

"I hope we shall meet again," I said: "he interests me very much."

"He will be at our farewell-party, this day fortnight," said the Earl. "Of course you will come? Muriel is anxious to gather all our friends around us once more, before we leave the place."

And then he explained to me—as Lady Muriel had left us together— that he was so anxious to get his daughter away from a place full of so many painful memories connected with the now-cancelled engagement with Major Lindon, that they had arranged to have the wedding in a month's time, after which Arthur and his wife were to go on a foreign tour.

"Don't forget Tuesday week!" he said as we shook hands at parting. "I only wish you could bring with you those charming children, that you introduced to us in the summer. Talk of the mystery of Mein Herr! That's nothing to the mystery that seems to attend them! I shall never forget those marvellous flowers!"

"I will bring them if I possibly can," I said. But how to fulfil such a promise, I mused to myself on my way back to our lodgings, was a problem entirely beyond my skill!

IN A SHADY PLACE

The ten days glided swiftly away: and, the day before the great party was to take place, Arthur proposed that we should stroll down to the Hall, in time for afternoon-tea.

"Hadn't you better go alone?" I suggested. "Surely I shall be very much de trop?"

"Well, it'll be a kind of experiment," he said. "Fiat experimentum in corpore vili!" he added, with a graceful bow of mock politeness towards the unfortunate victim. "You see I shall have to bear the sight, to-morrow night, of my lady-love making herself agreeable to everybody except the right person, and I shall bear the agony all the better if we have a dress-rehearsal beforehand!"

"My part in the play being, apparently, that of the sample wrong person?"

"Well, no," Arthur said musingly, as we set forth: "there's no such part in a regular company. 'Heavy Father'? That wo'n't do: that's filled already. 'Singing Chambermaid'? Well, the 'First Lady' doubles that part. 'Comic Old Man'? You're not comic enough. After all, I'm afraid there's no part for you but the 'Well-dressed Villain': only", with a critical side-glance, "I'm a leetle uncertain about the dress!"

We found Lady Muriel alone, the Earl having gone out to make a call, and at once resumed old terms of intimacy, in the shady arbour where the tea-things seemed to be always waiting. The only novelty in the arrangements (one which Lady Muriel seemed to regard as entirely a matter of course), was that two of the chairs were placed quite close together, side by side. Strange to say, I was not invited to occupy either of them!

"We have been arranging, as we came along, about letter-writing," Arthur began. "He will want to know how we're enjoying our Swiss tour: and of course we must pretend we are?"

"Of course," she meekly assented.

"And the skeleton-in-the-cupboard—" I suggested.

"—is always a difficulty", she quickly put in, "when you're travelling about, and when there are no cupboards in the hotels. However, ours is a very portable one; and will be neatly packed, in a nice leather case—"

"But please don't think about writing", I said, "when you've anything more attractive on hand. I delight in reading letters, but I know well how tiring it is to write them.

"It is, sometimes," Arthur assented. "For instance when you're very shy of the person you have to write to."

"Does that show itself in the letter?" Lady Muriel enquired. "Of course, when I hear any one talking—you, for instance—I can see how desperately shy he is! But can you see that in a letter?"

"Well, of course, when you hear any one talk fluently—you, for instance—you can see how desperately un-shy she is—not to say saucy! But the shyest and most intermittent talker must seem fluent in letter-writing. He may have taken half-an-hour to compose his second sentence but there it is, close after the first!"

"Then letters don't express all that they might express?"

"That's merely because our system of letter-writing is incomplete. A shy writer ought to be able to show that he is so. Why shouldn't he make pauses in writing, just as he would do in speaking? He might leave blank spaces—say half a page at a time. And a very shy girl—if there is such a thing—might write a sentence on the first sheet of her letter—then put in a couple of blank sheets—then a sentence on the fourth sheet: and so on."

"I quite foresee that we—I mean this clever little boy and myself—" Lady Muriel said to me, evidently with the kind wish to bring me into the conversation, "—are going to become famous—of course all our inventions are common property now—for a new Code of Rules for Letterwriting! Please invent some more, little boys"

"Well, another thing greatly needed, little girl, is some way of expressing that we don't mean anything."

"Explain yourself, little boy! Surely you can find no difficulty in expressing a total absence of meaning?"

I mean that you should be able, when you don't mean a thing to be taken seriously, to express that wish. For human nature is so constituted that whatever you write seriously is taken as a joke, and whatever you mean as a joke is taken seriously! At any rate, it is so in writing to a lady!"

"Ah, you're not used to writing to ladies!" Lady Muriel remarked, leaning back in her chair, and gazing thoughtfully into the sky. "You should try."

"Very good," said Arthur. "How many ladies may I begin writing to? As many as I can count on the fingers of both hands?"

"As many as you can count on the thumbs of one hand!" his lady-love replied with much severity. "What a very naughty little boy he is! Isn't he?" (with an appealing glance at me).

"He's a little fractious," I said. "Perhaps he's cutting a tooth." While to myself I said "How exactly like Sylvie talking to Bruno!"

"He wants his tea." (The naughty little boy volunteered the information.) "He's getting very tired, at the mere prospect of the great party to-morrow!"

"Then he shall have a good rest before-hand!" she soothingly replied. "The tea isn't made yet. Come, little boy, lean well back in your chair, and think about nothing—or about me, whichever you prefer!"

"All the same, all the same!" Arthur sleepily murmured, watching her with loving eyes, as she moved her chair away to the tea table, and began to make the tea. "Then he'll wait for his tea, like a good, patient little boy!"

"Shall I bring you the London Papers?" said Lady Muriel. "I saw them lying on the table as I came out, but my father said there was nothing in them, except that horrid murder-trial." (Society was just then enjoying its daily thrill of excitement in studying the details of a specially sensational murder in a thieve's den in the East of London.)

"I have no appetite for horrors," Arthur replied. "But hope we have learned the lesson they should teach us—though we are very apt to read it backwards!"

"You speak in riddles," said Lady Muriel. "Please explain yourself. See now," suiting the action to the word, "I am sitting at your feet, just as if you were a second Gamaliel! Thanks, no." (This was to me, who had risen to bring her chair back to its former place.) "Pray don't disturb yourself. This tree and the grass make a very nice easy-chair. What is the lesson that one always reads wrong?"

Arthur was silent for a minute. "I would like to be clear what it is I mean," he said, slowly and thoughtfully, "before I say anything to you— because you think about it."

Anything approaching to a compliment was so unusual an utterance for Arthur, that it brought a flush of pleasure to her cheek, as she replied "It is you, that give me the ideas to think about."

"One's first thought", Arthur proceeded, "in reading anything specially vile or barbarous, as done by a fellow-creature, is apt to be that we see a new depth of Sin revealed beneath us: and we seem to gaze down into that abyss from some higher ground, far apart from it."

"I think I understand you now. You mean that one ought to think—not 'God, I thank Thee that I am not as other men are'—but 'God, be merciful to me also, who might be, but for Thy grace, a sinner as vile as he!'"

"No," said Arthur. "I meant a great deal more than that."

She looked up quickly, but checked herself, and waited in silence.

"One must begin further back, I think. Think of some other man, the same age as this poor wretch. Look back to the time when they both began life—before they had sense enough to know Right from Wrong. Then, at any rate, they were equal in God's sight—"

She nodded assent.

"We have, then, two distinct epochs at which we may contemplate the two men whose lives we are comparing. At the first epoch they are, so far as moral responsibility is concerned, on precisely the same footing: they are alike incapable of doing right or wrong. At the second epoch the one man—I am taking an extreme case, for contrast —has won the esteem and love of all around him: his character is stainless, and his name will be held in honour hereafter: the other man's history is one unvaried record of crime, and his life is at last forfeited to the outraged laws of his country. Now what have been the causes, in each case, of each man's condition being what it is at the second epoch? They are of two kinds—one acting from within, the other from without. These two kinds need to be discussed separately—that is, if I have not already tired you with my prosing?"

"On the contrary," said Lady Muriel, "it is a special delight to me to have a question discussed in this way— analysed and arranged so that one can understand it. Some books, that profess to argue out a question, are to me intolerably wearisome, simply because the ideas are all arranged haphazard—a sort of 'first come, first served'."

"You are very encouraging," Arthur replied, with a pleased look. "The causes, acting from within, which make a man's character what it is at any given moment, are his successive acts of volition—that is, his acts of choosing whether he will do this or that."

"We are to assume the existence of Free-Will?" I said, in order to have that point made quite clear.

"If not," was the quiet reply, "cadit quaestio: and I have no more to say."

"We will assume it!" the rest of the audience—the majority, I may say, looking at it from Arthur's point of view—imperiously proclaimed. The orator proceeded.

"The causes, acting from without, are his surroundings—what Mr. Herbert Spencer calls his 'environment'. Now the point I want to make clear is this, that a man is responsible for his act of choosing, but not responsible for his environment. Hence, if these two men make, on some given occasion, when they are exposed to equal temptation, equal efforts to resist and to choose the right, their condition, in the sight of God, must be the same. If He is pleased in the one case, so will He be in the other, if displeased in the one case, so also in the other."

"That is so, no doubt: I see it quite clearly," Lady Muriel put in.

"And yet, owing to their different environments, the one may win a great victory over the temptation, while the other falls into some black abyss of crime."

"But surely you would not say those men were equally guilty in the sight of God?"

"Either that", said Arthur, "or else I must give up my belief in God's perfect justice. But let me put one more case, which will show my meaning even more forcibly. Let the one man be in a high social position—the other say, a common thief. Let the one be tempted to some trivial act of unfair dealing—something which he can do with the absolute certainty that it will never be discovered—something which he can with perfect ease forbear from doing—and which he distinctly knows to be a sin. Let the other be tempted to some terrible crime—as men would consider it—but, under an almost overwhelming pressure of motives—of course not quite overwhelming, as that would destroy all responsibility. Now, in this case, let the second man make a greater effort at resistance than the first. Also suppose both to fall under the temptation—I say that the second man is, in God's sight, less guilty than the other."

Lady Muriel drew a long breath. "It upsets all one's ideas of Right and Wrong—just at first! Why, in that dreadful murder-trial, you would say, I suppose, that it was possible that the least guilty man in the Court was the murderer, and that possibly the judge who tried him, by yielding to the temptation of making one unfair remark, had committed a crime outweighing the criminal's whole career!"

"Certainly I should," Arthur firmly replied. "It sounds like a paradox, I admit. But just think what a grievous sin it must be, in God's sight, to yield to some very slight temptation, which we could have resisted with perfect ease, and to do it deliberately, and in the full light of God's Law. What penance can atone for a sin like that?"

"I ca'n't reject your theory," I said. "But how it seems to widen the possible area of Sin in the world!"

"Is that so?" Lady Muriel anxiously enquired.

"Oh, not so, not so!" was the eager reply. "To me it seems to clear away much of the cloud that hangs over the world's history. When this view first made itself clear to me, I remember walking out into the fields, repeating to myself that line of Tennyson 'There seemed no room for sense of wrong!' The thought, that perhaps the real guilt of the human race was infinitely less than I fancied it— that the millions, whom I had thought of as sunk in hopeless depths of sin, were perhaps, in God's sight, scarcely sinning at all—was more sweet than words can tell! Life seemed more bright and beautiful, when once that thought had come! 'A livelier emerald twinkles in the grass, A purer sapphire melts into the sea!'" His voice trembled as he concluded, and the tears stood in his eyes.

Lady Muriel shaded her face with her hand, and was silent for a minute. "It is a beautiful thought," she said, looking up at last. "Thank you— Arthur, for putting it into my head!"

The Earl returned in time to join us at tea, and to give us the very unwelcome tidings that a fever had broken out in the little harbour-town that lay below us—a fever of so malignant a type that, though it had only appeared a day or two ago, there were already more than a dozen down in it, two or three of whom were reported to be in imminent danger.

In answer to the eager questions of Arthur—who of course took a deep scientific interest in the matter—he could give very few technical details, though he had met the local doctor. It appeared, however, that it was an almost new disease—at least in this century, though it might prove to be identical with the "Plague" recorded in History—very infectious, and frightfully rapid in its action. "It will not, however, prevent our party tomorrow," he said in conclusion. "None of the guests belong to the infected district, which is, as you know, exclusively peopled by fishermen: so you may come with out any fear."

Arthur was very silent, all the way back, and, on reaching our lodgings, immediately plunged into medical studies, connected with the alarming malady of whose arrival he had just heard.

THE FAREWELL-PARTY

On the following day, Arthur and I reached the Hall in good time, as only a few of the guests—it was to be a party of eighteen—had as yet arrived; and these were talking with the Earl, leaving us the opportunity of a few words apart with our hostess.

"Who is that very learned-looking man with the large spectacles?" Arthur enquired. "I haven't met him here before, have I?"

"No, he's a new friend of ours," said Lady Muriel: "a German, I believe. He is such a dear old thing! And quite the most learned man I ever met—with one exception, of course!" she added humbly, as Arthur drew himself up with an air of offended dignity.

"And the young lady in blue, just beyond him, talking to that foreign-looking man. Is she learned, too?"

"I don't know," said Lady Muriel. "But I'm told she's a wonderful piano-forte-player. I hope you'll hear her tonight. I asked that foreigner to take her in, because he's very musical, too. He's a French Count, I believe; and he sings splendidly!"

"Science—music—singing—you have indeed got a complete party!" said Arthur. "I feel quite a privileged person, meeting all these stars. I do love music!"

"But the party isn't quite complete!" said Lady Muriel. "You haven't brought us those two beautiful children," she went on, turning to me. "He brought them here to tea, you know, one day last summer," again addressing Arthur: "and they are such darlings!"

"They are, indeed," I assented.

"But why haven't you brought them with you? You promised my father you would."

"I'm very sorry," I said; "but really it was impossible to bring them with me." Here I most certainly meant to conclude the sentence: and it was with a feeling of utter amazement, which I cannot adequately describe, that I heard myself going on speaking. "—but they are to join me here in the course of the evening" were the words, uttered in my voice, and seeming to come from my lips.

"I'm so glad!" Lady Muriel joyfully replied. "I shall enjoy introducing them to some of my friends here! When do you expect them?"

I took refuge in silence. The only honest reply would rave been "That was not my remark. I didn't say it, and it isn't true!" But I had not the moral courage to make such a confession. The character of a "lunatic" is not, I believe, very difficult to acquire: but it is amazingly difficult to get rid of:

and it seemed quite certain that any such speech as that would quite justify the issue of a writ "de lunatico inquirendo".

Lady Muriel evidently thought I had failed to hear her question, and turned to Arthur with a remark on some other subject; and I had time to recover from my shock of surprise—or to awake out of my momentary "eerie" condition, whichever it was.

When things around me seemed once more to be real, Arthur was saying "I'm afraid there's no help for it: they must be finite in number."

"I should be sorry to have to believe it," said Lady Muriel. "Yet, when one comes to think of it, there are no new melodies, now-a-days. What people talk of as 'the last new song' always recalls to me some tune I've known as a child!"

"The day must come—if the world lasts long enough—" said Arthur, "when every possible tune will have been composed every possible pun perpetrated—" (Lady Muriel wrung her hands, like a tragedy-queen) "and worse than that, every possible book written! For the number of words is finite."

"It'll make very little difference to the authors," I suggested. "Instead of saying 'what book shall I write?' an author will ask himself 'which book shall I write?' A mere verbal distinction!"

Lady Muriel gave me an approving smile. "But lunatics would always write new books, surely?" she went on. They couldn't write the sane books over again!"

"True," said Arthur. "But their books would come to an end, also. The number of lunatic books is as finite as the number of lunatics."

"And that number is becoming greater every year," said a pompous man, whom I recognized as the self-appointed showman on the day of the picnic.

"So they say," replied Arthur. "And, when ninety per cent of us are lunatics," (he seemed to be in a wildly nonsensical mood) "the asylums will be put to their proper use."

"And that is?" the pompous man gravely enquired.

"To shelter the sane!" said Arthur. "We shall bar ourselves in. The lunatics will have it all their own way, outside. They'll do it a little queerly, no doubt. Railway-collisions will be always happening: steamers always blowing up: most of the towns will be burnt down: most of the ships sunk—"

"And most of the men killed!" murmured the pompous man, who was evidently hopelessly bewildered.

Certainly," Arthur assented. "Till at last there will be fewer lunatics than sane men. Then we come out: they go in: and things return to their normal condition!"

The pompous man frowned darkly, and bit his lip, and folded his arms, vainly trying to think it out. "He is jesting!" he muttered to himself at last, in a tone of withering contempt, as he stalked away.

By this time the other guests had arrived; and dinner was announced. Arthur of course took down Lady Muriel: and I was pleased to find myself seated at her other side, with a severe-looking old lady (whom I had not met before, and whose name I had, as is usual in introductions, entirely failed to catch, merely gathering that it sounded like a compound-name) as my partner for the banquet.

She appeared, however, to be acquainted with Arthur, and confided to me in a low voice her opinion that he was "a very argumentative young man". Arthur, for his part, seemed well inclined to show himself worthy of the character she had given him, and, hearing her say "I never take wine with my soup!" (this was not a confidence to me, but was launched upon Society, as a matter of general interest), he at once challenged a combat by asking her "when would you say that property commence in a plate of soup?"

"This is my soup," she sternly replied: "and what is before you is yours."

"No doubt," said Arthur: "but when did I begin to own it? Up to the moment of its being put into the plate, it was the property of our host: while being offered round the table, it was, let us say, held in trust by the waiter: did it become mine when I accepted it? Or when it was placed before me? Or when I took the first spoonful?"

"He is a very argumentative young man!" was all the old lady would say: but she said it audibly, this time, feeling that Society had a right to know it.

Arthur smiled mischievously. "I shouldn't mind betting you a shilling", he said, "that the Eminent Barrister next you" (It certainly is possible to say words so as to make them begin with capitals!) "ca'n't answer me!"

"I never bet," she sternly replied.

"Not even sixpenny points at whist?"

"Never!" she repeated. "Whist is innocent enough: but whist played for money!" She shuddered.

Arthur became serious again. "I'm afraid I ca'n't take that view," he said. "I consider that the introduction of small stakes for card-playing was one of the most moral acts Society ever did, as Society."

"How was it so?" said Lady Muriel.

"Because it took Cards, once for all, out of the category of games at which cheating is possible. Look at the way Croquet is demoralizing Society. Ladies are beginning to cheat at it, terribly: and, if they're found out, they only, laugh, and call it fun. But when there's money at stake that is out of the question. The swindler is not accepted as a wit. When a man sits down to cards, and cheats his friends out of their money, he doesn't get much fun out of it—unless he thinks it fun to be kicked down stairs!"

"If all gentlemen thought as badly of ladies as you do," my neighbour remarked with some bitterness, "there would be very few—very few—". She seemed doubtful how to end her sentence, but at last took "honeymoons" as a safe word.

"On the contrary," said Arthur, the mischievous smile returning to his face, "if only people would adopt my theory, the number of honeymoons— quite of a new kind —would be greatly increased!"

"May we hear about this new kind of honeymoon?" said Lady Muriel.

"Let X be the gentleman," Arthur began, in a slightly raised voice, as he now found himself with an audience of six, including "Mein Herr", who was seated at the other side of my polynomial partner. "Let X be the gentleman, and Y the lady to whom he thinks of proposing. He applies for an Experimental Honeymoon. It is granted. Forthwith the young couple accompanied by the great-aunt of Y, to act as chaperone—start for a month's tour, during which they have many a moonlight-walk, and many a tête-á-tête conversation, and each can form a more correct estimate of the other's character, in four weeks, than would have been possible in as many years, when meeting under the ordinary restrictions of Society. And it is only after their return that X finally decides whether he will, or will not, put the momentous question to Y!"

"In nine cases out of ten", the pompous man proclaimed, "he would decide to break it off!"

"Then in nine cases out of ten," Arthur rejoined, "an unsuitable match would be prevented, and both parties saved from misery!"

"The only really unsuitable matches", the old lady remarked, "are those made without sufficient Money. Love may come afterwards. Money is needed to begin with!"

This remark was cast loose upon Society, as a sort of general challenge; and, as such, it was at once accepted by several of those within hearing: Money became the keynote of the conversation for some time: and a fitful echo of it was again heard, when the dessert had been placed upon the table, the servants had left the room, and the Earl had started the wine in its welcome progress round the table.

"I'm very glad to see you keep up the old customs," I said to Lady Muriel as I filled her glass. "It's really delightful to experience, once more, the peaceful feeling that comes over one when the waiters have left the room—when one can converse without the feeling of being overheard, and without having dishes constantly thrust over one's shoulder. How much more sociable it is to be able to pour out the wine for the ladies, and to hand the dishes to those who wish for them!"

"In that case, kindly send those peaches down here," said a fat red-faced man, who was seated beyond our pompous friend. "I've been wishing for them—diagonally—for some time!"

"Yes, it is a ghastly innovation", Lady Muriel replied, "letting the waiters carry round the wine at dessert. For one thing, they always take it the wrong way round—which of course brings bad luck to everybody present!"

"Better go the wrong way than not go at all!" said our host. "Would you kindly help yourself?" (This was to the fat red-faced man.) "You are not a teetotaler, I think?"

"Indeed but I am!" he replied, as he pushed on the bottles. "Nearly twice as much money is spent in England on Drink, as on any other article of food. Read this card." (What faddist ever goes about without a pocketful of the appropriate literature?) "The stripes of different colours represent the amounts spent of various articles of food. Look at the highest three. Money spent on butter and on cheese, thirty-five millions: on bread, seventy millions: on intoxicating liquors, one hundred and thirty-six millions! If I had my way, I would close every public-house in the land! Look at that card, and read the motto. That's where all the money goes to!"

"Have you seen the Anti-Teetotal Card?" Arthur innocently enquired.

"No, Sir, I have not!" the orator savagely replied. "What is it like?"

"Almost exactly like this one. The coloured stripes are the same. Only, instead of the words 'Money spent on', it has 'Incomes derived from sale of'; and, instead of 'That's where all the money goes to', its motto is 'That's where all the money comes from!'"

The red-faced man scowled, but evidently considered Arthur beneath his notice. So Lady Muriel took up the cudgels. "Do you hold the theory", she enquired, "that people can preach teetotalism more effectually by being teetotalers themselves?"

"Certainly I do!" replied the red-faced man. "Now, here is a case in point," unfolding a newspaper-cutting: "let me read you this letter from a teetotaler. To the Editor. Sir, I was once a moderate drinker, and knew a man who drank to excess. I went to him. 'Give up this drink,' I said. 'It will ruin your health!' 'You drink,' he said: 'why shouldn't I?' 'Yes,' I said, 'but I know when to leave off.' He turned away from me. 'You drink in your way,' he said: 'let me drink in mine. Be off!' Then I saw that, to do any good with him, I must forswear drink. From that hour I haven't touched a drop!"

"There! What do you say to that?" He looked round triumphantly, while the cutting was handed round for inspection.

"How very curious!" exclaimed Arthur when it had reached him. "Did you happen to see a letter, last week, about early rising? It was strangely like this one."

The red-faced man's curiosity was roused. "Where did it appear?" he asked.

"Let me read it to you," said Arthur. He took some papers from his pocket, opened one of them, and read as follows. To the Editor. Sir, I was once a moderate sleeper, and knew a man who slept to excess. I pleaded with him. Give up this lying in bed,' I said. 'It will ruin your health!' You go to bed,' he said: 'why shouldn't I?' 'Yes,' I said, but I know when to get up in the morning.' He turned away from me. 'You sleep in your way,' he said: 'let me sleep in mine. Be off!' Then I saw that to do any good with him, I must forswear sleep. From that hour I haven't been to bed!"

Arthur folded and pocketed his paper, and passed on the newspaper-cutting. None of us dared to laugh, the red-faced man was evidently so angry. "Your parallel doesn't run on all fours!" he snarled.

"Moderate drinkers never do so!" Arthur quietly replied. Even the stern old lady laughed at this.

"But it needs many other things to make a perfect dinner!" said Lady Muriel, evidently anxious to change the subject. "Mein Herr! What is your idea of a perfect dinner party?"

The old man looked around smilingly, and his gigantic spectacles seemed more gigantic than ever. "A perfect dinner-party?" he repeated. "First, it must be presided over by our present hostess!"

"That of course!" she gaily interposed. "But what else, Mein Herr?"

"I can but tell you what I have seen," said Mein Herr, in mine own—in the country I have traveled in."

He paused for a full minute, and gazed steadily at the ceiling—with so dreamy an expression on his face, that I feared he was going off into a reverie, which seemed to be his normal state. However, after a minute, he suddenly began again.

"That which chiefly causes the failure of a dinner-party is the running-short—not of meat, nor yet of drink, but of conversation."

"In an English dinner-party", I remarked, "I have never known small-talk run short!"

"Pardon me," Mein Herr respectfully replied, "I did not say 'small-talk'. I said 'conversation'. All such topics as the weather, or politics, or local gossip, are unknown among us. They are either vapid or controversial. What we need for conversation is a topic of interest and of novelty. To secure these things we have tried various plans—Moving-Pictures, Wild-Creatures, Moving-Guests, and a Revolving-Humorist. But this last is only adapted to small parties."

"Let us have it in four separate Chapters, please!" said Lady Muriel, who was evidently deeply interested—as indeed, most of the party were, by this time: and, all down the table, talk had ceased, and heads were leaning forwards, eager to catch fragments of Mein Herr's oration.

"Chapter One! Moving-Pictures!" was proclaimed in the silvery voice of our hostess.

"The dining-table is shaped like a circular ring," Mein Herr began, in low dreamy tones, which, however, were perfectly audible in the silence. "The guests are seated at the inner side as well as the outer, having ascended to their places by a winding-staircase, from the room below. Along the middle of the table runs a little railway; and there is an endless train of trucks, worked round by machinery; and on each truck there are two pictures, leaning back to back. The train makes two circuits during dinner; and, when it has been once round, the waiters turn the pictures round in each truck, making em face the other way. Thus every guest sees every picture!"

He paused, and the silence seemed deader than ever. Lady Muriel looked aghast. "Really, if this goes on," she exclaimed, "I shall have to drop a pin! Oh, it's my fault, is it?" (In answer to an appealing look from Mein Herr.) "I was forgetting my duty. Chapter Two! Wild-Creatures!"

"We found the Moving-Pictures a little monotonous," said Mein Herr. "People didn't care to talk Art through a whole dinner; so we tried Wild-Creatures. Among the flowers, which we laid (just as you do) about the table, were to be seen, here a mouse, there a beetle; here a spider" (Lady Muriel shuddered), "there a wasp; here a toad, there a snake"; ("Father!" said Lady Muriel, plaintively. "Did you hear that?"); "so we had plenty to talk about!"

"And when you got stung—" the old lady began. "They were all chained-up, dear Madam!"

And the old lady gave a satisfied nod.

There was no silence to follow, this time. "Third Chapter!" Lady Muriel proclaimed at once. "Moving-Guests!"

"Even the Wild-Creatures proved monotonous," the orator proceeded. "So we left the guests to choose their own subjects; and, to avoid monotony, we changed them. we made the table of two rings; and the inner ring moved slowly round, all the time, along with the floor in the middle and the inner row of guests. Thus every dinner guest was brought face-to-face with every outer guest. It was a little confusing, sometimes, to have to begin a story to one friend and finish it to another; but every plan has its faults, you know."

"Fourth Chapter!" Lady Muriel hastened to announce. "The Revolving-Humorist!"

"For a small party we found it an excellent plan to have a round table, with a hole cut in the middle large enough to hold one guest. Here we placed our best talker. He revolved slowly, facing every other guest in turn: and he told lively anecdotes the whole time!"

"I shouldn't like it!" murmured the pompous man. "It would make me giddy, revolving like that! I should decline to—" here it appeared to dawn upon him that perhaps the assumption he was making was not warranted by the circumstances: he took a hasty gulp of wine, and choked himself.

But Mein Herr had relapsed into reverie, and made no further remark. Lady Muriel gave the signal, and the ladies left the room.

JABBERING AND JAM

When the last lady had disappeared, and the Earl taking his place at the head of the table, had issued the military order "Gentlemen! Close up the ranks, if you please!" and when, in obedience to his command, we had gathered ourselves compactly round him, the pompous man gave a deep sigh of relief, filled his glass to the brim, pushed on the wine, and began one of his favourite orations. "They are charming, no doubt! Charming, but very frivolous. They drag us down, so to speak, to a lower level. They—"

"Do not all pronouns require antecedent nouns?" the Earl gently enquired.

"Pardon me," said the pompous man, with lofty condescension. "I had overlooked the noun. The ladies. We regret their absence. Yet we console ourselves. Thought is free. With them, we are limited to trivial topics—Art Literature, Politics, and so forth. One can bear to discuss such paltry matters with a lady. But no man, in his senses —" (he looked sternly round the table, as if defying contradiction) "—ever yet discussed WINE with a lady!" He sipped his glass of port, leaned back in his chair, and slowly raised it up to his eye, so as to look through it at the lamp. "The vintage, my Lord?" he enquired, glancing at his host.

The Earl named the date.

"So I had supposed. But one likes to be certain. The tint is, perhaps, slightly pale. But the body is unquestionable. And as for the bouquet—"

Ah, that magic Bouquet! How vividly that magic word recalled the scene! The little beggar boy turning his somersault in the road—the sweet little crippled maiden in my arms—the mysterious evanescent nursemaid—all rushed tumultuously into my mind, like the creatures of a dream: and through this mental haze there still boomed on, like the tolling of a bell, the solemn voice of the great connoisseur of WINE!

Even his utterances had taken on themselves a strange and dream-like form. "No," he resumed—and why is it, I pause to ask, that, in taking up the broken thread of a dialogue, one always begins with this cheerless monosyllable? After much anxious thought, I have come to the conclusion that the object in view is the same as that of the schoolboy, when the sum he is working has got into a hopeless muddle, and when in despair he takes the sponge, washes it all out, and begins again. Just in the same way the bewildered orator, by the simple process of denying everything that has been hitherto asserted, makes a clean sweep of the whole discussion, and can "start fair" with a fresh theory. "No," he resumed: "there's nothing like cherry-jam, after all. That's what I say!"

"Not for all qualities!" an eager little man shrilly interposed. "For richness of general tone I don't say that it has a rival. But for delicacy of modulation—for what one may call the 'harmonics' of flavour—give me good old raspberry-jam—"

"Allow me one word!" The fat red-faced man, quite hoarse with excitement, broke into the dialogue. "It's too important a question to be settled by Amateurs! I can give you the views of a Professional—perhaps the most experienced jam-taster now living. Why, I've known him fix the age of strawberry-jam, to a day—and we all know what a difficult jam it is to give a date to—on a single tasting! Well, I put to him the very question you are discussing. His words were 'cherry-jam is best, for mere chiaroscuro of flavour: raspberry-jam lends itself best to those resolved discords that linger so lovingly on the tongue: but, for rapturous bitterness of saccharine perfection, it's apricot-jam first and the rest nowhere!' That was well put, wasn't it?"

"Consummately put!" shrieked the eager little man.

"I know your friend well," said the pompous man. "As a jam-taster, he has no rival! Yet I scarcely think—"

But here the discussion became general: and his words were lost in a confused medley of names, every guest sounding the praises of his own favourite jam. At length, through the din, our host's voice made itself heard. "Let us join the ladies!" These words seemed to recall me to waking life; and I felt sure that, for the last few minutes, I had relapsed into the "eerie" state.

"A strange dream!" I said to myself as we trooped upstairs. "Grown men discussing, as seriously as if they were matters of life and death, the hopelessly trivial details of mere delicacies, that appeal to no higher human function than the nerves of the tongue and palate! What a humiliating spectacle such a discussion would be in waking life!"

When, on our way to the drawing-room, I received from the housekeeper my little friends, clad in the daintiest of evening costumes, and looking, in the flush of expectant delight, more radiantly beautiful than I had ever seen them before. I felt no shock of surprise, but accepted the fact with the same unreasoning apathy with which one meets the events of a dream, and was merely conscious of a vague anxiety as to how they would acquit themselves in so novel a scene—forgetting that Court-life in Outland was as good training as they could need for Society in the more substantial world.

It would be best, I thought, to introduce them as soon as possible to some good-natured lady-guest, and I selected the young lady whose piano-forte-playing had been so much talked of. "I am sure you like children," I said. "May I introduce two little friends of mine? This is Sylvie—and this is Bruno."

The young lady kissed Sylvie very graciously. She would have done the same for Bruno, but he hastily drew back out of reach. "Their faces are new to me," she said. "Where do you come from, my dear?"

I had not anticipated so inconvenient a question; and, fearing that it might embarrass Sylvie, I answered for her. "They come from some distance. They are only here just for this one evening."

"How far have you come, dear?" the young lady persisted.

Sylvie looked puzzled. "A mile or two, I think," she said doubtfully.

"A mile or three," said Bruno.

"You shouldn't say 'a mile or three'," Sylvie corrected him.

The young lady nodded approval. "Sylvie's quite right. It isn't usual to say 'a mile or three'."

"It would be usual—if we said it often enough," said Bruno.

It was the young lady's turn to look puzzled now. "He's very quick, for his age!" she murmured. "You're not more than seven, are you, dear?" she added aloud.

"I'm not so many as that," said Bruno. "I'm one. Sylvie's one. Sylvie and me is two. Sylvie taught me to count."

"Oh, I wasn't counting you, you know!" the young lady laughingly replied.

"Hasn't oo learnt to count?" said Bruno.

The young lady bit her lip. "Dear! What embarrassing questions he does ask!" she said in a half-audible "aside".

"Bruno, you shouldn't!" Sylvie said reprovingly.

"Shouldn't what?" said Bruno.

"You shouldn't ask—that sort of questions."

"What sort of questions?" Bruno mischievously persisted.

"What she told you not," Sylvie replied, with a shy glance at the young lady, and losing all sense of grammar in her confusion.

"Oo ca'n't pronounce it!" Bruno triumphantly cried. And he turned to the young lady, for sympathy in his victory. "I knewed she couldn't pronounce 'umbrellasting'!"

The young lady thought it best to return to the arithmetical problem. "When I asked if you were seven, you know, I didn't mean 'how many children?' I meant 'how many years —'"

"Only got two ears," said Bruno. "Nobody's got seven ears."

"And you belong to this little girl?" the young lady continued, skilfully evading the anatomical problem.

"No I doosn't belong to her!" said Bruno. "Sylvie belongs to me!" And he clasped his arms round her as he added "She are my very mine!"

"And, do you know," said the young lady, "I've a little sister at home, exactly like your sister? I'm sure they'd love each other."

"They'd be very extremely useful to each other," Bruno said, thoughtfully. "And they wouldn't want no looking-glasses to brush their hair wiz."

"Why not, my child?"

"Why, each one would do for the other one's looking-glass a-course!" cried Bruno.

But here Lady Muriel, who had been standing by, listening to this bewildering dialogue, interrupted it to ask if the young lady would favour us with some music; and the children followed their new friend to the piano.

Arthur came and sat down by me. "If rumour speaks truly," he whispered, "we are to have a real treat!" And then, amid a breathless silence, the performance began.

She was one of those players whom Society talks of as "brilliant", and she dashed into the loveliest of Haydn's Symphonies in a style that was clearly the outcome of years of patient study under the best masters. At first it seemed to be the perfection of piano-forte-playing; but in a few minutes I began to ask myself, wearily, "What is it that is wanting? Why does one get no pleasure from it?"

Then I set myself to listen intently to every note; and the mystery explained itself. There was an almost perfect mechanical correctness—and there was nothing else! False notes, of course, did not occur: she knew the piece too well for that; but there was just enough irregularity of time to betray that the player had no real "ear" for music—just enough inarticulateness in the more elaborate passages to show that she did not think her audience worth taking real pains for—just enough mechanical monotony of accent to take all soul out of the heavenly modulations she was profaning—in short, it was simply irritating; and, when she had rattled off the finale and had struck the final chord as if, the instrument being now done with, it didn't matter how many wires she broke, I could not even affect to join in the stereotyped "Oh, thank you!" which was chorused around me.

Lady Muriel joined us for a moment. "Isn't it beautiful?" she whispered to Arthur, with a mischievous smile.

"No, it isn't!" said Arthur. But the gentle sweetness of his face quite neutralized the apparent rudeness of the reply.

"Such execution, you know!" she persisted.

"That's what she deserves," Arthur doggedly replied: "but people are so prejudiced against capital—"

"Now you're beginning to talk nonsense!" Lady Muriel cried. "But you do like Music, don't you? You said so just now."

"Do I like Music?" the Doctor repeated softly to himself. "My dear Lady Muriel, there is Music and Music. Your question is painfully vague. You might as well ask 'Do you like People?' "

Lady Muriel bit her lip, frowned, and stamped with one tiny foot. As a dramatic, representation of ill-temper, it was distinctly not a success. However, it took in one of her audience, and Bruno hastened to interpose, as peacemaker in a rising quarrel, with the remark "I likes Peoples!"

Arthur laid a loving hand on the little curly head. "What? All Peoples?" he enquired.

"Not all Peoples," Bruno explained. "Only but Sylvie—and Lady Muriel—and him—" (pointing to the Earl) 'and oo—and oo!"

"You shouldn't point at people," said Sylvie. "It's very rude."

"In Bruno's World," I said, "there are only four People—worth mentioning!"

"In Bruno's World!" Lady Muriel repeated thoughtfully. "A bright and flowery world. Where the grass is always green, where the breezes always blow softly, and the rain-clouds never gather; where there are no wild beasts, and no deserts—"

"There must be deserts," Arthur decisively remarked. "At least if it was my ideal world."

"But what possible use is there in a desert?" said Lady Muriel. "Surely you would have no wilderness in your ideal world?"

Arthur smiled. "But indeed I would!" he said. "A wilderness would be more necessary than a railway; and far more conducive to general happiness than church-bells!"

"But what would you use it for?"

"To practice music in," he replied. "All the young ladies, that have no ear for music, but insist on learning it, should be conveyed, every morning, two or three miles into the wilderness. There each would find a comfortable room provided for her, and also a cheap second-hand piano-forte, on which she might play for hours, without adding one needless pang to the sum of human misery!"

Lady Muriel glanced round in alarm, lest these barbarous sentiments should be overheard. But the fair musician was at a safe distance. "At any rate you must allow that she's a sweet girl?" she resumed.

"Oh, certainly. As sweet as cau sucre, if you choose—and nearly as interesting!"

"You are incorrigible!" said Lady Muriel, and turned to me. "I hope you found Mrs. Mills an interesting companion?"

"Oh, that's her name, is it?" I said. "I fancied there was more of it."

"So there is: and it will be 'at your proper peril' (whatever that may mean) if you ever presume to address her as 'Mrs. Mills'. She is 'Mrs. Ernest—Atkinson—Mills'!"

"She is one of those would-be grandees," said Arthur, "who think that, by tacking on to their surname all their spare Christian-names, with hyphens between, they can give it an aristocratic flavour. As if it wasn't trouble enough to remember one surname!"

By this time the room was getting crowded, as the guests, invited for the evening-party, were beginning to arrive, and Lady Muriel had to devote herself to the task of welcoming them, which she did with the sweetest grace imaginable. Sylvie and Bruno stood by her, deeply interested in the process.

"I hope you like my friends?" she said to them. "Specially my dear old friend, Mein Herr (What's become of him, I wonder? Oh, there he is!), that old gentleman in spectacles, with a long beard!"

"He's a grand old gentleman!" Sylvie said, gazing admiringly at "Mein Herr", who had settled down in a corner, from which his mild eyes beamed on us through a gigantic pair of spectacles. "And what a lovely beard!"

"What does he call his-self?" Bruno whispered.

"He calls himself 'Mein Herr'," Sylvie whispered in reply.

Bruno shook his head impatiently. "That's what he calls his hair, not his self, oo silly!" He appealed to me. "What doos he call his self, Mister Sir?"

"That's the only name I know of," I said. "But he looks very lonely. Don't you pity his grey hairs?"

"I pities his self," said Bruno, still harping on the misnomer; "but I doosn't pity his hair, one bit. His hair ca'n't feel!"

"We met him this afternoon," said Sylvie. "We'd been to see Nero, and we'd had such fun with him, making him invisible again! And we saw that nice old gentleman as we came back."

"Well, let's go and talk to him, and cheer him up a little," I said: "and perhaps we shall find out what he calls himself."

THE MAN IN THE MOON

The children came willingly. With one of them on each side of me, I approached the corner occupied by "Mein Herr". "You don't object to children, I hope?" I began.

"Crabbed age and youth cannot live together!" the old man cheerfully replied, with a most genial smile. "Now take a good look at me, my children! You would guess me to be an old man, wouldn't you?"

At first sight, though his face had reminded me so mysteriously of "the Professor", he had seemed to be decidedly a younger man: but, when I came to look into the wonderful depth of those large dreamy eyes, I felt, with a strange sense of awe, that he was incalculably older: he seemed to gaze at us out of some by-gone age, centuries away.

"I don't know if oo're an old man," Bruno answered, as the children, won over by the gentle voice, crept a little closer to him. "I thinks oo're eighty-three."

"He is very exact!" said Mein Herr.

"Is he anything like right?" I said.

"There are reasons," Mein Herr gently replied, "reasons which I am not at liberty to explain, for not mentioning definitely any Persons, Places, or Dates. One remark only I will permit myself to make—that the period of life, between the ages of a hundred-and-sixty-five and a hundred-and-seventy-five, is a specially safe one."

"How do you make that out?" I said.

"Thus. You would consider swimming to be a very safe amusement, if you scarcely ever heard of any one dying of it. Am I not right in thinking that you never heard of any one dying between those two ages?"

"I see what you mean," I said: "but I'm afraid you ca'n't prove swimming to be safe, on the same principle. It is no uncommon thing to hear of some one being drowned."

"In my country," said Mein Herr. "no one is ever drowned."

"Is there no water deep enough?"

"Plenty! But we ca'n't sink. We are all lighter than water. Let me explain," he added, seeing my look of surprise. "Suppose you desire a race of pigeons of a particular shape or colour, do you not select, from year to year, those that are nearest to the shape or colour you want, and keep those, and part with the others?"

"We do," I replied. "We call it 'Artificial Selection'."

"Exactly so," said Mein Herr. "Well, we have practised that for some centuries—constantly selecting the lightest people: so that, now, everybody is lighter than water."

"Then you never can be drowned at sea?"

"Never! It is only on the land—for instance, when attending a play in a theatre—that we are in such a danger."

"How can that happen at a theatre?"

"Our theatres are all underground. Large tanks of water are placed above. If a fire breaks out, the taps are turned, and in one minute the theatre is flooded, up to the very roof! Thus the fire is extinguished."

"And the audience, I presume?"

"That is a minor matter," Mein Herr carelessly replied. "But they have the comfort of knowing that, whether drowned or not, they are all lighter than water. We have not yet reached the standard of making people lighter than air: but we are aiming at it; and, in another thousand years or so—"

"What coos oo do wiz the peoples that's too heavy?" Bruno solemnly enquired.

"We have applied the same process," Mein Herr continued, not noticing Bruno's question, "to many other purposes. We have gone on selecting walking-sticks— always keeping those that walked best—till we have obtained some, that can walk by themselves! We have gone on selecting cotton-wool, till we have got some lighter than air! You've no idea what a useful material it is! We call it 'Imponderal'."

"What do you use it for?"

"Well, chiefly for packing articles, to go by Parcel-Post. It makes them weigh less than nothing, you know."

"And how do the Post Office people know what you have to pay?"

"That's the beauty of the new system!" Mein Herr cried exultingly. "They pay us: we don't pay them! I've often got as much as five shillings for sending a parcel."

"But doesn't your Government object?"

"Well, they do object a little. They say it comes so expensive, in the long run. But the thing's as clear as daylight, by their own rules. If I send a parcel, that weighs a pound more than nothing, I pay three-pence: so, of course, if it weighs a pound less than nothing, I ought to receive three-pence."

"It is indeed a useful article!" I said.

"Yet even 'Imponderal' has its disadvantages," he resumed. "I bought some, a few days ago, and put it into my hat, to carry it home, and the hat simply floated away!'

"Had oo some of that funny stuff in oor hat to-day?" Bruno enquired. "Sylvie and me saw oo in the road, and oor hat were ever so high up! Weren't it, Sylvie?"

"No, that was quite another thing," said Mein Herr. "There was a drop or two of rain falling: so I put my hat on the top of my stick—as an umbrella, you know. As I came along the road", he continued, turning to me, "I was overtaken by—"

"—a shower of rain?" said Bruno.

"Well, it looked more like the tail of a dog," Mein Herr replied. "It was the most curious thing! Something rubbed affectionately against my knee. And I looked down. And I could see nothing! Only, about a yard off, there was a dog's tail, wagging, all by itself!"

"Oh, Sylvie!" Bruno murmured reproachfully. "Oo didn't finish making him visible!"

"I'm so sorry!" Sylvie said, looking very penitent. "I meant to rub it along his back, but we were in such a hurry. We'll go and finish him to-morrow. Poor thing! Perhaps he'll get no supper to-night!"

"Course he won't!" said Bruno. "Nobody never gives bones to a dog's tail!"

Mein Herr looked from one to the other in blank astonishment. "I do not understand you," he said. "I had lost my way, and I was consulting a pocket-map, and somehow I had dropped one of my gloves, and this invisible Something, that had rubbed against my knee, actually brought it back to me!"

"Course he did!" said Bruno. "He's welly fond of fetching things."

Mein Herr looked so thoroughly bewildered that I thought it best to change the subject. "What a useful thing a pocket-map is!" I remarked.

"That's another thing we've learned from your Nation," said Mein Herr, "map-making. But we've carried it much further than you. What do you consider the largest map that would be really useful?"

"About six inches to the mile."

"Only six inches!" exclaimed Mein Herr. "We very soon got to six yards to the mile. Then we tried a hundred yards to the mile. And then came the grandest idea of all! We actually made a map of the country, on the scale of a mile to the mile!"

"Have you used it much?" I enquired.

"It has never been spread out, yet," said Mein Herr: "the farmers objected: they said it would cover the whole country, and shut out the sunlight! So we now use the country itself, as its own map, and I assure you it does nearly as well. Now let me ask you another question. What is the smallest world you would care to inhabit?"

"I know!" cried Bruno, who was listening intently. "I'd like a little teeny-tiny world, just big enough for Sylvie and me!"

"Then you would have to stand on opposite side of it," said Mein Herr. "And so you would never see your sister at all!"

"And I'd have no lessons," said Bruno.

"You don't mean to say you've been trying experiments in that direction!" I said.

"Well, not experiments exactly. We do not profess to construct planets. But a scientific friend of mine, who has made several balloon-voyages, assures me he has visited a planet so small that he could walk right round it in twenty minutes! There had been a great battle, just before his visit, which had ended rather oddly: the vanquished army ran away at full speed, and in a very few minutes found themselves face-to-face with the victorious army, who were marching home again, and who were so frightened at finding themselves between two armies, that they surrendered at once! Of course that lost them the battle, though, as a matter of fact, they had killed all the soldiers on the other side."

"Killed soldiers ca'n't run away," Bruno thoughtfully remarked.

"'Killed' is a technical word," replied Mein Herr. "In the little planet I speak of, the bullets were made of soft black stuff, which marked everything it touched. So, after a battle, all you had to do was to count how many soldiers on each side were 'killed'—that means 'marked on the back', for marks in front didn't count."

"Then you couldn't 'kill' any, unless they ran away?" I said.

"My scientific friend found out a better plan than that. He pointed out that, if only the bullets were sent the other way round the world, they would hit the enemy in the back. After that, the worst marksmen were considered the best soldiers; and the very worst of all always got First Prize."

"And how did you decide which was the very worst of all?"

"Easily. The best possible shooting is, you know, to hit what is exactly in front of you: so of course the worst possible is to hit what is exactly behind you."

"They were strange people in that little planet!" I said.

"They were indeed! Perhaps their method of government was the strangest of all. In this planet, I am told, a Nation consists of a number of Subjects, and one King: but, in the little planet I speak of, it consisted of a number of Kings, and one Subject!"

"You say you are 'told' what happens in this planet," I said. "May I venture to guess that you yourself are a visitor from some other planet?"

Bruno clapped his hands in his excitement. "Is oo the Man-in-the-Moon?" he cried.

Mein Herr looked uneasy. "I am not in the Moon, my child," he said evasively. "To return to what I was saying. I think that method of government ought to answer well. You see, the Kings would be sure to make Laws contradicting each other: so the Subject could never be punished, because, whatever he did he'd be obeying some Law."

"And, whatever he did, he'd be disobeying some Law!" cried Bruno. "So he'd always be punished!"

Lady Muriel was passing at the moment, and caught the last word. "Nobody's going to be punished here!" she said, taking Bruno in her arms. "This is Liberty-Hall! Would you lend me the children for a minute?"

"The children desert us, you see," I said to Mein Herr, as she carried them off: "so we old folk must keep each other company!"

The old man sighed. "Ah, well! We're old folk now and yet I was a child myself, once—at least I fancy so."

It did seem a rather unlikely fancy, I could not help owning to myself—looking at the shaggy white hair, and the long beard—that he could ever have been a child. You are fond of young people?" I said.

"Young men," he replied. "Not of children exactly. I used to teach young men—many a year ago—in my dear old University!"

"I didn't quite catch its name?" I hinted

"I did not name it," the old man replied mildly. "Nor would you know the name if I did. Strange tales I could tell you of all the changes I have witnessed there! But it would weary you, I fear."

"No, indeed!" I said. "Pray go on. What kind of changes?"

But the old man seemed to be more in a humour for questions than for answers. "Tell me," he said, laying his hand impressively on my arm, "tell me something. For I am a stranger in your land, and I know little of your modes of education: yet something tells me we are further on than you in the eternal cycle of change—and that many a theory we have tried and found to fail, you also will try, with a wilder enthusiasm: you also will find to fail, with a bitterer despair!"

It was strange to see how, as he talked, and his words flowed more and more freely, with a certain rhythmic eloquence, his features seemed to glow with an inner light, and the whole man seemed to be transformed, as if he had grown fifty years younger in a moment of time.

FAIRY-MUSIC

The silence that ensued was broken by the voice of the musical young lady, who had seated herself near us, and was conversing with one of the newly-arrived guests.

"Well!" she said in a tone of scornful surprise. We are to have something new in the way of music, it appears!"

I looked round for an explanation, and was nearly as much astonished as the speaker herself: it was Sylvie whom Lady Muriel was leading to the piano!

"Do try it, my darling!" she was saying. "I'm sure you can play very nicely!"

Sylvie looked round at me, with tears in her eyes. I tried to give her an encouraging smile, but it was evidently a great strain on the nerves of a child so wholly unused to be made an exhibition of, and she was frightened and unhappy. Yet here came out the perfect sweetness of her disposition: I could see that she was resolved to forget herself, and do her best to give pleasure to Lady Muriel and her friends. She seated herself at the instrument, and began instantly. Time and expression, so far as one could judge, were perfect: but her touch was one of such extraordinary lightness that it was at first scarcely possible, through the hum of conversation which still continued, to catch a note of what she was playing.

But in a minute the hum had died away into absolute silence, and we all sat, entranced and breathless, to listen to such heavenly music as none then present could ever forget.

Hardly touching the notes at first, she played a sort of introduction in a minor key—like an embodied twilight; one felt as though the lights were growing dim, and a mist were creeping through the room. Then there flashed through the gathering gloom the first few notes of a melody so lovely, so delicate, that one held one's breath, fearful to lose a single note of it. Ever and again the music dropped into the pathetic minor key with which it had begun, and, each time that the melody forced its way, so to speak, through the enshrouding gloom into the light of day, it was more entrancing, more magically sweet. Under the airy touch of the child, the instrument actually seemed to warble, like a bird. "Rise up, my love, my fair one," it seemed to sing, "and come away! For lo the winter is past, the rain is over and gone; the flowers appear on the earth, the time of the singing of birds is come!" One could fancy one heard the tinkle of the last few drops, shaken from the trees by a passing gust—that one saw the first glittering rays of the sun, breaking through the clouds.

The Count hurried across the room in great excitement. "I cannot remember myself", he exclaimed, "of the name of this so charming an air! It is of an opera most surely. Yet not even will the opera remind his name to me! What you call him, dear child?"

Sylvie looked round at him with a rapt expression of face. She had ceased playing, but her fingers still wandered fitfully over the keys. All fear and shyness had quite passed away now, and nothing remained but the pure joy of the music that had thrilled our hearts.

"The title of it!" the Count repeated impatiently. "How call you the opera?"

"I don't know what an opera is," Sylvie half-whispered.

"How, then, call you the air?"

"I don't know any, name for it," Sylvie replied, as she rose from the instrument.

"But this is marvellous!" exclaimed the Count, following the child, and addressing himself to me, as if I were the proprietor of this musical prodigy, and so must know the origin of her music. "You have heard her play this, sooner—I would say 'before this occasion'? How call you the air?"

I shook my head: but was saved from more questions by Lady Muriel, who came up to petition the Count for a song.

The Count spread out his hands apologetically, and ducked his head. "But, Milady, I have already respected—I would say prospected—all your songs; and there shall be none fitted to my voice! They are not for basso voices!"

"Wo'n't you look at them again?" Lady Muriel implored.

"Let's help him!" Bruno whispered to Sylvie. "Let's get him—you know!"

Sylvie nodded. "Shall we look for a song for you? she said sweetly to the Count.

"Mais oui!" the little man exclaimed.

"Of course we may!" said Bruno, while, each taking a hand of the delighted Count, they led him to the music-stand.

"There is still hope!" said Lady Muriel over her shoulder, as she followed them.

I turned to "Mein Herr", hoping to resume our interrupted conversation. "You were remarking—" I began: but at this moment Sylvie came to call Bruno who had returned to my side, looking unusually serious "Do come, Bruno!" she entreated. "You know we've nearly found it!" Then, in a whisper, "The locket's in my hand, now. I couldn't get it out while they were looking!"

But Bruno drew back. "The man called me names," he said with dignity.

"What names?" I enquired with some curiosity.

"I asked him", said Bruno, "which sort of song he liked. And he said 'A song of a man, not of a lady'. And I said 'Shall Sylvie and me find you the song of Mister Tottles And he said 'Wait, eel!' And I'm not an eel, oo know!"

"I'm sure he didn't mean it!" Sylvie said earnestly. "It's something French—you know he ca'n't talk English so well as—"

Bruno relented visibly. "Course he knows no better, he's Flench! Flenchmen never can speak English goodly as us!" And Sylvie led him away, a willing captive.

"Nice children!" said the old man, taking off his spectacles and rubbing them carefully. Then he put them on again, and watched with an approving smile, while the children tossed over the heap of music, and we just caught Sylvie's reproving words, "We're not making hay, Bruno!"

"This has been a long interruption to our conversation," I said. "Pray let us go on!"

"Willingly!" replied the gentle old man. "I was much interested in what you—" He paused a moment, and passed his hand uneasily across his brow. "One forgets," he murmured. "What was I saying? Oh! Something you were to tell me. Yes. Which of your teachers do you value the most highly, those whose words are easily understood, or those who puzzle you at every turn?"

I felt obliged to admit that we generally admired most the teachers we couldn't quite understand.

"Just so," said Mein Herr. "That's the way it begins. Well, we were at that stage some eighty years ago—or was it ninety? Our favourite teacher got more obscure every year; and every year we admired him more—just as your Art-fanciers call mist the fairest feature in a landscape, and admire a view with frantic delight when they can see nothing! Now I'll tell you how it ended. It was Moral Philosophy that our idol lectured on. Well, his pupils couldn't make head or tail of it, but they got it all by heart; and, when Examination-time came they wrote it down; and the Examiners said 'Beautiful! What depth!'"

"But what good was it to the young men afterwards?"

"Why, don't you see?" replied Mein Herr. "They became teachers in their turn, and they said all these things over again; and their pupils wrote it all down; and the Examiners accepted it; and nobody had the ghost of an idea what it all meant!"

"And how did it end?"

"It ended this way. We woke up one fine day, and found there was no one in the place that knew anything about Moral Philosophy. So we abolished it, teachers, classes, examiners, and all. And if any one wanted to learn anything about it, he had to make it out for himself, and after another twenty years or so there were several men that really knew something about it! Now tell me another thing. How long do you teach a youth before you examine him, in your Universities?"

I told him three or four years.

"Just so, just what we did!" he exclaimed. "We taught them a bit, and, just as they were beginning to take it in, took it all out again! We pumped our wells dry before they were a quarter full—we stripped our orchards while the apples were still in blossom—we applied the severe logic of arithmetic to our chickens, while peacefully slumbering in their shells! Doubtless it's the early bird that picks up the worm—but if the bird gets up so outrageously early that the worm is still deep underground, what then is its chance of a breakfast?"

Not much, I admitted.

"Now see how that works!" he went on eagerly. "If you want to pump your wells so soon—and I suppose you tell me that is what you must do?"

"We must," I said. "In an over-crowded country like this, nothing but Competitive Examinations—"

Mein Herr threw up his hands wildly. "What, again?" he cried. "I thought it was dead, fifty years ago! Oh this Upas tree of Competitive Examinations! Beneath whose deadly shade all the original genius, all the exhaustive research, all the untiring life-long diligence by which our forefathers have so advanced human knowledge, must slowly but surely wither away, and give place to a system of Cookery, in which the human mind is a sausage, and all we ask is, how much indigestible stuff can be crammed into it!"

Always, after these bursts of eloquence, he seemed to forget himself for a moment, and only to hold on to the thread of thought by some single word. "Yes, crammed," he repeated. "We went through all that stage of the disease—had it bad, I warrant you! Of course, as the Examination was all in all, we tried to put in just what was wanted—and the great thing to aim at was, that the Candidate should know absolutely nothing beyond the needs of the Examination! I don't say it was ever quite achieved: but one of my own pupils (pardon an old man's egotism) came very near it. After the Examination, he mentioned to me the few facts which he knew but had not been able to bring in, and I can assure you they were trivial, Sir, absolutely trivial!"

I feebly expressed my surprise and delight.

The old man bowed, with a gratified smile, and proceeded. "At that time, no one had hit on the much more rational plan of watching for the individual scintillations of genius, and rewarding them as they occurred. As it was, we made our unfortunate pupil into a Leyden-jar, charged him up to the eyelids—then applied the knob of a Competitive Examination, and drew off one magnificent spark, which very often cracked the jar! What mattered that? We labeled it 'First Class Spark', and put it away on the shelf."

"But the more rational system—?" I suggested.

"Ah, yes! that came next. Instead of giving the whole reward of learning in one lump, we used to pay for every good answer as it occurred. How well I remember lecturing in those days, with a heap of small coins at my elbow! It was 'A very good answer, Mr. Jones!' (that meant a shilling, mostly). 'Bravo, Mr. Robinson!' (that meant half-a-crown). Now I'll tell you how that worked. Not one single fact would any of them take in, without a fee! And when a clever boy came up from school, he got paid more for learning than we got paid for teaching him! Then came the wildest craze of all."

"What, another craze?" I said.

"It's the last one," said the old man. "I must have tired you out with my long story. Each College wanted to get the clever boys: so we adopted a system which we had heard was very popular in England: the Colleges competed against each other, and the boys let themselves out to the highest bidder! What geese we were! Why, they were bound to come to the University somehow. We needn't have paid 'em! And all our money went in getting clever boys to come to one College rather than another! The competition was so keen, that at last mere money-payments were not enough. Any College, that wished to secure some specially clever young man, had to waylay him at the Station, and hunt him through the streets. The first who touched him was allowed to have him."

"That hunting-down of the scholars, as they arrived, must have been a curious business," I said. "Could you give me some idea of what it was like?"

"Willingly!" said the old man. "I will describe to you the very last Hunt that took place, before that form of Sport (for it was actually reckoned among the Sports of the day: we called it 'Cub-Hunting') was finally abandoned. I witnessed it myself, as I happened to be passing by at the moment, and was what we called 'in at the death'. I can see it now!" he went on in an excited tone, gazing into vacancy with those large dreamy eyes of his "It seems like yesterday; and yet it happened—" He checked himself hastily, and the remaining words died away into a whisper.

"How many years ago did you say?" I asked, much interested in the prospect of at last learning some definite fact in his history.

"Many years ago," he replied. "The scene at the Railway-Station had been (so they told me) one of wild excitement. Eight or nine Heads of Colleges had assembled at the gates (no one was allowed inside), and the Station-Master had drawn a line on the pavement, and insisted on their all standing behind it. The gates were flung open! The young man darted through them, and fled like lightning down the street, while the Heads of Colleges actually yelled with excitement on catching sight of him! The Proctor gave the word, in the old statutory form, 'Semel! Bis! Ter! Currite!', and the Hunt began! Oh, it was a fine sight, believe me! At the first corner he dropped his Greek Lexicon: further on, his railway-rug: then various small articles: then his umbrella: lastly what I suppose he prized most, his hand-bag; but the game was up: the spherical Principal of—of—"

"Of which College?" I said.

"—of one of the Colleges", he resumed, "had put into operation the Theory—his own discovery—of Accelerated Velocity, and captured him just opposite to where I stood. I shall never forget that wild breathless struggle! But it was soon over. Once in those great bony hands; escape was impossible!"

"May I ask why you speak of him as the 'spherical' Principal?" I said.

"The epithet referred to his shape, which was a perfect sphere. You are aware that a bullet, another instance of a perfect sphere, when falling in a perfectly straight line, moves with Accelerated Velocity?"

I bowed assent.

"Well, my spherical friend (as I am proud to call him) set himself to investigate the causes of this. He found them to be three. One; that it is a perfect sphere. Two that it moves in a straight line. Three; that its direction is not upwards. When these three conditions are fulfilled, you get Accelerated Velocity."

"Hardly," I said: "if you will excuse my differing from you. Suppose we apply the theory to horizontal motion. If a bullet is fired horizontally, it—"

"—it does not move in a straight line," he quietly finished my sentence for me.

"I yield the point," I said. "What did your friend do next?"

"The next thing was to apply the theory, as you rightly suggest, to horizontal motion. But the moving body, ever tending to fall, needs constant support, if it is to move a true horizontal line. 'What, then,' he asked himself, will give constant support to a moving body?' And his answer was 'Human legs!' That was the discovery that immortalized his name!"

"His name being?" I suggested.

"I had not mentioned it," was the gentle reply of my most unsatisfactory informant. "His next step was an obvious one. He took to a diet of suet-dumplings, until his body had become a perfect sphere. Then he went out for his first experimental run—which nearly cost him his life!"

"How was that?"

"Well, you see, he had no idea of the tremendous new force in Nature that he was calling into play. He began too fast. In a very few minutes he found himself moving at a hundred miles an hour! And, if he had not had the presence of mind to charge into the middle of a haystack (which he scattered to the four winds) there can be no doubt that he would have left the Planet he belonged to, and gone right away into Space!"

"And how came that to be the last of the Cub-Hunts?" I enquired.

"Well, you see, it led to a rather scandalous dispute between two of the Colleges. Another Principal had laid his hand on the young one, so nearly at the same moment as the spherical one, that there was no knowing which had touched him first. The dispute got into print, and did us no credit, and, in short, Cub-Hunts came to an end. Now I'll tell you what cured us of that wild craze of ours, the bidding against each other, for the clever scholars, just as if they were articles to be sold by auction! Just when the craze had reached its highest point, and when one of the Colleges had actually advertised a Scholarship of one thousand pounds per annum, one of our tourists brought us the manuscript of an old African legend—I happen to have a copy of it in my pocket. Shall I translate it for you?"

"Pray go on," I said, though I felt I was getting very sleepy.

WHAT TOTTLES MEANT

Mein Herr unrolled the manuscript, but, to my great surprise, instead of reading it, he began to sing it, in a rich mellow voice that seemed to ring through the room.

"One thousand pounds per annuum
Is not so bad a figure, come!"
Cried Tottles. "And I tell you, flat,
A man may marry well on that!
To say 'the Husband needs the Wife'
Is not the way to represent it.
The crowning joy of Woman's life
Is Man!" said Tottles (and he meant it).
The blissful Honey-moon is past:
The Pair have settled down at last:
Mamma-in-law their home will share
And make their happiness her care.
"Your income is an ample one:
Go it, my children!" (And they went it).
"I rather think this kind of fun
Wo'n't last!" said Tottles (and he meant it).
They took a little country-box—
A box at Covent Garden also:
T hey lived a life of double-knocks
Acquaintances began to call so:
Their London house was much the same
(It took three hundred, clear, to rent it):
"Life is a very jolly game!"
Cried happy Tottles (and he meant it).
"Contented with a frugal lot"
(He always used that phrase at Gunter's)
He bought a handy little yacht—
A dozen serviceable hunters—
the fishing of a Highland Loch—
A sailing-boat to circumvent it—
"The sounding of that Gaelic 'och'
Beats me!" said Tottles (and he meant it).

Here, with one of those convulsive starts that wake one up in the very act of dropping off to sleep, I became conscious that the deep musical tones that thrilled me did not belong to Mein Herr, but to the French Count. The old man was still conning the manuscript.

"I beg your pardon for keeping you waiting!" he said. "I was just making sure that I knew the English for all the words. I am quite ready now." And he read me the following Legend:

"In a city that stands in the very centre of Africa, and is rarely visited by the casual tourist, the people had always bought eggs—a daily necessary in a climate where egg-flip was the usual diet—from a Merchant who came to their gates once a week. And the people always bid wildly against each other: so there was quite a lively auction every time the Merchant came, and the last egg in his basket used to fetch the value of two or three camels, or thereabouts. And eggs got dearer every week. And still they drank their egg-flip, and wondered where all their money went to.

"And there came a day when they put their heads together. And they understood what donkeys they had been.

"And next day, when the Merchant came, only one Man went forth. And he said 'Oh, thou of the hook-nose and the goggle-eyes, thou of the measureless beard, how much for that lot of eggs?'

"And the Merchant answered him 'I could let thee have that lot at ten thousand piastres the dozen'.

"And the Man chuckled inwardly, and said 'Ten piastres the dozen I offer thee, and no more, oh descendant of a distinguished grandfather!'

"And the Merchant stroked his beard, and said 'Hum! I will await the coming of thy friends.' So he waited. And the Man waited with him. And they waited both together."

"The manuscript breaks off here," said Mein Herr, as he rolled it up again; "but it was enough to open our eyes. We saw what simpletons we had been—buying our Scholars much as those ignorant savages bought their eggs—and the ruinous system was abandoned. If only we could have abandoned, along with it, all the other fashions we had borrowed from you, instead of carrying them to their logical results! But it was not to be. What ruined my country, and drove me from my home, was the introduction— into the Army, of all places—of your theory of Political Dichotomy!"

"Shall I trouble you too much," I said, "if I ask you to explain what you mean by 'the Theory of Political Dichotomy'?"

"No trouble at all!" was Mein Herr's most courteous reply. "I quite enjoy talking, when I get so good a listener. What started the thing, with us, was the report brought to us, by one of our most eminent statesmen, who had stayed some time in England, of the way affairs were managed there. It was a political necessity (so he assured us, and we believed him, though we had never discovered it till that moment) that there should be two Parties, in every affair and on every subject. In Politics, the two Parties, which you had found it necessary to institute, were called, he told us, 'Whigs' and 'Tories'."

"That must have been some time ago?" I remarked.

"It was some time ago," he admitted. "And this was the way the affairs of the British Nation were managed. (You will correct me if I misrepresent it. I do but repeat what our traveler told us.) These two Parties—which were in chronic hostility to each other—took turns in conducting the Government; and the Party, that happened not to be in power, was called the 'Opposition', I believe?"

"That is the right name," I said. "There have always, so long as we have had a Parliament at all, two Parties, one 'in', and one 'out'."

"Well, the function of the 'Ins' (if I may so call them) was to do the best they could for the national welfare—in such things as making war or peace, commercial, treaties, and so forth?"

Undoubtedly," I said.

"And the function of the 'Outs' was (so our traveler assured us, though we were very incredulous at first) to prevent the 'Ins' from succeeding in any of these things?"

"To criticize and to amend their proceedings," I corrected him. "It would be unpatriotic to hinder the Government in doing what was for the good of the Nation! We have always held a Patriot to be the greatest of heroes, and an unpatriotic spirit to be one of the worst of human ills!"

"Excuse me for a moment," the old gentleman courteously replied, taking out his pocket-book. "I have a few memoranda here, of a correspondence I had with our tourist, and, if you will allow me, I'll just refresh my memory—although I quite agree with you—it is, as you say, one of the worst of human ills—" And, here Mein Herr began singing again:

> But oh, the worst of human ills
> (Poor Tottles found) are "little bills"!
> And, with no balance in the Bank,
> What wonder that his spirits sank?
> Still, as the money flowed away,
> He wondered how on earth she spent it.
> "You cost me twenty pounds a day,
> At least!" cried Tottles (and he meant it).
> She sighed. "Those Drawing Rooms, you know!
> I really never thought about it:
> Mamma declared we ought to go—
> We should be Nobodies without it.
> That diamond-circlet for my brow—
> I quite believed that she had sent it,
> Until the Bill came in just now—"
> "Viper!" cried Tottles (and he meant it).
> Poor Mrs. T. could bear no more,
> But fainted flat upon the floor.
> Mamma-in-law, with anguish wild
> Seeks, all in vain, to rouse her child.
> "Quick! Take this box of smelling-salts!
> Don't scold her, James, or you'll repent it,
> She's a dear girl, with all her faults—"
> "She is!" groaned Tottles (and he meant it).
> "I was a donkey", Tottles cried,
> "To choose your daughter for my bride!
> 'Twas you that bid us cut a dash!
> 'Tis you have brought us to this smash!
> You don't suggest one single thing

That can in any way prevent it -"
"Then what's the use of arguing?"
"Shut up!" cried Tottles (and he meant it).

Once more I started into wakefulness, and realized that Mein Herr was not the singer. He was still consulting his memoranda.

"It is exactly what my friend told me," he resumed, after conning over various papers. "'Unpatriotic' is the very word I had used, in writing to him, and 'hinder' is the very word he used in his reply! Allow me to read you a portion of his letter:

"'I can assure you,' he writes, 'that unpatriotic as you may think it, the recognized function of the Opposition' is to hinder in every manner not forbidden by the Law, the action of the Government. This process is called 'Legitimate Obstruction': and the greatest triumph the 'Opposition' can ever enjoy, is when they are able to point out that, owing to their 'Obstruction' the Government have failed in everything they have tried to do for the good of the Nation!'"

"Your friend has not put it quite correctly," I said. "The Opposition would no doubt be glad to point out that the government had failed through their own fault; but not that they had failed on account of Obstruction!"

"You think so?" he gently replied. "Allow me now to read to you this newspaper-cutting, which my friend enclosed in his letter. It is part of the report of a public speech, made by a Statesman who was at the time a member of the 'Opposition':

"'At the close of the Session, he thought they had no reason to be discontented with the fortunes of the campaign. They had routed the enemy at every point. But the pursuit must be continued. They had only to follow up a disordered and dispirited foe.' "

"Now to what portion of your national history would you guess that the speaker was referring?"

"Really, the number of successful wars we have waged during the last century", I replied, with a glow of British pride, "is far too great for me to guess, with any chance of success, which it was we were then engaged in. However, I will name 'India' as the most probable. The Mutiny was no doubt, all but crushed, at the time that speech was made. What a fine, manly, patriotic speech it must have been!" I exclaimed in an outburst of enthusiasm.

"You think so?" he replied, in a tone of gentle pity. "Yet my friend tells me that the 'disordered and dispirited foe' simply meant the Statesmen who happened to be in power at the moment; that the 'pursuit' simply meant 'Obstruction'; and that the words 'they had routed the enemy' simply meant that the 'Opposition' had succeeded in hindering the Government from doing any of the work which the Nation had empowered them to do!"

I thought it best to say nothing.

"It seemed queer to us, just at first," he resumed, after courteously waiting a minute for me to speak: "but, when once we had mastered the idea, our respect for your Nation was so great that we carried it into every department of life! It was 'the beginning of the end' with us. My country never held up its head again!" And the poor old gentleman sighed deeply.

"Let us change the subject," I said. "Do not distress yourself, I beg!"

"No, no!" he said, with an effort to recover himself. "I had rather finish my story! The next step (after reducing our Government to impotence, and putting a stop to all useful legislation, which did not take us long to do) was to introduce what we called 'the glorious British Principle of Dichotomy' into Agriculture. We persuaded many of the well-to-do farmers to divide their staff of labourers into two Parties, and to set them one against the other. They were called, like our political Parties, the 'Ins' and the 'Outs': the business of the 'Ins' was to do as much of ploughing, sowing, or whatever might be needed, as they could manage in a day, and at night they were paid according to the amount they had done: the business of the 'Outs' was to hinder them, and they were paid for the amount they had hindered. The farmers found they had to pay only half as much wages as they did before, and they didn't observe that the amount of work done was only a quarter as much as was done before: so they took it up quite enthusiastically, at first."

"And afterwards?" I enquired.

"Well, afterwards they didn't like it quite so well. In a very short time, things settled down into a regular routine. No work at all was done. So the 'Ins' got no wages, and the 'Outs' got full pay. And the farmers never discovered, till most of them were ruined, that the rascals had agreed to manage it so, and had shared the pay between them! While the thing lasted, there were funny sights to be seen! Why, I've often watched a ploughman with two horses harnessed to the plough, doing his best to get it forwards; while the opposition-ploughman, with three donkeys harnessed at the other end, was doing his best to get it backwards! And the plough never moving an inch, either way!"

"But we never did anything like that!" I exclaimed.

"Simply because you were less logical than we were," replied Mein Herr. "There is sometimes an advantage in being a donk—Excuse me! No personal allusion intended. All this happened long ago, you know!"

"Did the Dichotomy-Principle succeed in any direction?" I enquired.

"In none," Mein Herr candidly confessed. "It had a very short trial in Commerce. The shop-keepers wouldn't take it up, after once trying the plan of having half the attendants busy in folding up and carrying away the goods which the other half were trying to spread out upon the counters. They said the Public didn't like it!"

"I don't wonder at it," I remarked.

"Well, we tried 'the British Principle' for some years. And the end of it all was—" His voice suddenly dropped, almost to a whisper; and large tears began to roll down his cheeks. "—the end was that we got involved in a war; and there was a great battle, in which we far out-numbered the enemy. But what could one expect, when only half of our soldiers were fighting, and the other half pulling them back? It ended in a crushing defeat—an utter rout. This caused a Revolution; and most of the Government were banished. I myself was accused of Treason, for having so strongly advocated 'the British Principle'. My property was all forfeited, and—and— I was driven into exile! 'Now the mischief's done,' they said, 'perhaps you'll kindly leave the country?' It nearly broke my heart, but I had to go!"

The melancholy tone became a wail: the wail became a chant: the chant became a song—though whether it was Mein Herr that was singing, this time, or somebody else, I could not feel certain.

"And now the mischief's done, perhaps
You'll kindly go and pack your traps?
Since two (your daughter and your son)
Are Company, but three are none.
A course of saving we'll begin:
When change is needed, I'll invent it:
Don't think to put your finger in
This pie!" cried Tottles (and he meant it).

The music seemed to die away. Mein Herr was again speaking in his ordinary voice. "Now tell me one thing more," he said. "Am I right in thinking that in your Universities, though a man may reside some thirty or forty years, you examine him, once for all, at the end of the first three or four?"

"That is so, undoubtedly," I admitted.

"Practically, then, you examine a man at the beginning of his career!" the old man said to himself rather than to me. "And what guarantee have you that he retains the knowledge for which you have rewarded him— beforehand, as we should say?"

"None," I admitted, feeling a little puzzled at the drift of his remarks. "How do you secure that object?"

"By examining him at the end of his thirty or forty years—not at the beginning," he gently replied. "On an average, the knowledge then found is about one-fifth of what it was at first—the process of forgetting going on at a very steady uniform rate—and he, who forgets least, gets most honour, and most rewards."

"Then you give him the money when he needs it no longer? And you make him live most of his life on nothing!"

"Hardly that. He gives his orders to the tradesmen: they supply him, for forty, sometimes fifty years, at their own risk: then he gets his Fellowship— which pays him in one year as much as your Fellowships pay in fifty— and then he can easily pay all his bills, with interest."

"But suppose he fails to get his Fellowship? That must occasionally happen."

"That occasionally happens." It was Mein Herr's turn, now, to make admissions.

"And what becomes of the tradesmen?"

"They calculate accordingly. When a man appears to be getting alarmingly ignorant, or stupid, they will sometimes refuse to supply him any longer. You have no idea with what enthusiasm a man will begin to rub up his ten sciences or languages, when his butcher has cut supply of beef and mutton!"

"And who are the Examiners?"

The young men who have just come, brimming over with knowledge. You would think it a curious sight," he went on, "to see mere boys examining such old men. I have known a man set to examine his own grandfather. It was a little painful for both of them, no doubt. The gentleman was as bald as a coot—"

"How bald would that be?" I've no idea why I asked this question. I felt I was getting foolish.

BRUNO'S PICNIC

"As bald as bald," was the bewildering reply. "Now, Bruno, I'll tell you a story."

"And I'll tell oo a story," said Bruno, beginning in a hurry for fear of Sylvie getting the start of him: "once there were a Mouse—a little tiny Mouse—such a little Mouse! Oo never saw such a tiny Mouse—"

"Did nothing ever happen to it, Bruno?" I asked. "Haven't you anything more to tell us, besides its being tiny?"

"Nothing never happened to it," Bruno solemnly replied.

"Why did nothing never happen to it?" said Sylvie, who was sitting, with her head on Bruno's shoulder, patiently waiting for a chance of beginning her story.

"It were too tiny," Bruno explained.

"That's no reason!" I said. "However tiny it was, things might happen to it."

Bruno looked pityingly at me, as if he thought me very stupid. "It were too tiny," he repeated. "If anything happened to it, it would die—it were so very tiny!"

"Really that's enough about its being tiny!" Sylvie put in. "Haven't you invented any more about it?"

"Haven't invented no more yet."

"Well, then, you shouldn't begin a story till you've invented more! Now be quiet, there's a good boy, and listen to my story."

And Bruno, having quite exhausted all his inventive faculty, by beginning in too great a hurry, quietly resigned himself to listening. "Tell about the other Bruno, please," he said coaxingly.

Sylvie put her arms round his neck, and began:—

"The wind was whispering among the trees," ("That wasn't good manners!" Bruno interrupted. "Never mind about manners," said Sylvie) "and it was evening—a nice moony evening, and the Owls were hooting—"

"Pretend they weren't Owls!" Bruno pleaded, stroking her cheek with his fat little hand. "I don't like Owls. Owls have such great big eyes. Pretend they were Chickens!"

"Are you afraid of their great big eyes, Bruno?" I said.

"Aren't 'fraid of nothing," Bruno answered in as careless a tone as he could manage: "they're ugly with their great big eyes. I think if they cried, the tears would be as big—oh, as big as the moon!" And he laughed merrily. "Doos Owls cry ever, Mister Sir?"

"Owls cry never," I said gravely, trying to copy Bruno's way of speaking: "they've got nothing to be sorry for, you know."

"Oh, but they have!" Bruno exclaimed. "They're ever so sorry, 'cause they killed the poor little Mouses!"

"But they're not sorry when they're hungry, I suppose?"

"Oo don't know nothing about Owls!" Bruno scornfully remarked. "When they're hungry, they're very, very sorry they killed the little Mouses, 'cause if they hadn't killed them there'd be sumfin for supper, oo know!"

Bruno was evidently getting into a dangerously inventive state of mind, so Sylvie broke in with "Now I'm going on with the story. So the Owls— the Chickens, I mean—were looking to see if they could find a nice fat Mouse for their supper—"

"Pretend it was a nice 'abbit!" said Bruno.

"But it wasn't a nice habit, to kill Mouses," Sylvie argued. "I ca'n't pretend that!"

"I didn't say 'habit', oo silly fellow!" Bruno replied with a merry twinkle in his eye. "'abbits—that runs about in the fields!"

"Rabbit? Well it can be a Rabbit, if you like. But you mustn't alter my story so much, Bruno. A Chicken couldn't eat a Rabbit!"

"But it might have wished to see if it could try to eat it."

"Well, it wished to see if it could try—oh, really, Bruno, that's nonsense! I shall go back to the Owls."

"Well, then, pretend they hadn't great eyes!"

"And they saw a little Boy," Sylvie went on, disdaining to make any further corrections. "And he asked them to tell him a story. And the Owls hooted and flew away—" ("Oo shouldn't say 'flewed'; oo should say 'flied'," Bruno whispered. But Sylvie wouldn't hear.) "And he met a Lion. And he asked the Lion to tell him a story. And the Lion said 'yes', it would. And, while the Lion was telling him the story, it nibbled some of his head off—"

"Don't say 'nibbled'!" Bruno entreated. "Only little things nibble—little thin sharp things, with edges—"

"Well, then, it 'nubbled'," said Sylvie. "And when it had nubbled all his head off, he went away, and he never said 'thank you'!"

"That were very rude," said Bruno. "If he couldn't speak, he might have nodded—no, he couldn't nod. Well, he might have shaked hands with the Lion!"

"Oh, I'd forgotten that part!" said Sylvie. "He did shake hands with it. He came back again, you know, and he thanked the Lion very much, for telling him the story."

"Then his head had growed up again?" said Bruno.

"Oh yes, it grew up in a minute. And the Lion begged pardon, and said it wouldn't nubble off little boys' heads —not never no more!"

Bruno looked much pleased at this change of events. "Now that are a really nice story!" he said. "Aren't it a nice story, Mister Sir?"

"Very," I said. "I would like to hear another story about that Boy."

"So would I," said Bruno, stroking Sylvie's cheek again. "Please tell about Bruno's Picnic; and don't talk about nubbly Lions!"

"I wo'n't, if it frightens you," said Sylvie.

"Flightens me!" Bruno exclaimed indignantly. "It isn't that! It's 'cause 'nubbly' 's such a grumbly word to say— when one person's got her head on another person's shoulder. When she talks like that," he exclaimed to me, "the talking goes down bofe sides of my face—all the way to my chin—and it doos tickle so! It's enough to make a beard grow, that it is!"

He said this with great severity, but it was evidently meant for a joke: so Sylvie laughed—a delicious musical little laugh, and laid her soft cheek on the top of her brother's curly head, as if it were a pillow, while she went on with the story. "So this Boy—"

"But it wasn't me, oo know!" Bruno interrupted. "And oo needn't try to look as if it was, Mister Sir!"

I represented, respectfully, that I was trying to look as if it wasn't.

"—he was a middling good Boy—"

"He were a welly good Boy!" Bruno corrected her. "And he never did nothing he wasn't told to do—"

"That doesn't make a good Boy!" Sylvie said contemptuously.

"That do make a good Boy!" Bruno insisted.

Sylvie gave up the point. "Well, he was a very good boy and he always kept his promises, and he had a big cupboard—"

"—for to keep all his promises in!" cried Bruno.

"If he kept all his promises," Sylvie said, with a mischievous look in her eyes, "he wasn't like some Boys I know of!"

"He had to put salt with them, a-course," Bruno said gravely: "oo ca'n't keep promises when there isn't any salt. And he kept his birthday on the second shelf."

"How long did he keep his birthday?" I asked. "I never can keep mine more than twenty-four hours."

"Why, a birthday stays that long by itself!" cried Bruno. "Oo doosn't know how to keep birthdays! This Boy kept his a whole year!"

"And then the next birthday would begin," said Sylvie. "So it would be his birthday always."

"So it were," said Bruno. "Doos oo have treats on oor birthday, Mister Sir?"

"Sometimes," I said.

"When oo're good, I suppose?"

"Why, it is a sort of treat, being good, isn't it?" I said.

"A sort of treat!" Bruno repeated. "It's a sort of punishment I think!"

"Oh, Bruno!" Sylvie interrupted, almost sadly. "How can you?"

"Well, but it is," Bruno persisted. "Why, look here, Mister Sir! This is being good!" And he sat bolt upright, and put on an absurdly solemn face. "First oo must sit up as straight as pokers—"

"—as straight as a poker," Sylvie corrected him.

"—as straight as pokers," Bruno firmly repeated. "Then oo must clasp oor hands—so. Then— 'Why hasn't oo brushed oor hair? Go and brush it toreckly!' Then—'Oh, Bruno, oo mustn't dog's-ear the daisies!' Did oo learn oor spelling wiz daisies, Mister Sir?"

"I want to hear about that Boy's Birthday," I said.

Bruno returned to the story instantly. "Well, so this Boy said 'Now it's my Birthday!' And so—I'm tired!" he suddenly broke off, laying his head in Sylvie's lap. "Sylvie knows it best. Sylvie's grown-upper than me. Go on, Sylvie!"

Sylvie patiently took up the thread of the story again. "So he said 'Now it's my Birthday. Whatever shall I do to keep my Birthday?' All good little Boys—" (Sylvie turned away from Bruno, and made a great presence of whispering to me) "—all good little Boys—Boys that learn their lessons quite perfect—they always keep their birthdays, you know. So of course this little Boy kept his Birthday."

"Oo may call him Bruno, if oo like," the little fellow carelessly remarked. "It weren't me, but it makes it more interesting."

"So Bruno said to himself 'The properest thing to do is to have a Picnic, all by myself, on the top of the hill. And I'll take some Milk, and some Bread, and some Apples: and first and foremost, I want some Milk!' So, first and foremost, Bruno took a milk-pail—"

"And he went and milkted the Cow!" Bruno put in.

"Yes," said Sylvie, meekly accepting the new verb. "And the Cow said 'Moo! What are you going to do with all that Milk?' And Bruno said 'Please'm, I want it for my Picnic.' And the Cow said 'Moo! But I hope you wo'n't boil any of it?' And Bruno said 'No, indeed I wo'n't! New Milk's so nice and so warm, it wants no boiling!'"

"It doesn't want no boiling,' Bruno offered as an amended version.

"So Bruno put the Milk in a bottle. And then Bruno said 'Now I want some Bread!' So he went to the Oven, and he took out a delicious new Loaf. And the Oven—".

"—ever so light and so puffy!" Bruno impatiently corrected her. "Oo shouldn't leave out so many words!"

Sylvie humbly apologized. "—a delicious new Loaf, ever so light and so puffy. And the Oven said—" Here Sylvie made a long pause. "Really I don't know what an Oven begins with, when it wants to speak!"

Both children looked appealingly at me; but I could only say, helplessly, "I haven't the least idea! I never heard an Oven speak!"

For a minute or two we all sat silent; and then Bruno said, very softly, "Oven begins wiz 'O'."

"Good little boy!" Sylvie exclaimed. "He does his spelling very nicely. He's cleverer than he knows!" she added, aside, to me. "So the Oven said 'O! What are you going to do with all that Bread?' And Bruno said 'Please—' Is an Oven 'Sir' or 'm', would you say?" She looked to me for a reply. "Both, I think," seemed to me the safest thing to say.

Sylvie adopted the suggestion instantly. "So Bruno said 'Please, Sirm, I want it for my Picnic.' And the Oven said 'O! But I hope you wo'n't toast any of it?' And Bruno said, 'No, indeed I wo'n't! New Bread's so light and so puffy, it wants no toasting!'"

"It never doesn't want no toasting," said Bruno. "I wiss oo wouldn't say it so short!"

"So Bruno put the Bread in the hamper. Then Bruno said 'Now I want some Apples!' So he took the hamper, and he went to the Apple-Tree, and he picked some lovely ripe Apples. And the Apple-Tree said—" Here followed another long pause.

Bruno adopted his favourite expedient of tapping his forehead; while Sylvie gazed earnestly upwards, as if she hoped for some suggestion from the birds, who were singing merrily among the branches overhead. But no result followed.

"What does an Apple-Tree begin with, when it wants to speak?" Sylvie murmured despairingly, to the irresponsive birds.

At last, taking a leaf out of Bruno's book, I ventured on a remark. "Doesn't 'Apple-Tree' always begin with 'Eh!'?"

"Why, of course it does! How clever of you!" Sylvie cried delightedly.

Bruno jumped up, and patted me on the head. I tried not to feel conceited.

"So the Apple-Tree said 'Eh! What are you going to do with all those Apples?' And Bruno said 'Please, Sir, I want them for my Picnic.' And the Apple-Tree said 'Eh! But I hope you wo'n't bake any of them?' And Bruno said 'No, indeed I wo'n't! Ripe Apples are so nice and so sweet, they want no baking!'"

"They never doesn't—" Bruno was beginning, but Sylvie corrected herself before he could get the words out.

"'They never doesn't nohow want no baking.' So Bruno put the Apples in the hamper, along with the Bread, and the bottle of Milk. And he set off to have a Picnic, on the top of the hill, all by himself—"

"He wasn't greedy, oo know, to have it all by himself," Bruno said, patting me on the cheek to call my attention; "'cause he hadn't got no brothers and sisters."

"It was very sad to have no sisters, wasn't it?" I said.

"Well, I don't know," Bruno said thoughtfully, "'cause he hadn't no lessons to do. So he didn't mind."

Sylvie went on. "So, as he was walking along the road he heard behind him such a curious sort of noise—a sort of a Thump! Thump! Thump! 'Whatever is that?' said Bruno. 'Oh, I know!' said Bruno. 'Why, it's only my Watch a-ticking!'"

"Were it his Watch a-ticking?" Bruno asked me, with eyes that fairly sparkled with mischievous delight.

"No doubt of it!" I replied. And Bruno laughed exultingly.

"Then Bruno thought a little harder. And he said 'No! it ca'n't be my Watch a-ticking; because I haven't got a Watch!'"

Bruno peered up anxiously into my face, to see how I took it. I hung my head, and put a thumb into my mouth, to the evident delight of the little fellow.

"So Bruno went a little further along the road. And then he heard it again, that queer noise—Thump! Thump! Thump! 'Whatever is that?' said Bruno. 'Oh, I know!' said Bruno. 'Why, it's only the Carpenter amending my Wheelbarrow!'"

"Were it the Carpenter a-mending his Wheelbarrow?" Bruno asked me.

I brightened up, and said "It must have been!" in a tone of absolute conviction.

Bruno threw his arms round Sylvie's neck. "Sylvie!" he said, in a perfectly audible whisper. "He says it must have been!"

"Then Bruno thought a little harder. And he said 'No! It ca'n't be the Carpenter a-mending my Wheelbarrow, because I haven't got a Wheelbarrow!'"

This time I hid my face in my hands, quite unable to meet Bruno's look of triumph.

"So Bruno went a little further along the road. And then he heard that queer noise again—Thump! Thump! Thump! So he thought he'd look round, this time, just to see what it was. And what should it be but a great Lion!'"

"A great big Lion," Bruno corrected her.

"A great big Lion. And Bruno was ever so frightened, and he ran—"

"No, he wasn't flightened a bit!" Bruno interrupted. (He was evidently anxious for the reputation of his namesake.) "He runned away to get a good look at the Lion; 'cause he wanted to see if it were the same Lion what used to nubble little Boys' heads off; and he wanted to know how big it was!"

"Well, he ran away, to get a good look at the Lion. And the Lion trotted slowly after him. And the Lion called after him, in a very gentle voice, 'Little Boy, little Boy, You needn't be afraid of me! I'm a very gentle old Lion now. I never nubble little Boys' heads off, as I used to do.' And so Bruno said 'Don't you really, Sir? Then what do you live on?' And the Lion—"

"Oo see he weren't a bit flightened!" Bruno said to me, patting my cheek again. "'cause he remembered to call it Sir', oo know."

I said that no doubt that was the real test whether a person was frightened or not.

"And the Lion said 'Oh, I live on bread-and-butter, and cherries, and marmalade, and plum-cake—"

"—and apples!" Bruno put in.

"Yes, 'and apples'. And Bruno said "wo'n't you with me to my Picnic?' And the Lion said 'Oh, I should like it very much indeed!' And Bruno and the Lion went away together." Sylvie stopped suddenly.

"Is that all?" I asked, despondingly.

"Not quite all," Sylvie slily replied "There's a sentence or two more. Isn't there, Bruno?"

"Yes," with a carelessness that was evidently put on "just a sentence or two more."

"And, as they were walking along, they looked over a hedge, and who should they see but a little black Lamb! And the Lamb was ever so frightened. And it ran—"

"It were really flightened!" Bruno put in.

"It ran away. And Bruno ran after it. And he called 'Little Lamb! You needn't be afraid of this Lion! It never kills things! It lives on cherries, and marmalade—'"

"—and apples!" said Bruno. 'Oo always forgets the apples!"

"And Bruno said 'Wo'n't you come with us to my Picnic?' And the Lamb said 'Oh, I should like it very much indeed, if my Ma will let me!' And Bruno said 'Let's go and ask your Ma!' And they went to the old Sheep. And Bruno said 'Please, may your little Lamb come to my Picnic?' And the Sheep said 'Yes, if it's learnt all its lessons.' And the Lamb said 'Oh yes, Ma! I've learnt all my lessons!'"

"Pretend it hadn't any lessons!" Bruno earnestly pleaded.

"Oh, that would never do!" said Sylvie. "I ca'n't leave out all about the lessons! And the old Sheep said 'Do you know your A B C yet? Have you learnt A?' And the Lamb said 'Oh yes, Ma! I went to the A-field, and I helped them to make A!' 'Very good, my child! And have you learnt B?' 'Oh yes, Ma! I went to the B-hive, and the B gave me some honey!' 'Very good, my child! And have you learnt C?' 'Oh yes, Ma! I went to the C-side, and I saw the ships sailing on the C!' 'Very good, my child! You may go to Bruno's Picnic.'"

"So they set off. And Bruno walked in the middle so that the Lamb mightn't see the Lion—"

"It were flightened," Bruno explained.

"Yes, and it trembled so; and it got paler and paler; and, before they'd got to the top of the hill, it was a white little Lamb—as white as snow!"

"But Bruno weren't flightened!" said the owner of that name. "So he staid black!"

"No, he didn't stay black! He staid pink!" laughed Sylvie. "I shouldn't kiss you like this, you know, if you were black!"

"Oo'd have to!" Bruno said with great decision. "Besides, Bruno wasn't Bruno, oo know—I mean, Bruno wasn't me—I mean—don't talk nonsense, Sylvie!"

"I wo'n't do it again!" Sylvie said very humbly. "And so, as they went along, the Lion said 'Oh, I'll tell you what I used to do when I was a young Lion. I used to hide behind trees, to watch for little boys.'" (Bruno cuddled a little closer to her.) "'And, if a little thin scraggy Boy came by, why, I used to let him go. But, if a little fat juicy—'"

Bruno could bear no more. "Pretend he wasn't juicy!" he pleaded, half-sobbing.

"Nonsense, Bruno!" Sylvie briskly replied. "It'll be done in a moment! '—if a little fat juicy Boy came by, why, I used to spring out and gobble him up! Oh, you've no idea what a delicious thing it is—a little juicy Boy!' And Bruno said 'Oh, if you please, Sir, don't talk about eating little boys! It makes me so shivery!

The real Bruno shivered, in sympathy with the hero.

"And the Lion said 'Oh, well, we wo'n't talk about it, then! I'll tell you what happened on my wedding day—"

"I like this part better," said Bruno, patting my cheek to keep me awake.

"'There was, oh, such a lovely wedding-breakfast! At one end of the table there was a large plum-pudding. And at the other end there was a nice roasted Lamb! Oh, you've no idea what a delicious thing it is—a nice roasted Lamb!' And the Lamb said 'Oh, if you please, Sir, don't talk about eating Lambs! It makes me so shivery!' And the Lion said 'Oh, well, we wo'n't talk about it, then!'"

THE LITTLE FOXES

"So, when they got to the top of the hill, Bruno opened the hamper: and he took out the Bread, and the Apples and the Milk: and they ate, and they drank. And when they'd finished the Milk, and eaten half the Bread and half the Apples, the Lamb said 'Oh, my paws is so sticky! I want to wash my paws!' And the Lion said 'Well, go down the hill, and wash them in the brook, yonder. We'll wait for you!'"

"It never comed back!" Bruno solemnly whispered to me.

But Sylvie overheard him. "You're not to whisper, Bruno! It spoils the story! And when the Lamb had been gone a long time, the Lion said to Bruno 'Do go and see after that silly little Lamb! It must have lost its way.' And Bruno went down the hill. And when he got to the brook, he saw the Lamb sitting on the bank. and who should be sitting by it but an old Fox!"

"Don't know who should be sitting by it," Bruno said thoughtfully to himself. "A old Fox were sitting by it."

"And the old Fox were saying," Sylvie went on, for once conceding the grammatical point. "'Yes, my dear, you'll be ever so happy with us, if you'll only come and I've got three little Foxes there, and we do love lambs so dearly!' And the Lamb said 'But you never eat them, do you, Sir?' And the Fox said 'Oh, no! eat a Lamb? We never dream of doing such a thing!' So the Lamb said 'Then I'll come with you. And off they went, hand in hand."

"That Fox were welly extremely wicked, weren't it?" said Bruno.

"No, no!" said Sylvie, rather shocked at such violent language. "It wasn't quite so bad as that!"

"Well, I mean, it wasn't nice," the little fellow corrected himself.

"And so Bruno went back to the Lion. 'Oh, come quick!' he said. 'The Fox has taken the Lamb to his house with him! I'm sure he means to eat it!' And the Lion said 'I'll come as quick as ever I can!' And they trotted down the hill."

"Do oo think he caught the Fox, Mister Sir?" said Bruno. I shook my head, not liking to speak: and Sylvie went on.

"And when they got to the house, Bruno looked in at the window. And there he saw the three little Foxes sitting round the table, with their clean pinafores on, and spoons in their hands—"

"Spoons in their hands!" Bruno repeated in an ecstasy of delight.

"And the Fox had got a great big knife—all ready to kill the poor little Lamb—" ("Oo needn't be flightened, Mister Sir!" Bruno put in, in a hasty whisper.)

"And just as he was going to do it, Bruno heard a great ROAR—" (The real Bruno put his hand into mine, and held tight), "and the Lion came bang through the door, and the next moment it had bitten off the old Fox's head! And Bruno jumped in at the window, and went leaping round the room, and crying out 'Hooray! Hooray! The old Fox is dead! The old Fox is dead!'"

Bruno got up in some excitement. "May I do it now?" he enquired.

Sylvie was quite decided on this point. "Wait till afterwards," she said. "The speeches come next, don't you know? You always love the speeches, don't you?"

"Yes, I doos," said Bruno: and sat down again.

"The Lion's speech. 'Now, you silly little Lamb, go home to your mother, and never listen to old Foxes again. And be very good and obedient.'"

"The Lamb's speech. 'Oh, indeed, Sir, I will, Sir!' and the Lamb went away." ("But oo needn't go away!" Bruno explained. "It's quite the nicest part—what's coming now!" Sylvie smiled. She liked having an appreciative audience.)

"The Lion's speech to Bruno. 'Now, Bruno, take those little Foxes home with you, and teach them to be good obedient little Foxes! Not like that wicked old thing there, that's got no head!'" ("That hasn't got no head," Bruno repeated.)

"Bruno's speech to the Lion. 'Oh, indeed, Sir, I will Sir!' And the Lion went away." ("It gets betterer and betterer, now," Bruno whispered to me, "right away to the end!")

"Bruno's speech to the little Foxes. 'Now, little Foxes, you're going to have your first lesson in being good—I'm going to put you into the hamper, along with the Apples and the Bread: and you're not to eat the Apples: and you're not to eat the Bread: and you're not to eat anything—till we get to my house: and then you'll have your supper.'"

"The little Foxes' speech to Bruno. The little Foxes said nothing.

"So Bruno put the Apples into the hamper—and the little Foxes—and the Bread—" ("They had picnicked all the Milk," Bruno explained in a whisper) "—and he set off to go to his house." ("We're getting near the end now, said Bruno.)

"And, when he had got a little way, he thought would look into the hamper, and see how the little Foxes were getting on."

"So he opened the door—" said Bruno.

"Oh, Bruno!" Sylvie exclaimed, "you're not telling the story! So he opened the door, and behold, there were no Apples! So Bruno said 'Eldest little Fox, have you been eating the Apples?' And the eldest little Fox said No no no!'" (It is impossible to give the tone in which Sylvie repeated this rapid little 'No no no!' The nearest I can come to it is to say that it was much as if a young and excited duck had tried to quack the words. It was too quick for a quack, and yet too harsh to be anything else.) "Then he said 'Second little Fox, have you been eating the Apples?' And the second little Fox said 'No no no!' Then he said 'Youngest little Fox, have you been eating the Apples?' And the youngest little Fox tried to say 'No no no!' but its mouth was so full, it couldn't, and it only said 'Wauch! Wauch! Wauch!' And Bruno looked into its mouth. And its mouth was full of Apples. And Bruno shook his head, and he said 'Oh dear, oh dear! What bad creatures these Foxes are!'"

Bruno was listening intently: and, when Sylvie paused to take breath, he could only just gasp out the words "About the Bread?"

"Yes," said Sylvie, "the Bread comes next. So he shut the door again; and he went a little further; and then he thought he'd just peep in once more. And behold, there was no Bread!" "What do 'behold' mean?" said Bruno. "Hush!" said Sylvie.) "And he said Eldest little Fox, have you been eating the Bread?' And the eldest little Fox said 'No no no!' 'Second little Fox, have you been eating the Bread?' And the second little Fox only said 'Wauch! Wauch! Wauch!' And Bruno looked into its mouth, and its mouth was full of Bread!' (It might have chokeded it," said Bruno.) "So he said 'Oh dear, oh dear! What shall I do with these Foxes?' And he went a little further—" ("Now comes the most interesting part," Bruno whispered.)

"And when Bruno opened the hamper again, what do you think he saw?" ("Only two Foxes!" Bruno cried in a great hurry.) "You shouldn't tell it so quick. However he did see only two Foxes. And he said 'Eldest little Fox have you been eating the youngest little Fox?' And the eldest little Fox said 'No no no!' 'Second little Fox, have you been eating the youngest little Fox?' And the second little Fox did its very best to say 'No no no!' but it could only say 'Weuchk! Weuchk! Weuchk!' And when Bruno looked into its mouth, it was half full of Bread, and half full of Fox!' (Bruno said nothing in the pause this time. He was beginning to pant a little, as he knew the crisis was coming.)

"And when he'd got nearly home, he looked once more into the hamper, and he saw—"

"Only—" Bruno began, but a generous thought struck him, and he looked at me. "Oo may say it, this time, Mister Sir!" he whispered. It was a noble offer, but I wouldn't rob him of the treat. "Go on, Bruno," I said, "you say it much the best." "Only—but—one—Fox!" Bruno said with great solemnity.

"'Eldest little Fox,'" Sylvie said, dropping the narrative-form in her eagerness, "'you've been so good that I can hardly believe you've been disobedient: but I'm afraid you've been eating your little sister?' And the eldest little Fox said 'Whihuauch! Whihuauch!' and then it choked. And Bruno looked into its mouth, and it was full! (Sylvie paused to take breath, and Bruno lay back among the daisies, and looked at me triumphantly. "Isn't it grand, Mister Sir?" said he. I tried hard to assume a critical tone. "It's grand," I said: "but it frightens one so! Oo may sit a little closer to me, if oo like," said Bruno.)

"And so Bruno went home: and took the hamper into the kitchen, and opened it. And he saw—" Sylvie looked at me, this time, as if she thought I had been rather neglected and ought to be allowed one guess, at any rate.

"He ca'n't guess!" Bruno cried eagerly. "I 'fraid I must tell him! There weren't nuffin in the hamper!" I shivered in terror, and Bruno clapped his hands with delight. 'He is flightened, Sylvie! Tell the rest!"

"So Bruno said 'Eldest little Fox, have you been eating yourself, you wicked little Fox?' And the eldest little fox said 'Whihuauch!' And then Bruno saw there was only its mouth in the hamper! So he took the mouth, and he opened it, and shook, and shook! And at last he shook the little Fox out of its own mouth! And then he said 'Open your mouth again, you wicked little thing!' And he shook, and shook! And he shook out the second little Fox! And he said 'Now open your mouth!' And he shook, and shook! And he shook out the youngest little Fox, and all the Apples, and all the Bread!

"And then Bruno stood the little Foxes up against the wall: and he made them a little speech. 'Now, little Foxes, you've begun very wickedly—and you'll have to be punished. First you'll go up to the nursery, and wash your faces, and put on clean pinafores. Then you'll hear the bell ring for supper. Then you'll come down: and you wo'n't have any supper: but you'll have a good whipping! Then you'll go to bed. Then in the morning you'll hear the bell ring for breakfast. But you wo'n't have any breakfast! You'll have a good whipping! Then you'll have your lessons. And, perhaps, if you're very good, when dinner-time comes, you'll have a little dinner, and no more whipping!'" ("How very kind he was!" I whispered to Bruno. "Middling kind," Bruno corrected me gravely.)

"So the little Foxes ran up to the nursery. And soon Bruno went into the hall, and rang the big bell. 'Tingle, tingle, tingle! Supper, supper, supper!' Down came the little Foxes, in such a hurry for their supper! Clean pinafores! Spoons in their hands! And, when they got into the dining-room, there was ever such a white table-cloth on the table! But there was nothing on it but a big whip. And they had such a whipping!" (I put my handkerchief to my eyes, and Bruno hastily climbed upon my knee and stroked my face. "Only one more whipping, Mister Sir!" he whispered. "Don't cry more than oo ca'n't help!")

"And the next morning early, Bruno rang the big bell again. 'Tingle, tingle, tingle! Breakfast, breakfast, breakfast!' Down came the little Foxes! Clean pinafores! Spoons in their hands! No breakfast! Only the big whip! Then came lessons," Sylvie hurried on, for I still had my handkerchief to my eyes. "And the little Foxes were ever so good! And they learned their lessons backwards, and forwards, and upside-down. And at last Bruno rang the big bell again. 'Tingle, tingle, tingle! Dinner, dinner, dinner! And when the little Foxes came down—" ("Had they clean pinafores on?" Bruno enquired. "Of course!" said Sylvie. "And spoons?" "Why, you know they had!" "Couldn't be certain," said Bruno.) "—they came as slow as slow! And they said 'Oh! There'll be no dinner! There'll only be the big whip!' But, when they got into the room, they saw the most lovely dinner!" ("Buns?" cried Bruno, clapping his hands.) "Buns, and cake, and—" ("—and jam?" said Bruno.) "Yes, jam—and soup—and—" ("—and sugar plums!" Bruno put in once more; and Sylvie seemed satisfied.)

"And ever after that, they were such good little Foxes! They did their lessons as good as gold—and they never did what Bruno told them not to—and they never ate each other any more and they never ate themselves!"

The story came to an end so suddenly, it almost took my breath away; however I did my best to make a pretty speech of thanks. "I'm sure it's very—very—very much so, I'm sure!" I seemed to hear myself say.

BEYOND THESE VOICES

"I didn't quite catch what you said!" were the next words that reached my ear, but certainly not in the voice either of Sylvie or of Bruno, whom I could just see, through the crowd of guests, standing by the piano, and listening to the Count's song. Mein Herr was the speaker. "I didn't quite catch what you said!" he repeated. But I've no doubt you take my view of it. Thank you very much for your kind attention. There is only but one verse left to be sung!" These last words were not in the gentle voice of Mein Herr, but in the deep bass of the French Count. And, in the silence that followed, the final stanza of "Tottles" rang through the room.

See now this couple settled down
In quiet lodgings, out of town:
Submissively the tearful wife
Accepts a plain and humble life:
Yet begs one boon on bended knee:
"My ducky-darling, don't resent it!
Mamma might come for two or three—"

"NEVER!" yelled Tottles. And he meant it.

The conclusion of the song was followed by quite a chorus of thanks and compliments from all parts of the room, which the gratified singer responded to by bowing low in all directions. "It is to me a great privilege", he said to Lady Muriel, "to have met with this so marvellous a song. The accompaniment to him is so strange, so mysterious: it is as if a new music were to be invented. I will play him once again so as that to show you what I mean." He returned to the piano, but the song had vanished.

The bewildered singer searched through the heap of music lying on an adjoining table, but it was not there, either. Lady Muriel helped in the search: others soon joined: the excitement grew. "What can have become of it?" exclaimed Lady Muriel. Nobody knew: one thing only was certain, that no one had been near the piano since the Count had sung the last verse of the song.

"Nevare mind him!" he said, most good-naturedly. "I shall give it you with memory alone!" He sat down, and began vaguely fingering the notes; but nothing resembling the tune came out. Then he, too, grew excited. "But what oddness! How much of singularity! That I might lose, not the words alone, but the tune also—that is quite curious, I suppose?"

We all supposed it, heartily.

"It was that sweet little boy, who found it for me," the Count suggested. "Quite perhaps he is the thief?"

"Of course he is!" cried Lady Muriel. "Bruno! Where are you, my darling?"

But no Bruno replied: it seemed that the two children had vanished as suddenly, and as mysteriously, as the song.

"They are playing us a trick?" Lady Muriel gaily exclaimed. "This is only an ex tempore game of Hide-and-Seek! That little Bruno is an embodied Mischief!"

The suggestion was a welcome one to most of us, for some of the guests were beginning to look decidedly uneasy. A general search was set on foot with much enthusiasm: curtains were thrown back and shaken, cupboards opened, and ottomans turned over; but the number of possible hiding-places proved to be strictly limited; and the search came to an end almost as soon as it had begun.

"They must have run out, while we were wrapped up in the song," Lady Muriel said, addressing herself to the Count, who seemed more agitated than the others; "and no doubt they've found their way back to the housekeeper's room."

"Not by this door!" was the earnest protest of a knot of two or three gentlemen, who had been grouped round the door (one of them actually leaning against it) for the last half-hour, as they declared. "This door has not been opened since the song began!"

An uncomfortable silence followed this announcement. Lady Muriel ventured no further conjectures, but quietly examined the fastenings of the windows, which opened as doors. They all proved to be well fastened, inside.

Not yet at the end of her resources, Lady Muriel rang the bell. "Ask the housekeeper to step here, she said, "and to bring the children's walking-things with her."

"I've brought them, my Lady," said the obsequious housekeeper, entering after another minute of silence. "I thought the young lady would have come to my room to put on her boots. Here's your boots, my love' she added cheerfully, looking in all directions for the children. There was no answer, and she turned to Lady Muriel with a puzzled smile. "Have the little darlings hid themselves?"

"I don't see them, just now," Lady Muriel replied, rather evasively. "You can leave their things here, Wilson. I'll dress them, when they're ready to go."

The two little hats, and Sylvie's walking-jacket, were handed round among the ladies, with many exclamations of delight. There certainly was a sort of witchery of beauty about them. Even the little boots did not miss their share of favourable criticism. "Such natty little things!" the musical young lady exclaimed, almost fondling them as she spoke. "And what tiny tiny feet they must have!"

Finally, the things were piled together on the centre-ottoman, and the guests, despairing of seeing the children again, began to wish good-night and leave the house.

There were only some eight or nine left—to whom the Count was explaining, for the twentieth time, how he had had his eye on the children during the last verse of the song; how he had then glanced round the room, to see what effect "de great chest-note" had had upon his audience; and how, when he looked back again, they had both disappeared—when exclamations of dismay began to be heard on all sides, the Count hastily bringing his story to an end to join in the outcry.

The walking-things had all disappeared!

After the utter failure of the search for the children there was a very half-hearted search made for their apparel. The remaining guests seemed only too glad to get away, leaving only the Count and our four selves.

The Count sank into an easy-chair, and panted a little.

Who then are these dear children, I pray you?" he said. Why come they, why go they, in this so little ordinary a fashion? That the music should make itself vanish—that the hats, the boots, should make themselves to vanish— how is it, I pray you?"

"I've no idea where they are!" was all I could say, on finding myself appealed to, by general consent, for an explanation.

The Count seemed about to ask further questions, but checked himself.

"The hour makes himself to become late," he said. "I wish to you a very good night, my Lady. I betake myself to my bed—to dream—if that indeed I be not dreaming now!" And he hastily left the room.

"Stay awhile, stay awhile!" said the Earl, as I was about to follow the Count. "You are not a guest, you know! Arthur's friend is at home here!"

"Thanks!" I said, as with true English instincts, we drew our chairs together round the fire-place, though no fire was burning—Lady Muriel having taken the heap of music on her knee, to have one more search for the strangely-vanished song.

"Don't you sometimes feel a wild longing", she said addressing herself to me, "to have something more to do with your hands, while you talk, than just holding a cigar, and now and then knocking off the ash? Oh, I know all that you're going to say!" (This was to Arthur, who appeared about to interrupt her.) "The Majesty of Thought supersedes the work of the fingers. A Man's severe thinking, plus the shaking-off a cigar-ash, comes to the same total as a Woman's trivial fancies, plus the most elaborate embroidery. That's your sentiment, isn't it, only better expressed?"

Arthur looked into the radiant, mischievous face, with a grave and very tender smile. "Yes," he said resignedly: that is my sentiment, exactly."

"Rest of body, and activity of mind," I put in. "Some writer tells us that is the acme of human happiness."

"Plenty of bodily rest, at any rate!" Lady Muriel agreed, glancing at the three recumbent figures around her. "But what you call activity of mind—"

"—is the privilege of young Physicians only," said the Earl. "We old men have no claim to be active. What can old man do but die?"

"A good many other things, I should hope," Arthur said earnestly.

"Well, maybe. Still you have the advantage of me in any ways, dear boy! Not only that your day is dawning while mine is setting, but your interest in Life—somehow I ca'n't help envying you that. It will be many a year before you lose your hold of that."

"Yet surely many human interests survive human Life?" I said.

"Many do, no doubt. And some forms of Science; but only some, I think. Mathematics, for instance: that seems to possess an endless interest: one ca'n't imagine any form of Life, or any race of intelligent beings, where Mathematical truth would lose its meaning. But I fear Medicine stands on a different footing. Suppose you discover a remedy for some disease hitherto supposed to be incurable. Well, it is delightful for the moment, no doubt—full of interest—perhaps it brings you fame and fortune. But what then? Look on, a few years, into a life where disease has no existence. What is your discovery worth, then? Milton makes Jove promise too much. 'Of so much fame in heaven expect thy need.' Poor comfort when one's 'fame' concerns matters that will have ceased to have a meaning!"

"At any rate one wouldn't care to make any fresh medical discoveries," said Arthur. "I see no help for that—though I shall be sorry to give up my favourite studies. Still, medicine, disease, pain, sorrow, sin—I fear they're all linked together. Banish sin, and you banish them all!"

"Military science is a yet stronger instance," said the Earl. Without sin, war would surely be impossible. Still any mind, that has had in this life any keen interest, not in itself sinful, will surely find itself some congenial line of work hereafter. Wellington may have no more battles to fight—and yet—

We doubt not that, for one so true,

There must be other, nobler work to do,

Than when he fought at Waterloo,

And Victor he must ever be!'"

He lingered over the beautiful words, as if he loved them: and his voice, like distant music, died away into silence.

After a minute or two he began again. "If I'm not wearying you, I would like to tell you an idea of the future Life which has haunted me for years, like a sort of waking nightmare—I ca'n't reason myself out of it."

"Pray do," Arthur and I replied, almost in a breath. Lady Muriel put aside the heap of music, and folded her hands together.

"The one idea", the Earl resumed, "that has seemed to me to overshadow all the rest, is that of Eternity—involving, as it seems to do, the necessary exhaustion of all subjects of human interest. Take Pure Mathematics, for instance—a Science independent of our present surroundings. I have studied it, myself, a little. Take the subject of circles and ellipses—what we call 'curves of the second degree'. In a future Life, it would only be a question of so many years (or hundreds of years, if you like) for a man to work out all their properties. Then he might go to curves of the third degree. Say that took ten times as long (you see we have unlimited time to deal with). I can hardly imagine his interest in the subject holding out even for those; and, though there is no limit to the degree of the curves he might study, yet surely the time, needed to exhaust all the novelty and interest of the subject, would be absolutely finite? And so of all other branches of Science. And, when I transport myself, in thought, through some thousands or millions of years, and fancy myself possessed of as much Science as one created reason can carry, I ask myself 'What then? With nothing more to learn, can one rest content on knowledge, for the eternity yet to be lived through?' It has been a very wearying thought to me. I have sometimes fancied one might, in that event, say 'It is better not to be', and pray for personal annihilation—the Nirvana of the Buddhists."

"But that is only half the picture," I said. "Besides working for oneself, may there not be the helping of others?"

"Surely, surely!" Lady Muriel exclaimed in a tone of relief, looking at her father with sparkling eyes.

"Yes," said the Earl, "so long as there were any others needing help. But, given ages and ages more, surely all created reasons would at length reach the same dead level of satiety. And then what is there to look forward to?"

"I know that weary feeling," said the young Doctor. "I have gone through it all, more than once. Now let me tell you how I have put it to myself. I have imagined a little child, playing with toys on his nursery-floor, and yet able to reason, and to look on, thirty years ahead. Might he not say to himself 'By that time I shall have had enough of bricks and ninepins. How weary Life will be!' Yet, if we look forward through those thirty years, we find him a great statesman, full of interests and joys far more intense than his baby-life could give—joys wholly inconceivable to his baby-mind—joys such as no baby-language could in the faintest degree describe. Now, may not our life, a million years hence, have the same relation, to our life now, that the man's life has to the child's? And, just as one might try, all in vain, to express to that child, in the language of bricks and ninepins, the meaning of 'politics', so perhaps all those descriptions of Heaven, with its music, and its feasts, and its streets of gold, may be only attempts to describe, in our words, things for which we really have no words at all. Don't you think that in your picture of another life, you are in fact transplanting that child into political life, without making any allowance for his growing up?"

"I think I understand you," said the Earl. "The music of Heaven may be something beyond our powers of thought. Yet the music of Earth is sweet! Muriel, my child, sing us something before we go to bed!"

"Do," said Arthur, as he rose and lit the candles on the cottage-piano, lately banished from the drawing-room to make room for a "semi-grand". "There is a song here, that I have never heard you sing.

'Hail to thee, blithe spirit!
Bird thou never wert,
That from Heaven, or near it,
Pourest thy full heart!'"

he read from the page he had spread open before her.

"And our little life here", the Earl went on, "is, to that grand time, like a child's summer-day! One gets tired as night draws on," he added, with a touch of sadness in his voice, "and one gets to long for bed! For those welcome words 'Come, child, 'tis bed-time!'"

TO THE RESCUE

"It isn't bed-time!" said a sleepy little voice. "The owls hasn't gone to bed, and I s'a'n't go to seep wizout oo sings to me!"

"Oh, Bruno!" cried Sylvie. "Don't you know the owls have only just got up? But the frogs have gone to bed, ages ago."

"Well, I aren't a frog," said Bruno.

"What shall I sing?" said Sylvie, skilfully avoiding the argument.

"Ask Mister Sir," Bruno lazily replied, clasping his hands behind his curly head, and lying back on his fern-leaf, till it almost bent over with his weight. "This aren't a comfable leaf, Sylvie. Find me a comfabler—please!" he added, as an after-thought, in obedience to a warning finger held up by Sylvie. "I doosn't like being feet-upwards!"

It was a pretty sight to see the motherly way in which the fairy-child gathered up her little brother in her arms, and laid him on a stronger leaf. She gave it just a touch to set it rocking, and it went on vigorously by itself, as if it contained some hidden machinery. It certainly wasn't the wind, for the evening-breeze had quite died away again, and not a leaf was stirring over our heads.

"Why does that one leaf rock so, without the others?" I asked Sylvie. She only smiled sweetly and shook her head. "I don't know why," she said. "It always does, if it's got a fairy-child on it. It has to, you know."

"And can people see the leaf rock, who ca'n't see the Fairy on it?"

"Why, of course!" cried Sylvie. "A leaf's a leaf, and everybody can see it; but Bruno's Bruno, and they ca'n't see him, unless they're eerie, like you."

Then I understood how it was that one sometimes sees —going through the woods in a still evening—one fern-leaf rocking steadily on, all by itself. Haven't you ever seen that? Try if you can see the fairy-sleeper on it, next time; but don't pick the leaf, whatever you do; let the little one sleep on!

But all this time Bruno was getting sleepier and sleepier. "Sing, sing!" he murmured fretfully, Sylvie looked to me for instructions. "What shall it be?" she said. "Could you sing him the nursery-song you once told me of? I suggested. "The one that had been put through the mind-mangle, you know. 'The little man that had a little gun,' I think it was."

"Why, that are one of the Professor's songs!" cried Bruno. "I likes the little man; and I likes the way they spinned him—like a teetle-totle-tum." And he turned a loving look on the gentle old man who was sitting at the other side of his leaf-bed, and who instantly began to sing, accompanying himself on his Outlandish guitar, while the snail, on which he sat, waved its horns in time to the music.

In stature the Manlet was dwarfish—
No burly big Blunderbore he:
And he wearily gazed on the crawfish
His Wifelet had dressed for his tea.
"Now reach me, sweet Atom, my gunlet,
And hurl the old shoelet for luck:
Let me hie to the bank of the runlet,
And shoot thee a Duck!
She has reached him his minikin gunlet:
She has hurled the old shoelet for luck:
She is busily baking a bunlet
To welcome him home with his Duck.
On he speeds, never wasting a wordlet
Though thoughtlets cling, closely as wax
To the spot where the beautiful birdlet
So quietly quacks.

Where the Lobsterlet lurks, and the Crablet
So slowly and sleepily crawls:
Where the Dolphin's at home, and the Dablet
Pays long ceremonious calls:
Where the Grublet is sought by the Froglet:
Where the Frog is pursued by the Duck:
Where the Ducklet is chased by the Doglet—
So runs the world's luck!

He has loaded with bullet and powder:
His footfall is noiseless as air:
But the Voices grow louder and louder,
And bellow, and bluster, and blare.
They bristle before him and after,
They flutter above and below,
Shrill shriekings of lubberly laughter,
Weird wailings of woe!
They echo without him, within him:
They thrill through his whiskers and beard:
Like a teetotum seeming to spin him,
With sneers never hitherto sneered.
"Avengement," they cry, "on our Foelet!
Let the Manikin weep for our wrongs!
Let us drench him, from toplet to toelet,
With Nursery-Songs!

"He shall muse upon 'Hey! Diddle! Diddle!'
On the Cow that surmounted the Moon:
He shall rave of the Cat and the Fiddle,
And the Dish that eloped with the Spoon:
And his soul shall be sad for the Spider,
When Miss Muffet was sipping her whey,
That so tenderly sat down beside her,
And scared her away!
"The music of Midsummer-madness
Shall sting him with many a bite,
Till, in rapture of rollicking sadness,
He shall groan with a gloomy delight:
He shall swathe him, like mists of the morning,
In platitudes luscious and limp,
Such as deck, with a deathless adorning,
The Song of the Shrimp!
"When the Ducklet's dark doom is decided,
We will trundle him home in a trice:
And the banquet, so plainly provided,
Shall round into rose-buds and rice:
In a blaze of pragmatic invention
He shall wrestle with Fate, and shall reign:
But he has not a friend fit to mention,
So hit him again!"
He has shot it, the delicate darling!
And the Voices have ceased from their strife:
Not a whisper of sneering or snarling,
as he carries it home to his wife:
Then, cheerily champing the bunlet
His spouse was so skilful to bake,
He hies him once more to the runlet,
To fetch her the Drake!

"He's sound asleep now," said Sylvie, carefully tucking in the edge of a violet-leaf, which she had been spreading over him as a sort of blanket: "good night!"

"Good night!" I echoed.

"You may well say 'good night'!" laughed Lady Muriel, rising and shutting up the piano as she spoke. "When you've been nid—nid—nodding all the time I've been singing for your benefit! What was it all about, now?" she demanded imperiously.

"Something about a duck?" I hazarded. "Well, a bird of some kind?" I corrected myself, perceiving at once that that guess was wrong, at any rate.

"Something about a bird of some kind!" Lady Muriel repeated, with as much withering scorn as her sweet face was capable of conveying. "And that's the way he speaks of Shelley's Sky-Lark, is it? When the Poet particularly says 'Hail to thee, blithe spirit! Bird thou never wert!'"

She led the way to the smoking-room, where, ignoring all the usages of Society and all the instincts of Chivalry, the three Lords of the Creation reposed at their ease in low rocking-chairs, and permitted the one lady who was present to glide gracefully about among us, supplying our wants in the form of cooling drinks, cigarettes, and lights. Nay, it was only one of the three who had the chivalry to go beyond the common-place "thank you", and to quote the Poet's exquisite description of how Geraint, when waited on by Enid, was moved

"To stoop and kiss the tender little thumb
That crossed the platter as she laid it down,"

and to suit the action to the word—an audacious liberty for which, I feel bound to report, he was not duly reprimanded.

As no topic of conversation seemed to occur to any one, and as we were, all four, on those delightful terms with one another (the only terms, I think, on which any friendship, that deserves the name of intimacy, can be maintained) which involve no sort of necessity for speaking for mere speaking's sake, we sat in silence for some minutes.

At length I broke the silence by asking "Is there any fresh news from the harbour about the Fever?"

"None since this morning," the Earl said, looking very grave. "But that was alarming enough. The Fever is spreading fast: the London doctor has taken fright and left the place, and the only one now available isn't a regular doctor at all: he is apothecary, and doctor, and dentist, and I don't know what other trades, all in one. It's a bad outlook for those poor fishermen—and a worse one for all the women and children."

"How many are there of them altogether?" Arthur asked.

"There were nearly one hundred, a week ago," said the Earl: "but there have been twenty or thirty deaths since then."

"And what religious ministrations are there to be had?"

"There are three brave men down there," the Earl replied, his voice trembling with emotion, "gallant heroes as ever won the Victoria Cross! I am certain that no one of the three will ever leave the place merely to save his own life. There's the Curate: his wife is with him: they have no children. Then there's the Roman Catholic Priest. And there's the Wesleyan Minister. They go amongst their own flocks mostly; but I'm told that those who are dying like to have any of the three with them. How slight the barriers seem to be that part Christian from Christian when one has to deal with the great facts of Life and the reality of Death!"

"So it must be, and so it should be—" Arthur was beginning, when the front-door bell rang, suddenly and violently.

We heard the front-door hastily opened, and voices outside: then a knock at the door of the smoking-room, and the old house-keeper appeared, looking a little scared.

"Two persons, my Lord, to speak with Dr. Forester."

Arthur stepped outside at once, and we heard his cheery "Well, my men?" but the answer was less audible, the only words I could distinctly catch being "ten since morning, and two more just—"

"But there is a doctor there?" we heard Arthur say and a deep voice, that we had not heard before, replied "Dead, Sir. Died three hours ago."

Lady Muriel shuddered, and hid her face in her hands: but at this moment the front-door was quietly closed, and we heard no more.

For a few minutes we sat quite silent: then the Earl left the room, and soon returned to tell us that Arthur had gone away with the two fishermen, leaving word that he would be back in about an hour. And, true enough, at the end of that interval—during which very little was said, none of us seeming to have the heart to talk—the front-door once more creaked on its rusty hinges, and a step was heard in the passage, hardly to be recognized as Arthur's, so slow and uncertain was it, like a blind man feeling his way.

He came in, and stood before Lady Muriel, resting one hand heavily on the table, and with a strange look in his eyes, as if he were walking in his sleep.

"Muriel—my love—" he paused, and his lips quivered: but after a minute he went on more steadily. "Muriel—my darling—they—want me—down in the harbour."

"Must you go?" she pleaded, rising and laying her hands on his shoulders, and looking up into his face with great eyes brimming over with tears. "Must you go, Arthur? It may mean—death!"

He met her gaze without flinching. "It does mean death," he said, in a husky whisper: "but—darling—I am called. And even my life itself—" His voice failed him, and he said no more.

For a minute she stood quite silent, looking upwards in a helpless gaze, as if even prayer were now useless, while her features worked and quivered with the great agony she was enduring. Then a sudden inspiration seemed to come upon her and light up her face with a strange sweet smile. "Your life?" she repeated. "It is not yours to give!"

Arthur had recovered himself by this time, and could reply quite firmly, "That is true," he said. "It is not mine give. It is yours, now, my—wife that is to be! And you—do you forbid me to go? Will you not spare me, my own beloved one?"

Still clinging to him, she laid her head softly on his breast. She had never done such a thing in my presence before, and I knew how deeply she must be moved. "I will spare you", she said, calmly and quietly, "to God."

"And to God's poor," he whispered.

"And to God's poor," she added. "When must it be, sweet love?"

"To-morrow morning," he replied. "And I have much to do before then."

And then he told us how he had spent his hour of absence. He had been to the Vicarage, and had arranged for the wedding to take place at eight the next morning (there was no legal obstacle, as he had, some time before this, obtained a Special Licence) in the little church we knew so well. "My old friend here", indicating me, "will act as 'Best Man', I know: your father will be there to give you away: and—and—you will dispense with bride's-maids, my darling?"

She nodded: no words came.

"And then I can go with a willing heart—to do God's work—knowing that we are one—and that we are together in spirit, though not in bodily presence—and are most of all together when we pray! Our prayers will go up together—"

"Yes, yes!" sobbed Lady Muriel. "But you must not stay longer now, my darling! Go home and take some rest. You will need all your strength to-morrow—"

"Well, I will go," said Arthur. "We will be here in good time to-morrow. Good night, my own own darling!"

I followed his example, and we two left the house together. As we walked back to our lodgings, Arthur sighed deeply once or twice, and seemed about to speak—but no words came, till we had entered the house, and had lit our candles, and were at our bedroom-doors. Then Arthur said "Good night, old fellow! God bless you!"

"God bless you!" I echoed from the very depths of my heart.

We were back again at the Hall by eight in the morning, and found Lady Muriel and the Earl, and the old Vicar, waiting for us. It was a strangely sad and silent party that walked up to the little church and back, and I could not help feeling that it was much more like a funeral than a wedding: to Lady Muriel it was in fact, a funeral rather than a wedding, so heavily did the presentiment weigh upon her (as she told us afterwards) that her newly-won husband was going forth to his death.

Then we had breakfast; and, all too soon, the vehicle was at the door, which was to convey Arthur, first to his lodgings, to pick up the things he was taking with him and then as far towards the death-stricken hamlet as it was considered safe to go. One or two of the fishermen were to meet him on the road, to carry his things the rest of the way.

"And are you quite sure you are taking all that you need?" Lady Muriel asked. "All that I shall need as a doctor, certainly. And my personal needs are few: I shall not even take any of own wardrobe—there is a fisherman's suit, ready-made, that is waiting for me at my lodgings. I shall only take my watch, and a few books, and—stay—there is one book I should like to add, a pocket-Testament—to use at the bedsides of the sick and dying—"

Take mine!" said Lady Muriel: and she ran upstairs to fetch it. "It has nothing written in it but 'Muriel'," she said as she returned with it: "shall I inscribe—" ', my own one," said Arthur, taking it from her. "What could you inscribe better than that? Could any human name mark it more clearly as my own individual property? Are you not mine? Are you not," (with all the old playfulness of manner) "as Bruno would say, 'my very mine'?"

He bade a long and loving adieu to the Earl and to me, and left the room, accompanied only by his wife, who was bearing up bravely, and was—outwardly, at least—less overcome than her old father. We waited in the room a minute or two, till the sounds of wheels had told us that Arthur had driven away; and even then we waited still, for the step of Lady Muriel, going upstairs to her room, to die away in the distance. Her step, usually so light and joyous, now sounded slow and weary, like one who plods on under a load of hopeless misery; and I felt almost as hopeless, and almost as wretched as she. "Are we four destined ever to meet again, on this side the grave?" I asked myself, as I walked to my home. And the tolling of a distant bell seemed to answer me, "No! No! No!"

A NEWSPAPER-CUTTING

EXTRACT FROM THE "FAYFIELD CHRONICLE"

Our readers will have followed with painful interest, the accounts we have from time to time published of the terrible epidemic which has, during the last two months, carried off most of the inhabitants of the little fishing-harbour adjoining the village of Elveston. The last survivors, numbering twenty-three only, out of a population which, three short months ago exceeded one hundred and twenty, were removed on Wednesday last, under the authority of the Local Board, and safely lodged in the County Hospital: and the place is now veritably "a city of the dead", without a single human voice to break its silence.

The rescuing party consisted of six sturdy fellows—fishermen from the neighbourhood—directed by the resident Physician of the Hospital, who came over for that purpose, heading a train of hospital-ambulances. The six men had been selected—from a much larger number who had volunteered for this peaceful "forlorn hope"—for their strength and robust health, as the expedition was considered to be, even now, when the malady has expended its chief force, not unattended with danger.

Every precaution that science could suggest, against the risk of infection, was adopted: and the sufferers were tenderly carried on litters, one by one, up the steep hill, and placed in the ambulances which, each provided with a hospital nurse, were waiting on the level road. The fifteen miles, to the Hospital, were done at a walking-pace, as some of the patients were in too prostrate a condition to bear jolting, and the journey occupied the whole afternoon.

The twenty-three patients consist of nine men, six women and eight children. It has not been found possible to identify them all, as some of the children—left with no surviving relatives—are infants: and two men and one woman are not yet able to make rational replies, the brain-powers being entirely in abeyance. Among a more well-to-do race, there would no doubt have been names marked on the clothes; but here no such evidence is forthcoming.

Besides the poor fishermen and their families, there were but five persons to be accounted for: and it was ascertained, beyond a doubt, that all five are numbered with the dead. It is a melancholy pleasure to place on record the names of these genuine martyrs—than whom none, surely, are more worthy to be entered on the glory-roll of England's heroes! They are as follows:

The Rev. James Burgess, M.A., and Emma his wife. He was the Curate at the Harbour, not thirty years old, and had been married only two years. A written record was found in their house, of the dates of their deaths.

Next to theirs we will place the honoured name of Dr. Arthur Forester, who, on the death of the local physician, nobly faced the imminent peril of death, rather than leave these poor folk uncared for in their last extremity. No record of his name, or of the date of his death, was found: but the corpse was easily identified, although dressed in the ordinary fisherman's suit (which he was known to have adopted when he went down there), by a copy of the New Testament, the gift of his wife, which was found, placed next his heart, with his hands crossed over it. It was not thought prudent to remove the body, for burial elsewhere: and accordingly it was at once committed to the ground, along with four others found in different houses, with all due reverence. His wife, whose maiden name was Lady Muriel Orme, had been married to him on the very morning on which he undertook his self-sacrificing mission.

Next we record the Rev. Walter Saunders, Wesleyan Minister. His death is believed to have taken place two or three weeks ago, as the words "Died October 5" were found written on the wall of the room which he is known to have occupied—the house being shut up, and apparently not having been entered for some time.

Last—though not a whit behind the other four in glorious self-denial and devotion to duty—let us record the name of Father Francis, a young Jesuit Priest who had been only a few months in the place. He had not been dead many hours when the exploring party came upon the body, which was identified, beyond the possibility of doubt, by the dress, and by the crucifix which was, like the young Doctor's Testament, clasped closely to his heart.

Since reaching the hospital, two of the men and one of the children have died. Hope is entertained for all the others: though there are two or three cases where the vital powers seem to be so entirely exhausted that it is but "hoping against hope" to regard ultimate recovery as even possible.

A FAIRY-DUET

The year—what an eventful year it had been for me,— was drawing to a close, and the brief wintry day hardly gave light enough to recognize the old familiar objects bound up with so many happy memories, as the train glided round the last bend into the station, and the hoarse cry of "Elveston! Elveston!" resounded along the platform.

It was sad to return to the place, and to feel that I should never again see the glad smile of welcome, that had awaited me here so few months ago. "And yet, if I were to find him here," I muttered, as in solitary state I followed the porter, who was wheeling my luggage on a barrow, "and if he were to 'strike a sudden hand in mine, And ask a thousand things of home,' I should not—no, 'I should not feel it to be strange'!"

Having given directions to have my luggage taken to my old lodgings, I strolled off alone, to pay a visit, before settling down in my own quarters, to my dear old friends—for such I indeed felt them to be, though it was barely half a year since first we met—the Earl and his widowed daughter.

The shortest way, as I well remembered, was to cross through the churchyard. I pushed open the little wicket-gate and slowly took my way among the solemn memorials of the quiet dead, thinking of the many who had during the past year, disappeared from the place, and had gone to "join the majority". A very few steps brought me in sight of the object of my search. Lady Muriel, dressed in the deepest mourning, her face hidden by a long crepe veil, was kneeling before a little marble cross, round which she was fastening a wreath of flowers.

The cross stood on a piece of level turf, unbroken by any mound, and I knew that it was simply a memorial cross, for one whose dust reposed elsewhere, even before reading the simple inscription:

In loving Memory of
ARTHUR FORESTER, M.D.
whose mortal remains lie buried by the sea:
whose spirit has returned to God who gave it.
"GREATER LOVE HATH NO MAN THAN THIS, THAT
A MAN LAY DOWN HIS LIFE FOR HIS FRIENDS."

She threw back her veil on seeing me approach, and came forwards to meet me, with a quiet smile, and far more self-possessed than I could have expected.

"It is quite like old times, seeing you here again!" she said, in tones of genuine pleasure. "Have you been to see my father?"

"No," I said: "I was on my way there, and came through here as the shortest way. I hope he is well, and you also?"

"Thanks, we are both quite well. And you? Are you any better yet?"

"Not much better, I fear: but no worse, I am thankful to say."

"Let us sit here awhile, and have a quiet chat," she said. The calmness—almost indifference—of her manner quite took me by surprise. I little guessed what a fierce restraint she was putting upon herself.

"One can be so quiet here," she resumed. "I come here every—every day."

"It is very peaceful," I said.

"You got my letter?"

"Yes, but I delayed writing. It is so hard to say—on paper "

"I know. It was kind of you. You were with us when we saw the last of—" She paused a moment, and went on more hurriedly. "I went down to the harbour several times, but no one knows which of those vast graves it is. However, they showed me the house he died in: that was some comfort. I stood in the very room where—where—" She struggled in vain to go on. The flood-gates had given way at last, and the outburst of grief was the most terrible I had ever witnessed. Totally regardless of my presence, she flung herself down on the turf, burying her face in the grass, and with her hands clasped round the little marble cross. "Oh, my darling, my darling!" she sobbed. "And God meant your life to be so beautiful!"

I was startled to hear, thus repeated by Lady Muriel, the very words of the darling child whom I had seen weeping so bitterly over the dead hare. Had some mysterious influence passed, from that sweet fairy-spirit, ere she went back to Fairyland, into the human spirit that loved her so dearly? The idea seemed too wild for belief. And yet, are there not "more things in heaven and earth than are dreamt of in our philosophy"?

"God meant it to be beautiful," I whispered, "and surely it was beautiful? God's purpose never fails!" I dared say no more, but rose and left her. At the entrance-gate to the Earl's house I waited, leaning on the gate and watching the sun set, revolving many memories—some happy, some sorrowful—until Lady Muriel joined me.

She was quite calm again now. "Do come in," she said. "My father will be so pleased to see you!"

The old man rose from his chair, with a smile, to welcome me; but his self-command was far less than his daughter's, and the tears coursed down his face as he grasped both my hands in his, and pressed them warmly.

My heart was too full to speak; and we all sat silent for a minute or two. Then Lady Muriel rang the bell for tea. "You do take five o'clock tea, I know!" she said to me, with the sweet playfulness of manner I remembered so well, "even though you ca'n't work your wicked will on the Law of

Gravity, and make the teacups descend into Infinite Space, a little faster than the tea!"

This remark gave the tone to our conversation. By a tacit mutual consent, we avoided, during this our first meeting after her great sorrow, the painful topics that filled our thoughts, and talked like light-hearted children who had never known a care.

"Did you ever ask yourself the question," Lady Muriel began, à propos of nothing, "what is the chief advantage of being a Man instead of a Dog?"

"No, indeed," I said: "but I think there are advantages on the Dog's side of the question as well.

"No doubt," she replied, with that pretty mock-gravity that became her so well: "but, on Man's side, the chief advantage seems to me to consist in having pockets! It was borne in upon me—upon us, I should say; for my father and I were returning from a walk—only yesterday. We met a dog carrying home a bone. What it wanted it for, I've no idea: certainly there was no meat on it—"

A strange sensation came over me, that I had heard all this, or something exactly like it, before: and I almost expected her next words to be "perhaps he meant to make a cloak for the winter?" However what she really said was "and my father tried to account for it by some wretched joke about pro bono publico. Well, the dog laid down the bone—not in disgust with the pun, which would have shown it to be a dog of taste but simply to rest its jaws, poor thing! I did pity it so! Won't you join my Charitable Association for supplying dogs with pockets' How would you like to have to carry your walking-stick in your mouth?"

Ignoring the difficult question as to the raison d'être of a walking-stick, supposing one had no hands, I mentioned a curious instance, I had once witnessed, of reasoning by a dog. A gentleman, with a lady, and child, and a large dog, were down at the end of a pier on which I was walking. To amuse his child, I suppose, the gentleman put down on the ground his umbrella and the lady's parasol, and then led the way to the other end of the pier, from which he sent the dog back for the deserted articles. I was watching with some curiosity. The dog came racing back to where I stood, but found an unexpected difficulty in picking up the things it had come for. With the umbrella in its mouth, its jaws were so far apart that it could get no firm grip on the parasol. After two or three failures, it paused and considered the matter.

Then it put down the umbrella and began with the parasol. Of course that didn't open its jaws nearly so wide and it was able to get a good hold of the umbrella, and galloped off in triumph. One couldn't doubt that it had gone through a real train of logical thought.

I entirely agree with you," said Lady Muriel. "but don't orthodox writers condemn that view, as putting Man on the level of the lower animals? Don't they draw a sharp boundary-line between Reason and Instinct?"

"That certainly was the orthodox view, a generation ago," said the Earl. "The truth of Religion seemed ready to stand or fall with the assertion that Man was the only reasoning animal. But that is at an end now. Man can still claim certain monopolies—for instance, such a use of language as enables us to utilize the work of many, by division of labour'. But the belief, that we have a monopoly of Reason, has long been swept away. Yet no catastrophe has followed. As some old poet says, 'God is where he was'."

"Most religious believers would now agree with Bishop Butler," said I, "and not reject a line of argument, even if it led straight to the conclusion that animals have some kind of soul, which survives their bodily death."

"I would like to know that to be true!" Lady Muriel exclaimed. "If only for the sake of the poor horses. Sometimes I've thought that, if anything could make me cease to believe in a God of perfect justice, it would be the sufferings of horses—without guilt to deserve it, and without any compensation!"

"It is only part of the great Riddle," said the Earl, "why innocent beings ever suffer. It is a great strain on Faith—but not a breaking strain, I think."

The sufferings of horses", I said, "are chiefly caused by Man's cruelty. So that is merely one of the many instances of Sin causing suffering to others than the Sinner himself. But don't you find a greater difficulty in sufferings inflicted by animals upon each other? For instance, a cat playing with a mouse. Assuming it to have no moral responsibility, isn't that a greater mystery than a man over-driving a horse?"

"I think it is," said Lady Muriel, looking a mute appeal to her father.

"What right have we to make that assumption?" said the Earl. "Many of our religious difficulties are merely deductions from unwarranted assumptions. The wisest answer to most of them, is, I think, 'behold, we know not anything'."

"You mentioned 'division of labour', just now," I said. "Surely it is carried to a wonderful perfection in a hive of bees?"

"So wonderful—so entirely super-human—" said the Earl, "and so entirely inconsistent with the intelligence they show in other ways—that I feel no doubt at all that it is pure Instinct, and not, as some hold, a very high order of Reason. Look at the utter stupidity of a bee, trying to find its way out of an open window! It doesn't try, in any reasonable sense of the word: it simply bangs itself about! We should call a puppy imbecile, that behaved so. And yet we are asked to believe that its intellectual level is above Sir Isaac Newton!"

"Then you hold that pure Instinct contains no Reason at all?"

"On the contrary," said the Earl, "I hold that the work of a bee-hive involves Reason of the highest order. But none of it is done by the Bee. God has reasoned it all out, and has put into the mind of the Bee the conclusions, only, of the reasoning process."

"But how do their minds come to work together?" I asked.

"What right have we to assume that they have minds?"

"Special pleading, special pleading!" Lady Muriel cried, in a most unfilial tone of triumph. "Why, you yourself said, just now, 'the mind of the Bee'!"

"But I did not say 'minds', my child," the Earl gently replied. "It has occurred to me, as the most probable solution of the 'Bee'-mystery, that a swarm of Bees have only one mind among them. We often see one mind animating a most complex collection of limbs and organs, when joined together. How do we know that any material connection is necessary? May not mere neighbourhood be enough? If so, a swarm of bees is simply a single animal whose many limbs are not quite close together!"

"It is a bewildering thought," I said, "and needs a night's rest to grasp it properly. Reason and Instinct both tell me I ought to go home. So, good-night!"

"I'll 'set' you part of the way," said Lady Muriel. "I've had no walk to-day. It will do me good, and I have more to say to you. Shall we go through the wood? It will be pleasanter than over the common, even though it is getting a little dark."

We turned aside into the shade of interlacing boughs, which formed an architecture of almost perfect symmetry, grouped into lovely groined arches, or running out, far as the eye could follow, into endless aisles, and chancels, and naves, like some ghostly cathedral, fashioned out of the dream of a moon-struck poet.

"Always, in this wood," she began after a pause (silence seemed natural in this dim solitude), "I begin thinking of Fairies! May I ask you a question?" she added hesitatingly. "Do you believe in Fairies?"

The momentary impulse was so strong to tell her of my experiences in this very wood, that I had to make a real effort to keep back the words that rushed to my lips. "If you mean, by 'believe', 'believe in their possible existence', I say 'Yes'. For their actual existence, of course, one would need evidence."

"You were saying, the other day", she went on, "that you would accept anything, on good evidence, that was not à priori impossible. And I think you named Ghosts as an instance of a provable phenomenon. Would Fairies be another instance?"

"Yes, I think so." And again it was hard to check the wish to say more: but I was not yet sure of a sympathetic listener.

"And have you any theory as to what sort of place they would occupy in Creation? Do tell me what you think about them! Would they, for instance (supposing such beings to exist), would they have any moral responsibility? I mean" (and the light bantering tone suddenly changed to one of deep seriousness) "would they be capable of sin?"

"They can reason—on a lower level, perhaps, than men and women—never rising, I think, above the faculties of a child; and they have a moral sense, most surely. Such a being, without free will, would be an absurdity. So I am driven to the conclusion that they are capable of sin."

"You believe in them?" she cried delightedly, with a sudden motion as if about to clap her hands. "Now tell me, have you any reason for it?"

And still I strove to keep back the revelation I felt sure was coming. "I believe that there is life everywhere —not material only, not merely what is palpable to our senses—but immaterial and invisible as well; We believe in our own immaterial essence—call it 'soul, or spirit, or what you will. Why should not other similar essences exist around us, not linked on to a visible and material body? Did not God make this swarm of happy insects, to dance in this sunbeam for one hour of bliss, for no other object, that we can imagine, than to swell the sum of conscious happiness? And where shall we dare to draw the line, and say 'He has made all these and no more'?"

"Yes, yes"! she assented, watching me with sparkling eyes. "But these are only reasons for not denying. You have more reasons than this, have you not?"

"Well, yes," I said, feeling I might safely tell all now. "And I could not find a fitter time or place to say it. I have seen them—and in this very wood!"

Lady Muriel asked no more questions. Silently she paced at my side, with head bowed down and hands clasped tightly together. Only, as my tale went on, she drew a little short quick breath now and then, like a child panting with delight. And I told her what I had never yet breathed to any other listener, of my double life, and, more than that (for mine might have been but a noonday-dream), of the double life of those two dear children.

And when I told her of Bruno's wild gambols, she laughed merrily; and when I spoke of Sylvie's sweetness and her utter unselfishness and trustful love, she drew a deep breath, like one who hears at last some precious tidings for which the heart has ached for a long while and the happy tears chased one another down her cheeks.

I have often longed to meet an angel," she whispered so low that I could hardly catch the words. "I'm so glad I've seen Sylvie! My heart went out to the child the first moment that I saw her—Listen!" she broke off suddenly. That's Sylvie singing! I'm sure of it! Don't you know her voice?"

"I have heard Bruno sing, more than once," I said: "but I never heard Sylvie."

"I have only heard her once," said Lady Muriel. "It was that day when you brought us those mysterious flowers. The children had run out into the garden; and I saw Eric coming in that way, and went to the window to meet him: and Sylvie was singing, under the trees, a song I had never heard before. The words were something like 'I think it is Love, I feel it is Love'. Her voice sounded far away, like a dream, but it was beautiful beyond all words—as sweet as an infant's first smile, or the first gleam of the white cliffs when one is coming home after weary years—a voice that seemed to fill one's whole being with peace and heavenly thoughts—Listen!" she cried, breaking off again in her excitement. "That is her voice, and that's the very song!"

I could distinguish no words, but there was a dreamy sense of music in the air that seemed to grow ever louder and louder, as if coming nearer to us. We stood quite silent, and in another minute the two children appeared, coming straight towards us through an arched opening among the trees. Each had an arm round the other, and the setting sun shed a golden halo round their heads, like what one sees in pictures of saints. They were looking in our direction, but evidently did not see us, and I soon made out that Lady Muriel had for once passed into a condition familiar to me, that we were both of us "eerie", and that, though we could see the children so plainly, we were quite invisible to them.

The song ceased just as they came into sight: but, to my delight, Bruno instantly said "Let's sing it all again, Sylvie! It did sound so pretty!" And Sylvie replied "Very well. It's you to begin, you know."

So Bruno began, in the sweet childish treble I knew so well:

"Say, what is the spell, when her fledgelings are cheeping,
That lures the bird home to her nest?
Or wakes the tired mother, whose infant is weeping,
To cuddle and croon it to rest;
What's the magic that charms the glad babe in her arms,
Till it cooes with the voice of the dove?"

And now ensued quite the strangest of all the strange experiences that marked the wonderful year whose history I am writing—the experience of first hearing Sylvie's voice in song. Her part was a very short one—only a few words—and she sang it timidly, and very low indeed, scarcely audibly, but the sweetness of her voice was simply indescribable; I have never heard any earthly music like it.

"'Tis a secret, and so let us whisper it low
And the name of the secret is Love!"

On me the first effect of her voice was a sudden sharp pang that seemed to pierce through one's very heart. (I had felt such a pang only once before in my life, and it had been from seeing what, at the moment, realized one's idea of perfect beauty—it was in a London exhibition where, in making my way through a crowd, I suddenly met, face to face, a child of quite unearthly beauty.) Then came a rush of burning tears to the eyes, as though one could weep one's soul away for pure delight. And lastly there fell on me a sense of awe that was almost terror— some such feeling as Moses must have had when he heard the words "Put off thy shoes from off thy feet, for the place whereon thou standest is holy ground" The figures of the children became vague and shadowy, like glimmering meteors: while their voices rang together in exquisite harmony as they sang:

"For I think it is Love
For I feel it is Love,
For I'm sure it is nothing but Love!"

By this time I could see them clearly once more. Bruno again sang by himself:

"Say, whence is the voice that, when anger is burning,
Bids the whirl of the tempest to cease?
That stirs the vexed soul with an aching—a yearning
For the brotherly hand-grip of peace;
Whence the music that fills all our being—that thrills
Around us, beneath, and above?"

Sylvie sang more courageously, this time: the words seemed to carry her away, out of herself:

"'Tis a secret: none knows how it comes, how it goes
But the name of the secret is Love!"

And clear and strong the chorus rang out:

"For I think it is Love,
For I feel it is Love,
For I'm sure it is nothing but Love!"

Once more we heard Bruno's delicate little voice alone:

"Say whose is the skill that paints valley and hill,
Like a picture so fair to the sight?
That pecks the green meadow with sunshine and shadow,
Till the little lambs leap with delight?"

And again uprose that silvery voice, whose angelic sweetness I could hardly bear:

"'Tis a secret untold to hearts cruel and cold,
Though 'tis sung, by the angels above,
In notes that ring clear for the ears that can hear—
And the name of the secret is Love!"

And then Bruno joined in again with

"For I think it is Love,
For I feel it is Love,
For I'm sure it is nothing but Love!"

"That are pretty!" the little fellow exclaimed, as the children passed us— so closely that we drew back a little to make room for them, and it seemed we had only to reach out a hand to touch them: but this we did not attempt.

"No use to try and stop them!" I said, as they passed away into the shadows. "Why, they could not even see us!"

"No use at all," Lady Muriel echoed with a sigh. "One would like to meet them again, in living form! But I feel, somehow, that can never be. They have passed out of our lives!" She sighed again; and no more was said, till we came out into the main road, at a point near my lodgings.

"Well; I will leave you here," she said. "I want to get back before dark: and I have a cottage-friend to visit, first. Good night, dear friend! Let us see you soon—and often!" she added, with an affectionate warmth that went to my very heart. "For those are few we hold as dear!

"Good night!" I answered. "Tennyson said that of a worthier friend than me."

"Tennyson didn't know what he was talking about!" she saucily rejoined, with a touch of her old childish gaiety; and we parted.

GAMMON AND SPINACH

My landlady's welcome had an extra heartiness about it: and though, with a rare delicacy of feeling, she made no direct allusion to the friend whose companionship had done so much to brighten life for me, I felt sure that it was a kindly sympathy with my solitary state that made her so specially anxious to do all she could think of to ensure my comfort, and make me feel at home.

The lonely evening seemed long and tedious: yet I lingered on, watching the dying fire, and letting Fancy mould the red embers into the forms and faces belonging to bygone scenes. Now it seemed to be Bruno's roguish smile that sparkled for a moment, and died away: now it was Sylvie's rosy cheek: and now the Professor's jolly round face, beaming with delight. "You're welcome, my little ones!" he seemed to say. And then the red coal, which for the moment embodied the dear old Professor began to wax dim, and with its dying lustre the words seemed to die away into silence. I seized the poker, and with an artful touch or two revived the waning glow, while Fancy—no coy minstrel she—sang me once again the magic strain I loved to hear.

"You're welcome, little ones!" the cheery voice repeated. "I told them you were coming. Your rooms are all ready for you. And the Emperor and the Empress— well, I think they're rather pleased than otherwise! In fact, Her Highness said 'I hope they'll be in time for the Banquet!' Those were her very words, I assure you!"

"Will Uggug be at the Banquet?" Bruno asked. And both children looked uneasy at the dismal suggestion.

"Why, of course he will!" chuckled the Professor. "Why, it's his birthday, don't you know? And his health will be drunk, and all that sort of thing. What would the Banquet be without him?"

"Ever so much nicer," said Bruno. But he said it in a very low voice, and nobody but Sylvie heard him.

The Professor chuckled again. "It'll be a jolly Banquet, now you've come, my little man! I am so glad to see you again!"

"I 'fraid we've been very long in coming," Bruno politely remarked.

"Well, yes," the Professor assented. "However, you're very short, now you've come: that's some comfort." And he went on to enumerate the plans for the day. The Lecture comes first," he said. "That the Empress insists on. She says people will eat so much at the Banquet, they'll be too sleepy to attend to the Lecture afterwards— and perhaps she's right. There'll just be a little refreshment, when the people first arrive as a kind of surprise for the

Empress, you know. Ever since she's been—well, not quite so clever as she once was—we've found it desirable to concoct little surprises for her. Then comes the Lecture—"

"What? The Lecture you were getting ready ever so long ago?" Sylvie enquired.

"Yes—that's the one," the Professor rather reluctantly admitted. "It has taken a goodish time to prepare. I've got so many other things to attend to. For instance, I'm Court-Physician. I have to keep all the Royal Servants in good health—and that reminds me!" he cried, ringing the bell in a great hurry. "This is Medicine-Day! We only give Medicine once a week. If we were to begin giving it every day, the bottles would soon be empty!"

"But if they were ill on the other days?" Sylvie suggested.

"What, ill on the wrong day!" exclaimed the Professor. "Oh, that would never do! A Servant would be dismissed at once, who was ill on the wrong day! This is the Medicine for to-day, he went on, taking down a large jug from a shelf. I mixed it, myself, first thing this morning. Taste it!" he said, holding out the jug to Bruno. "Dip in your finger, and taste it!"

Bruno did so, and made such an excruciatingly wry face that Sylvie exclaimed in alarm, "Oh, Bruno, you mustn't!"

"It's welly extremely nasty!" Bruno said, as his face resumed its natural shape.

"Nasty?" said the Professor. "Why, of course it is! What would Medicine be, if it wasn't nasty?"

"Nice," said Bruno.

"I was going to say—" the Professor faltered, rather taken aback by the promptness of Bruno's reply, "—that that would never do! Medicine has to be nasty, you know. Be good enough to take this jug, down into the Servants' Hall, he said to the footman who answered the bell "and tell them it's their Medicine for to-day."

"Which of them is to drink it?" the footman asked as he carried off the jug.

"Oh, I've not settled that yet!" the Professor briskly replied. "I'll come and settle that, soon. Tell them not to begin, on any account, till I come! It's really wonderful", he said, turning to the children, "the success I've had in curing Diseases! Here are some of my memoranda." He took down from the shelf a heap of little bits of paper pinned together in twos and threes. "Just look at this set, now. Under-Cook Number Thirteen recovered from Common Fever—Febris Communis.' And now see what's pinned to it. 'Gave Under-Cook Number Thirteen a Double Dose of Medicine.' That's something to be proud of, isn't it?"

"But which happened first?" said Sylvie, looking very much puzzled.

The Professor examined the papers carefully. "They are not dated, I find," he said with a slightly dejected air: "so I fear I ca'n't tell you. But they both happened: there's no doubt of that. The Medicine's the great thing, you know. The Diseases are much less important. You can keep a Medicine, for years and years: but nobody ever wants to keep a Disease! By the way, come and look at the platform. The Gardener asked me to come and see if it would do. We may as well go before it gets dark."

"We'd like to, very much!" Sylvie replied. "Come, Bruno, put on your hat. Don't keep the dear Professor waiting!"

"Ca'n't find my hat!" the little fellow sadly replied. "I were rolling it about. And it's rolled itself away!"

"Maybe it's rolled in there," Sylvie suggested, pointing to a dark recess, the door of which stood half open: and Bruno ran in to look. After a minute he came slowly out again, looking very grave, and carefully shut the cupboard door after him.

"It aren't in there," he said, with such unusual solemnity, that Sylvie's curiosity was aroused.

"What is in there, Bruno?"

"There's cobwebs—and two spiders—" Bruno thoughtfully replied, checking off the catalogue on his fingers, "—and the cover of a picture-book—and a tortoise—and a dish of nuts—and an old man."

"An old man!" cried the Professor, trotting across the room in great excitement. "Why, it must be the Other Professor, that's been lost for ever so long!"

He opened the door of the cupboard wide: and there he was, the Other Professor, sitting in a chair, with a book on his knee, and in the act of helping himself to a nut from a dish, which he had taken down off a shelf just within his reach. He looked round at us, but said nothing till he had cracked and eaten the nut. Then he asked the old question. "Is the Lecture all ready?"

"It'll begin in an hour," the Professor said, evading the question. "First, we must have something to surprise the Empress. And then comes the Banquet—"

"The Banquet!" cried the Other Professor, springing up, and filling the room with a cloud of dust. Then I'd better go and—and brush myself a little. What a state I'm in!"

"He does want brushing!" the Professor said, with a critical air. "Here's your hat, little man! I had put it on by mistake. I'd quite forgotten I had one on, already. Let's go and look at the platform."

"And there's that nice old Gardener singing still!" Bruno exclaimed in delight, as we went out into the garden. I do believe he's been singing that very song ever since we went away!"

"Why, of course he has!" replied the Professor. "It wouldn't be the thing to leave off, you know."

"Wouldn't be what thing?" said Bruno: but the Professor thought it best not to hear the question. "What are you doing with that hedgehog?" he shouted at the Gardener, whom they found standing upon one foot, singing softly to himself, and rolling a hedgehog up and down with the other foot.

"Well, I wanted fur to know what hedgehogs lives on: so I be a-keeping this here hedgehog—fur to see if it eats potatoes—"

"Much better keep a potato," said the Professor, "and see if hedgehogs eat it!"

"That be the roight way, sure-ly!" the delighted Gardener exclaimed. "Be you come to see the platform?"

"Aye, aye!" the Professor cheerily replied. "And the children have come back, you see!"

The Gardener looked round at them with a grin. Then he led the way to the Pavilion; and as he went he sang:

"He looked again, and found it was
A Double Rule of Three:
'And all its Mystery', he said,
'Is clear as day to me!'"

"You've been months over that song," said the Professor. "Isn't it finished yet?"

"There be only one verse more," the Gardener sadly replied. And, with tears streaming down his cheeks, he sang the last verse:

"He thought he saw an Argument
That proved he was the Pope:
He looked again, and found it was
A Bar of Mottled Soap.
'A fact so dread', he faintly said,
'Extinguishes all hope!'"

Choking with sobs, the Gardener hastily stepped on a few yards ahead of the party, to conceal his emotion.

"Did he see the Bar of Mottled Soap?" Sylvie enquired, as we followed.

"Oh, certainly!" said the Professor. "That song is his own history, you know."

Tears of an ever-ready sympathy glittered in Bruno's eyes. "I's welly sorry he isn't the Pope!" he said. "Aren't you sorry, Sylvie?"

"Well—I hardly know," Sylvie replied in the vaguest manner. "Would it make him any happier?' she asked the Professor

"It wouldn't make the Pope any happier," said the Professor. "Isn't the platform lovely?" he asked, as we entered the Pavilion.

"I've put an extra beam under it!" said the Gardener, patting it affectionately as he spoke. "And now it's that strong, as—as a mad elephant might dance upon it!"

"Thank you very much!" the Professor heartily rejoined. "I don't know that we shall exactly require—but it's convenient to know." And he led the children upon the platform, to explain the arrangements to them. Here are three seats, you see, for the Emperor and the Empress and Prince Uggug. But there must be two more chairs here!" he said, looking down at the Gardener. "One for Lady Sylvie, and one for the smaller animal!"

"And may I help in the Lecture?" said Bruno. "I can do some conjuring tricks."

"Well, it's not exactly a conjuring lecture," the Professor said, as he arranged some curious-looking machines on the table. "However, what can you do? Did you ever go through a table, for instance?"

"Often!" said Bruno. "Haven't I, Sylvie?"

The Professor was evidently surprised, though he tried not to show it. "This must be looked into," he muttered to himself, taking out a note-book. "And first—what kind of table?"

"Tell him!" Bruno whispered to Sylvie, putting his arms round her neck.

"Tell him yourself," said Sylvie

"Ca'n't," said Bruno. "It's a bony word."

"Nonsense!" laughed Sylvie. "You can say it well enough, if you only try. Come!"

"Muddle—" said Bruno. "That's a bit of it."

"What does he say?" cried the bewildered Professor.

"He means the multiplication-table," Sylvie explained.

The Professor looked annoyed, and shut up his notebook again. "Oh, that's quite another thing," he said.

"It are ever so many other things," said Bruno. "Aren't it, Sylvie?"

A loud blast of trumpets interrupted this conversation "Why, the entertainment has begun!" the Professor exclaimed, as he hurried the children into the Reception Saloon. "I had no idea it was so late!"

A small table, containing cake and wine, stood in a corner of the Saloon; and here we found the Emperor and Empress waiting for us. The rest of the Saloon had been cleared of furniture, to make room for the guests. I was much struck by the great change a few months had made in the faces of the Imperial Pair. A vacant stare was now the Emperor's usual expression; while over the face of the Empress there flitted, ever and anon, a meaningless smile.

"So you're come at last!" the Emperor sulkily remarked, as the Professor and the children took their places. It was evident that he was very much out of temper: and we were not long in learning the cause of this. He did not consider the preparations, made for the Imperial party, to be such as suited their rank. A common mahogany table!" he growled, pointing to it contemptuously with his thumb. "Why wasn't it made of gold, I should like to know?"

"It would have taken a very long—" the Professor began, but the Emperor cut the sentence short.

"Then the cake! Ordinary plum! Why wasn't it made of—of—" He broke off again. "Then the wine! Merely old Madeira! Why wasn't it—? Then this chair! That s worst of all. Why wasn't it a throne? One might excuse the other omissions, but I ca'n't get over the chair!"

"What I ca'n't get over", said the Empress, in eager sympathy with her angry husband, "is the table!"

"Pooh!" said the Emperor.

"It is much to be regretted!" the Professor mildly replied, as soon as he had a chance of speaking. After a moment's thought he strengthened the remark. Everything", he said, addressing Society in general, "is very much to be regretted!"

A murmur of "Hear, hear!" rose from the crowded Saloon.

There was a rather awkward pause: the Professor evidently didn't know how to begin. The Empress leant forwards, and whispered to him. "A few jokes, you know, Professor—just to put people at their ease!

"True, true, Madam!" the Professor meekly replied. "This little boy—"

"Please don't make any jokes about me!" Bruno exclaimed, his eyes filling with tears.

"I wo'n't if you'd rather I didn't," said the kind-hearted Professor. "It was only something about a Ship's Buoy—a harmless pun—but it doesn't matter." Here he turned to the crowd and addressed them in a loud voice. Learn your A's!" he shouted. "Your B's! Your C's! and your D's, Then you'll be at your ease!"

There was a roar of laughter from all the assembly, and then a great deal of confused whispering. "What was it he said? Something about bees, I fancy—"

The Empress smiled in her meaningless way, and fanned herself. The poor Professor looked at her timidly: he was clearly at his wits' end again, and hoping for another hint. The Empress whispered again.

"Some spinach, you know, Professor, as a surprise."

The Professor beckoned to the Head-Cook, and said something to him in a low voice. Then the Head-Cook left the room, followed by all the other cooks.

"It's difficult to get things started," the Professor remarked to Bruno. "When once we get started, it'll go on all right, you'll see."

"If oo want to startle people", said Bruno, "oo should put live frogs on their backs."

Here the cooks all came in again, in a procession, the Head-Cook coming last and carrying something, which the others tried to hide by waving flags all round it. "Nothing but flags, Your Imperial Highness! Nothing but flags!" he kept repeating, as he set it before her. Then all the flags were dropped in a moment, as the Head Cook raised the cover from an enormous dish.

"What is it?" the Empress said faintly, as she put her spy-glass to her eye. "Why, it's Spinach, I declare!"

"Her Imperial Highness is surprised," the Professor explained to the attendants: and some of them clapped their hands. The Head-Cook made a low bow, and in doing so dropped a spoon on the table, as if by accident, just within reach of the Empress, who looked the other way and pretended not to see it.

"I am surprised!" the Empress said to Bruno. "Aren't you?"

"Not a bit," said Bruno. "I heard—" but Sylvie put her hand over his mouth, and spoke for him. "He's rather tired, I think. He wants the Lecture to begin."

"I want the supper to begin," Bruno corrected her.

The Empress took up the spoon in an absent manner, and tried to balance it across the back of her hand, and in doing this she dropped it into the dish: and, when she took it out again, it was full of spinach. "How curious!" she said, and put it into her mouth. "It tastes just like real spinach! I thought it was an imitation—but I do believe it's real!" And she took another spoonful.

"It wo'n't be real much longer," said Bruno.

But the Empress had had enough spinach by this time, and somehow— I failed to notice the exact process—we all found ourselves in the Pavilion, and the Professor in the act of beginning the long-expected Lecture.

THE PROFESSOR'S LECTURE

"In Science—in fact, in most things—it is usually best to begin at the beginning. In some things, of course, it's better to begin at the other end. For instance, if you wanted to paint a dog green, it might be best to begin with the tail, as it doesn't bite at that end. And so—"

"May I help oo?" Bruno interrupted.

"Help me to do what?" said the puzzled Professor, looking up for a moment, but keeping his finger on the book he was reading from, so as not to lose his place.

"To paint a dog green!" cried Bruno. "Oo can begin wiz its mouf, and I'll—"

"No, no!" said the Professor. "We haven't got to the Experiments yet. And so", returning to his note-book, "I'll give you the Axioms of Science. After that I shall exhibit some Specimens. Then I shall explain a Process or two. And I shall conclude with a few Experiments. An Axiom, you know, is a thing that you accept without contradiction. For instance, if I were to say 'Here we are", that would be accepted without any contradiction, and it's a nice sort of remark to begin a conversation with. So it would be an Axiom. Or again, supposing I were to say, 'Here we are not!', that would be—"

"—a fib!" cried Bruno.

"Oh, Bruno!" said Sylvie in a warning whisper. "Of course it would be an Axiom, if the Professor said it!"

"—that would be accepted, if people were civil," continued the Professor; "so it would be another Axiom."

"It might be an Axledum," Bruno said: "but it wouldn't be true!"

"Ignorance of Axioms", the Lecturer continued, "is a great drawback in life. It wastes so much time to have to say them over and over again. For instance, take the Axiom, 'Nothing is greater than itself'; that is, 'Nothing can contain itself.' How often you hear people say 'He was so excited, he was quite unable to contain himself.' Why, of course he was unable! The excitement had nothing to do with it!"

"I say, look here, you know!" said the Emperor, who was getting a little restless. "How many Axioms are you going to give us? At this rate, we sha'n't get to the Experiments till to-morrow-week!"

"Oh, sooner than that, I assure you!" the Professor replied, looking up in alarm. "There are only," (he referred to his notes again) "only two more, that are really necessary."

"Read 'em out, and get on to the Specimens," grumbled the Emperor.

"The First Axiom", the Professor read out in a great hurry, "consists of these words, 'Whatever is, is.' And the Second consists of these words, 'Whatever isn't, isn't.' We will now go on to the Specimens. The first tray contains Crystals and other Things." He drew it towards him, and again referred to his notebook. "Some of the labels—owing to insufficient adhesion—" Here he stopped again, and carefully examined the page with his eyeglass. "I ca'n't read the rest of the sentence," he said at last, "but it means that the labels have come loose, and the Things have got mixed—"

"Let me stick 'em on again!" cried Bruno eagerly, and began licking them, like postage-stamps, and dabbing them down upon the Crystals and the other Things. But the Professor hastily moved the tray out of his reach. "They might get fixed to the wrong Specimens, you know!" he said.

"Oo shouldn't have any wrong peppermints in the tray!" Bruno boldly replied. "Should he, Sylvie?"

But Sylvie only shook her head.

The Professor heard him not. He had taken up one of the bottles, and was carefully reading the label through his eye-glass. "Our first Specimen—" he announced, as he placed the bottle in front of the other Things, "is— that is, it is called—" here he took it up, and examined the label again, as if he thought it might have changed since he last saw it, "is called Aqua Pura—common water—the fluid that cheers—"

"Hip! Hip! Hip!" the Head-Cook began enthusiastically.

"—but not inebriates!" the Professor went on quickly, but only just in time to check the "Hooroar!" which was beginning.

"Our second Specimen", he went on, carefully opening a small jar, "is— " here he removed the lid, and a large beetle instantly darted out, and with an angry buzz went straight out of the Pavilion, "—is—or rather, I should say," looking sadly into the empty jar, "it was— a curious kind of Blue Beetle. Did anyone happen to remark—as it went past—three blue spots under each wing?"

Nobody had remarked them.

"Ah, well!" the Professor said with a sigh. "It's a pity. Unless you remark that kind of thing at the moment, it's very apt to get overlooked! The next Specimen, at any rate, will not fly away! It is—in short, or perhaps, more correctly, at length—an Elephant. You will observe—" Here he beckoned to the Gardener to come up on the platform, and with his help began putting together what looked like an enormous dog-kennel, with short tubes projecting out of it on both sides.

"But we've seen Elephants before," the Emperor grumbled.

"Yes, but not through a Megaloscope!" the Professor eagerly replied. "You know you ca'n't see a Flea, properly, without a magnifying-glass— what we call a Microscope. Well, just in the same way, you ca'n't see an Elephant, properly—without a minimifying-glass. There's one in each of these little tubes. And this is a Megaloscope The Gardener will now bring in the next Specimen. Please open both curtains, down at the end there, and make way for the Elephant!"

There was a general rush to the sides of the Pavilion and all eyes were turned to the open end, watching for the return of the Gardener, who had gone away singing "He thought he saw an Elephant That practiced on a Fife!" There was silence for a minute: and then his harsh voice was heard again in the distance. "He looked again—come up then! He looked again, and found it was—woe back! and found it was A letter from his— make way there! He's a-coming!"

And in marched or waddled—it is hard to say which is the right word— an Elephant, on its hind-legs, and playing on an enormous fife which it held with its fore-feet.

The Professor hastily threw open a large door at the end of the Megaloscope, and the huge animal, at a signal from the Gardener, dropped the fife, and obediently trotted into the machine, the door of which was at once shut by the Professor. "The Specimen is now ready for observation!" he proclaimed. "It is exactly the size of the common Mouse—Mus Communis!"

There was a general rush to the tubes, and the spectators watched with delight the minikin creature, as it playfully coiled its trunk round the Professor's extended finger, finally taking its stand upon the palm of his hand while he carefully lifted it out, and carried it off to exhibit to the Imperial party.

"Isn't it a darling?" cried Bruno. "May I stroke it, please? I'll touch it welly gently!"

The Empress inspected it solemnly with her eye-glass. "It is very small," she said in a deep voice. "Smaller than elephants usually are, I believe?"

The Professor gave a start of delighted surprise. "Why, that's true!" he murmured to himself. Then louder, turning to the audience, "Her Imperial Highness has made a remark which is perfectly sensible!" And a wild cheer arose from that vast multitude.

"The next Specimen", the Professor proclaimed, after carefully placing the little elephant in the tray, among the Crystals and other things, "is a Flea, which we will enlarge for the purposes of observation." Taking a small pill-box from the tray, he advanced to the Megaloscope, and reversed all the tubes. "The Specimen is ready!" he cried, with his eye at one of the tubes, while he carefully emptied the pill-box through a little hole at the side. "It is now the size of the Common Horse—Equis Communis!

There was another general rush, to look through the tubes, and the Pavilion rang with shouts of delight; through which the Professor's anxious tones could scarcely be heard. "Keep the door of the Microscope shut!" he cried. "If the creature were to escape, this size, it would—" But the mischief was done. The door had swung open, and in another moment the Monster had got out, and was trampling down the terrified, shrieking spectators.

But the Professor's presence of mind did not desert him. "Undraw those curtains!" he shouted. It was done. The Monster gathered its legs together, and in one tremendous bound vanished into the sky.

"Where is it?" said the Emperor, rubbing his eyes.

"In the next Province, I fancy," the Professor replied. "That jump would take it at least five miles! The next thing is to explain a Process or two. But I find there is hardly room enough to operate—the smaller animal is rather in my way—"

"Who does he mean?" Bruno whispered to Sylvie.

"He means you!" Sylvie whispered back. "Hush!"

"Be kind enough to move—angularly—to this corner," the Professor said, addressing himself to Bruno.

Bruno hastily moved his chair in the direction indicated. "Did I move angrily enough?" he inquired. But the Professor was once more absorbed in his Lecture, which he was reading from his note-book.

"I will now explain the process of—the name is blotted, I'm sorry to say. It will be illustrated by a number of— of—" here he examined the pages for some time, and at last said "It seems to be either 'Experiments' or 'Specimens'—"

"Let it be Experiments," said the Emperor. "We've seen plenty of Specimens."

"Certainly, certainly!" the Professor assented. "We will have some Experiments."

"May I do them?" Bruno eagerly asked.

"Oh dear no!" The Professor looked dismayed. "I really don't know what would happen if you did them!"

"Nor nobody doosn't know what'll happen if oo doos them!" Bruno retorted.

"Our First Experiment requires a Machine. It has two knobs—only two—you can count them, if you like."

The Head-Cook stepped forwards, counted them, and retired satisfied.

"Now you might press those two knobs together—but that's not the way to do it. Or you might turn the Machine upside-down—but that's not the way to do it!"

"What are the way to do it?" said Bruno, who was listening very attentively.

The Professor smiled benignantly. "Ah, yes!" he said, in a voice like the heading of a chapter. "The Way To Do It! Permit me!" and in a moment he had whisked Bruno upon the table. "I divide my subject", he began, "into three parts—"

"I think I'll get down!" Bruno whispered to Sylvie. "It aren't nice to be divided!"

"He hasn't got a knife, silly boy!" Sylvie whispered in reply. "Stand still! You'll break all the bottles!"

"The first part is to take hold of the knobs," putting them into Bruno's hands. "The second part is—" Here he turned the handle, and, with a loud "Oh!", Bruno dropped both the knobs, and began rubbing his elbows.

The Professor chuckled in delight. "It had a sensible effect. Hadn't it?" he enquired.

"No, it hadn't a sensible effect!" Bruno said indignantly. "It were very silly indeed. It jingled my elbows, and it banged my back, and it crinkled my hair, and it buzzed among my bones!"

"I'm sure it didn't!" said Sylvie. "You're only inventing,"

"Oo doesn't know nuffin about it!" Bruno replied. "Oo wasn't there to see. Nobody ca'n't go among my bones. There isn't room!"

"Our Second Experiment", the Professor announced, as Bruno returned to his place, still thoughtfully rubbing his elbows, "is the production of that seldom-seen-but greatly-to-be-admired phenomenon, Black Light! You have seen White Light, Red Light, Green Light, and so on: but never, till this wonderful day, have any eyes but mine seen Black Light! This box", carefully lifting it upon the table, and covering it with a heap of blankets, "is quite full of it. The way I made it was this—I took a lighted candle into a dark cupboard and shut the door. Of course the cupboard was then full of Yellow Light. Then I took a bottle of Black ink, and poured it over the candle: and, to my delight, every atom of the Yellow Light turned Black! That was indeed the proudest moment of my life! Then I filled a box with it. And now —would anyone like to get under the blankets and see it?"

Dead silence followed this appeal: but at last Bruno said "I'll get under, if it won't jingle my elbows."

Satisfied on this point, Bruno crawled under the blankets, and, after a minute or two, crawled out again, very hot and dusty, and with his hair in the wildest confusion.

"What did you see in the box?" Sylvie eagerly enquired.

"I saw nuffin!" Bruno sadly replied. "It were too dark!"

He has described the appearance of the thing exactly!" the Professor exclaimed with enthusiasm. "Black Light and Nothing, look so extremely alike, at first sight, that I don t wonder he failed to distinguish them! We will now proceed to the Third Experiment."

The Professor came down, and led the way to where a post had been driven firmly into the ground. To one side of the post was fastened a chain, with an iron weight hooked on to the end of it, and from the other side projected a piece of whalebone, with a ring at the end of it. This is a most interesting Experiment!" the Professor announced. "It will need time, I'm afraid: but that is a trifling disadvantage. Now observe. If I were to unhook this weight, and let go, it would fall to the ground. You do not deny that?"

Nobody denied it.

"And in the same way, if I were to bend this piece of whalebone round the post—thus—and put the ring over this hook—thus—it stays bent: but, if I unhook it, it straightens itself again. You do not deny that?"

Again, nobody denied it.

"Well, now, suppose we left things just as they are, for a long time. The force of the whalebone would get exhausted, you know, and it would stay bent, even when you unhooked it. Now, why shouldn't the same thing happen with the weight? The whalebone gets so used to being bent, that it ca'n't straighten itself any more. Why shouldn't the weight get so used to being held up, that it ca'n't fall any more? That's what I want to know!"

"That's what we want to know!" echoed the crowd.

"How long must we wait?" grumbled the Emperor.

The Professor looked at his watch. "Well, I think a thousand years will do to begin with," he said. "Then we will cautiously unhook the weight:

and, if it still shows (as perhaps it will) a slight tendency to fall, we will hook it on to the chain again, and leave it for another thousand years."

Here the Empress experienced one of those flashes of Common Sense which were the surprise of all around her. "Meanwhile there'll be time for another Experiment," she said.

"There will indeed!" cried the delighted Professor. "Let us return to the platform, and proceed to the Fourth Experiment!"

"For this concluding Experiment, I will take a certain Alkali, or Acid—I forget which. Now you'll see what will happen when I mix it with Some—" here he took up a bottle, and looked at it doubtfully, "—when I mix it with—with Something—"

Here the Emperor interrupted. "What's the name of the stuff?" he asked.

"I don't remember the name," said the Professor: "and the label has come off." He emptied it quickly into the other bottle, and, with a tremendous bang, both bottles flew to pieces, upsetting all the machines, and filling the Pavilion with thick black smoke. I sprang to my feet in terror, and—and found myself standing before my solitary hearth, where the poker, dropping at last from the hand of the sleeper, had knocked over the tongs and the shovel, and had upset the kettle, filling the air with clouds of steam. With a weary sigh, I betook myself to bed.

THE BANQUET

"Heaviness may endure for a night: but joy cometh in the morning." The next day found me quite another being. Even the memories of my lost friend and companion were sunny as the genial weather that smiled around me. I did not venture to trouble Lady Muriel, or her father, with another call so soon: but took a walk into the country, and only turned homewards when the low sunbeams warned me that day would soon be over.

On my way home, I passed the cottage where the old man lived, whose face always recalled to me the day when I first met Lady Muriel; and I glanced in as I passed, half-curious to see if he were still living there.

Yes: the old man was still alive. He was sitting out in the porch, looking just as he did when I first saw him at Fayfield Junction—it seemed only a few days ago!

"Good evening!" I said, pausing.

"Good evening, Maister!" he cheerfully responded. "Wo'n't ee step in?"

I stepped in, and took a seat on the bench in the porch. "I'm glad to see you looking so hearty," I began. "Last time, I remember, I chanced to pass just as Lady Muriel was coming away from the house. Does she still come to see you?"

"Ees," he answered slowly. "She has na forgotten me. I don't lose her bonny face for many days together. Well I mind the very first time she come, after we'd met at Railway Station. She told me as she come to mak' amends. Dear child! Only think o' that! To mak' amends!"

"To make amends for what?" I enquired. "What could she have done to need it?"

"Well, it were loike this, you see? We were both on us a-waiting fur t' train at t' Junction. And I had settee mysen down upat t' bench. And Station-Maister, he comes and he orders me off—fur t' mak' room for her Ladyship, you understand?"

"I remember it all," I said. "I was there myself; that day."

"Was you, now? Well, an' she axes my pardon fur 't. Think o' that, now! My pardon! An owd ne'er-do-weel like me! Ah! She's been here many a time, sin' then. Why, she were in here only yestere'en, as it were, a-sittin', as it might be, where you're a-sitting now, an' lookin' sweeter and kinder nor an angel! An' she says 'You've not got your Minnie, now,' she says, 'to fettle for ye.' Minnie was my grand-daughter, Sir, as lived wi' me. She died, a matter of two months ago—or it may be three. She was a bonny lass—and a good lass, too. Eh, but life has been rare an' lonely without her!"

He covered his face in his hands: and I waited a minute or two, in silence, for him to recover himself.

"So she says, 'Just tak' me fur your Minnie!' she says. 'Didna Minnie mak' your tea fur you?' says she. 'Ay,' says I. An' she mak's the tea. 'An' didna Minnie light your pipe?' says she. 'Ay,' says I. An' she lights the pipe for me. 'An' didna Minnie set out your tea in t' porch?' An' I says 'My dear,' I says, 'I'm thinking you're Minnie hersen!' An' she cries a bit. We both on us cries a bit—"

Again I kept silence for a while.

"An' while I smokes my pipe, she sits an' talks to me—as loving an' as pleasant! I'll be bound I thowt it were Minnie come again! An' when she gets up to go, I says 'Winnot ye shak' hands wi' me?' says I. An' she says 'Na,' she says: 'a cannot shak' hands wi' thee!" she says."

"I'm sorry she said that," I put in, thinking it was the only instance I had ever known of pride of rank showing itself in Lady Muriel.

"Bless you, it werena pride!" said the old man, reading my thoughts. "She says 'Your Minnie never shook hands wi' you!' she says. 'An' I'm your Minnie now,' she says. An' she just puts her dear arms about my neck—and she kisses me on t' cheek—an' may God in Heaven bless her!" And here the poor old man broke down entirely, and could say no more.

"God bless her!" I echoed. "And good night to you!" I pressed his hand, and left him. "Lady Muriel," I said softly to myself as I went homewards, "truly you know how to 'mak' amends'!"

Seated once more by my lonely fireside, I tried to recall the strange vision of the night before, and to conjure up the face of the dear old Professor among the blazing coals. "That black one—with just a touch of red—would suit him well," I thought. "After such a catastrophe, it would be sure to be covered with black stains—and he would say:

"The result of that combination—you may have noticed?—was an Explosion! Shall I repeat the Experiment?"

"No, no! Don't trouble yourself!" was the general cry. And we all trooped off, in hot haste, to the Banqueting Hall, where the feast had already begun.

No time was lost in helping the dishes, and very speedily every guest found his plate filled with good things.

"I have always maintained the principle," the Professor began, "that it is a good rule to take some food— occasionally. The great advantage of dinner-parties—" he broke off suddenly. "Why, actually here's the Other Professor!" he cried. "And there's no place left for him!"

The Other Professor came in reading a large book, which he held close to his eyes. One result of his not looking where he was going was that he tripped up, as he crossed the Saloon, flew up into the air, and fell heavily on his face in the middle of the table.

"What a pity!" cried the kind-hearted Professor, as he helped him up.

"It wouldn't be me, if I didn't trip," said the Other Professor.

The Professor looked much shocked. "Almost anything would be better than that!" he exclaimed. "It never does", he added, aside to Bruno, "to be anybody else, does it?"

To which Bruno gravely replied "I's got nuffin on my plate."

The Professor hastily put on his spectacles, to make sure that the facts were all right, to begin with: then he turned his jolly round face upon the unfortunate owner of the empty plate. "And what would you like next, my little man?"

"Well," Bruno said, a little doubtfully, "I think I'll take some plum-pudding, please—while I think of it."

"Oh, Bruno!" (This was a whisper from Sylvie.) "It isn't good manners to ask for a dish before it comes!"

And Bruno whispered back "But I might forget to ask for some, when it comes, oo know—I do forget things, sometimes," he added, seeing Sylvie about to whisper more.

And this assertion Sylvie did not venture to contradict.

Meanwhile a chair had been placed for the Other Professor, between the Empress and Sylvie. Sylvie found him a rather uninteresting neighbour: in fact, she couldn't afterwards remember that he had made more than one remark to her during the whole banquet, and that was "What a comfort a Dictionary is!" (She told Bruno, afterwards, that she had been too much afraid of him to say more than "Yes, Sir" in reply: and that had been the end of their conversation. On which Bruno expressed a very decided opinion that that wasn't worth calling a "conversation" at all. "Oo should have asked him a riddle!" he added triumphantly. "Why, I asked the Professor three riddles! One was that one you asked me in the morning, 'How many pennies is there in two shillings?' And another was—" "Oh, Bruno!" Sylvie interrupted. "That wasn't a riddle!" "It were!" Bruno fiercely replied.)

By this time a waiter had supplied Bruno with a plateful of something, which drove the plum-pudding out of his head.

"Another advantage of dinner-parties", the Professor cheerfully explained, for the benefit of anyone that would listen, "is that it helps you to see your friends. If you want to see a man, offer him something to eat. It's the same rule with a mouse."

"This Cat's very kind to the Mouses," Bruno said, stooping to stroke a remarkably fat specimen of the race, that had just waddled into the room, and was rubbing itself affectionately against the leg of his chair. "Please, Sylvie, pour some milk in your saucer. Pussie's ever so thirsty!"

"Why do you want my saucer?" said Sylvie. "You've got one yourself!"

"Yes, I know," said Bruno: "but I wanted mine for to give it some more milk in."

Sylvie looked unconvinced: however it seemed quite impossible for her ever to refuse what her brother asked so she quietly filled her saucer with milk, and handed it to Bruno, who got down off his chair to administer it to the cat.

"The room's very hot, with all this crowd," the Professor said to Sylvie. "I wonder why they don't put some lumps of ice in the grate? You fill it with lumps of coal in the winter, you know, and you sit around it and enjoy the warmth. How jolly it would be to fill it now with lumps of ice, and sit round it and enjoy the coolth!"

Hot as it was, Sylvie shivered a little at the idea. "It's very cold outside," she said. "My feet got almost frozen to-day."

"That's the shoemaker's fault!" the Professor cheerfully replied. "How often I've explained to him that he ought to make boots with little iron frames under the soles to hold lamps! But he never thinks. No one would suffer from cold, if only they would think of those little things. I always use hot ink, myself, in the winter. Very few people ever think of that! Yet how simple it is!"

"Yes, it's very simple," Sylvie said politely. "Has the cat had enough?" This was to Bruno, who had brought back the saucer only half-emptied.

But Bruno did not hear the question. "There's somebody scratching at the door and wanting to come m," he said. And he scrambled down off his chair, and went and cautiously peeped out through the door-way.

"Who was it wanted to come in?" Sylvie asked, as he returned to his place.

"It were a Mouse," said Bruno. "And it peepted in. And it saw the Cat. And it said 'I'll come in another day.' And I said 'Oo needn't be flightened. The Cat's welly kind to Mouses.' And it said 'But I's got some imporkant business, what I must attend to.' And it said 'I'll call again to-morrow.' And it said 'Give my love to the Cat.'"

"What a fat cat it is!" said the Lord Chancellor, leaning across the Professor to address his small neighbour. "It's quite a wonder!"

"It was awfully fat when it camed in," said Bruno: "so it would be more wonderfuller if it got thin all in a minute."

"And that was the reason, I suppose," the Lord Chancellor suggested, "why you didn't give it the rest of the milk?"

"No," said Bruno. "It was a betterer reason. I tooked the saucer up 'cause it were so discontented!"

"It doesn't look so to me," said the Lord Chancellor. "What made you think it was discontented?"

"'Cause it grumbled in its throat."

"Oh, Bruno!" cried Sylvie. "Why, that's the way cats show they're pleased!"

Bruno looked doubtful. "It's not a good way," he objected. "Oo wouldn't say I were pleased, if I made that noise in my throat!"

"What a singular boy!" the Lord Chancellor whispered to himself: but Bruno had caught the words.

"What do it mean to say 'a singular boy'?" he whispered to Sylvie.

"It means one boy," Sylvie whispered in return. "And plural means two or three."

"Then I's welly glad I is a singular boy!" Bruno said with great emphasis. "It would be horrid to be two or three boys! P'raps they wouldn't play with me!"

"Why should they?" said the Other Professor, suddenly waking up out of a deep reverie. "They might be asleep, you know."

"Couldn't, if I was awake," Bruno said cunningly.

"Oh, but they might indeed!" the Other Professor protested. "Boys don't all go to sleep at once, you know. So these boys—but who are you talking about?"

"He never remembers to ask that first!" the Professor whispered to the children.

"Why, the rest of me, a-course!" Bruno exclaimed triumphantly. "Supposing I was two or three boys!"

The Other Professor sighed, and seemed to be sinking back into his reverie; but suddenly brightened up again, and addressed the Professor. "There's nothing more to be done now, is there?"

"Well, there's the dinner to finish," the Professor said with a bewildered smile: "and the heat to bear. I hope you'll enjoy the dinner—such as it is; and that you wo'n't mind the heat—such as it isn't."

The sentence sounded well, but somehow I couldn't quite understand it; and the Other Professor seemed to be no better off. "Such as it isn't what?" he peevishly enquired.

"It isn't as hot as it might be," the Professor replied, catching at the first idea that came to hand.

"Ah, I see what you mean now!" the Other Professor graciously remarked. "It's very badly expressed, but I quite see it now! Thirteen minutes and a half ago," he went on, looking first at Bruno and then at his watch as he spoke, "you said 'this Cat's very kind to the Mouses.' It must be a singular animal!"

"So it are," said Bruno, after carefully examining the Cat, to make sure how many there were of it.

"But how do you know it's kind to the Mouses—or, more correctly speaking, the Mice?"

"'Cause it plays with the Mouses," said Bruno; "for to amuse them, oo know."

"But that is just what I don't know," the Other Professor rejoined. "My belief is, it plays with them to kill them!"

"Oh, that's quite a accident!" Bruno began, so eagerly, that it was evident he had already propounded this very difficulty to the Cat. "It 'sprained all that to me, while it were drinking the milk. It said 'I teaches the Mouses new games: the Mouses likes it ever so much.' It said 'Sometimes little accidents happens: sometimes the Mouses kills themselves.' It said 'I's always welly sorry, when the Mouses kills theirselves.' It said—"

"If it was so very sorry," Sylvie said, rather disdainfully, "it wouldn't eat the Mouses after they'd killed themselves!"

But this difficulty, also, had evidently not been lost sight of in the exhaustive ethical discussion just concluded. "It said—" (the orator constantly omitted, as superfluous, his own share in the dialogue, and merely gave us the replies of the Cat) "It said 'Dead Mouses never objecks to be eaten.' It said 'There's no use wasting good Mouses.' It said 'Wifful—' sumfinoruvver. It said 'And oo may live to say "How much I wiss I had the Mouse that then I frew away!"'It said—

"It hadn't time to say such a lot of things!" Sylvie interrupted indignantly.

"Oo doesn't know how Cats speaks!" Bruno rejoined contemptuously. "Cats speaks welly quick!"

THE PIG-TALE

By this time the appetites of the guests seemed to be nearly satisfied, and even Bruno had the resolution to say, when the Professor offered him a fourth slice of plum-pudding, "I thinks three helpings is enough!"

Suddenly the Professor started as if he had been electrified. "Why, I had nearly forgotten the most important part of the entertainment! The Other Professor is to recite a Tale of a Pig—I mean a Pig-Tale," he corrected himself. "It has Introductory Verses at the beginning, and at the end."

"It ca'n't have Introductory Verses at the end, can it?" said Sylvie.

"Wait till you hear it," said the Professor: "then you'll see. I m not sure it hasn't some in the middle, as well." Here he rose to his feet, and there was an instant silence through the Banqueting-Hall: they evidently expected a speech.

"Ladies, and gentlemen," the Professor began, "the Other Professor is so kind as to recite a Poem. The title of it is 'The Pig-Tale'. He never recited it before!" (General cheering among the guests.) "He will never recite it again!" (Frantic excitement, and wild cheering all down the hall, the Professor himself mounting the table in hot haste, to lead the cheering, and waving his spectacles in one hand and a spoon in the other.)

Then the Other Professor got up, and began:

<blockquote>
Little Birds are dining
Warily and well,
Hid in mossy cell:
Hid, I say, by waiters
Gorgeous in their gaiters—
I've a Tale to tell.
Little Birds are feeding
Justices with jam,
Rich in frizzled ham:
Rich, I say, in oysters
Haunting shady cloisters—
That is what I am.
Little Birds are teaching
Tigresses to smile,
Innocent of guile:
Smile, I say, not smirkle—
Mouth a semicircle,
That's the proper style.
</blockquote>

Little Birds are sleeping
All among the pins,
Where the loser wins:
Where, I say, he sneezes
When and how he pleases—
So the Tale begins.
There was a Pig that sat alone
Beside a ruined Pump:
By day and night he made his moan—
It would have stirred a heart of stone
To see him wring his hoofs and groan,
Because he could not jump.
A certain Camel heard him shout—
A Camel with a hump.
"Oh, is it Grief, or is it Gout?
What is this bellowing about?"
That Pig replied, with quivering snout,
"Because I cannot jump!"
That Camel scanned him, dreamy-eyed.
"Methinks you are too plump.
I never knew a Pig so wide—
That wobbled so from side to side—
Who could, however much he tried,
Do such a thing as jump!
"Yet mark those trees, two miles away,
All clustered in a clump:
If you could trot there twice a day,
Nor ever pause for rest or play,
In the far future—Who can say—
You may be fit to jump."

That Camel passed, and left him there,
Beside the ruined Pump.
Oh, horrid was that Pig's despair!
His shrieks of anguish filled the air.
He wrung his hoofs, he rent his hair,
Because he could not jump.
There was a Frog that wandered by—
A sleek and shining lump:
Inspected him with fishy eye,
And said "O Pig, what makes you cry?"
And bitter was that Pig's reply,
"Because I cannot jump!"
That Frog he grinned a grin of glee,
And hit his chest a thump.
"O Pig," he said, "be ruled by me,
And you shall see what you shall see.
This minute, for a trifling fee,
I'll teach you how to jump!
"You may be faint from many a fall,
And bruised by many a bump:
But, if you persevere through all,

163

And practice first on something small,
Concluding with a ten-foot wall,
You'll find that you can jump!"
That Pig looked up with joyful start:
"Oh Frog, you are a trump!
Your words have healed my inward smart—
Come, name your fee and do your part:
Bring comfort to a broken heart
By teaching me to jump!"
"My fee shall be a mutton-chop,
My goal this ruined Pump.
Observe with what an airy flop
I plant myself upon the top!
Now bend your knees and take a hop,
For that's the way to jump!"

Uprose that Pig, and rushed, full whack,
    Against the ruined Pump:
Rolled over like an empty sack
And settled down upon his back
While all his bones at once went "Crack!"
    It was a fatal jump.

When the Other Professor had recited this Verse, he went across to the fire-place, and put his head up the chimney. In doing this, he lost his balance, and fell head first into the empty grate, and got so firmly fixed there that it was some time before he could be dragged out again.

Bruno had had time to say "I thought he wanted to see how many peoples was up the chimbley."

And Sylvie had said "Chimney—not chimbley."

And Bruno had said "Don't talk 'ubbish!"

All this, while the Other Professor was being extracted.

"You must have blacked your face!" the Empress said anxiously. "Let me send for some soap?"

"Thanks, no," said the Other Professor, keeping his face turned away. "Black's quite a respectable colour. Besides, soap would be no use without water—"

Keeping his back well turned away from the audience, he went on with the Introductory Verses:

Little Birds are writing
    Interesting books,
    To be read by cooks:
Read, I say, not roasted—
Letterpress, when toasted,
    Loses its good looks.
Little Birds are playing
    Bagpipes on the shore,
Where the tourists snore:
"Thanks!" they cry. "'Tis thrilling!
Take, oh take this shilling!
    Let us have no more!"
Little Birds are bathing
    Crocodiles in cream,
    Like a happy dream:
Like, but not so lasting—
Crocodiles, when fasting,
    Are not all they seem!

165

That Camel passed, as Day grew dim
Around the ruined Pump.
"O broken heart! O broken limb!
It needs", that Camel said to him
"Something more fairy-like and slim,
To execute a jump!"
That Pig lay still as any stone
And could not stir a stump:
Nor ever, if the truth were known
Was he again observed to moan
Nor ever wring his hoofs and groan,
Because he could not jump.
That Frog made no remark, for he
Was dismal as a dump:
He knew the consequence must be
That he would never get his fee—
And still he sits, in miserie
Upon that ruined Pump!

"It's a miserable story!" said Bruno. "It begins miserably, and it ends miserablier. I think I shall cry. Sylvie, please lend me your handkerchief."

"I haven't got it with me," Sylvie whispered

'Then I wo'n't cry," said Bruno manfully.

There are more Introductory Verses to come," said the Other Professor, "but I'm hungry." He sat down, cut a large slice of cake, put it on Bruno's plate, and gazed at his own empty plate in astonishment

"Where did you get that cake?" Sylvie whispered to Bruno.

"He gived it me," said Bruno.

"But you shouldn't ask for things! You know you shouldn't!"

"I didn't ask," said Bruno, taking a fresh mouthful: "he gived it me."

Sylvie considered this for a moment: then she saw her way out of it. "Well, then, ask him to give me some!"

"You seem to enjoy that cake?" the Professor remarked.

"Doos that mean 'munch'?" Bruno whispered to Sylvie.

Sylvie nodded. "It means 'to munch' and 'to like to munch'."

Bruno smiled at the Professor. "I doos enjoy it," he said.

The Other Professor caught the word. "And I hope you're enjoying yourself, little Man?" he enquired.

Bruno's look of horror quite startled him. "No, indeed I aren't!" he said.

The Other Professor looked thoroughly puzzled. "Well, well!" he said. "Try some cowslip wine!" And he filled a glass and handed it to Bruno. "Drink this, my dear, and you'll be quite another man!"

"Who shall I be?" said Bruno, pausing in the act of putting it to his lips.

"Don't ask so many questions!" Sylvie interposed, anxious to save the poor old man from further bewilderment. "Suppose we get the Professor to tell us a story."

Bruno adopted the idea with enthusiasm. Please do. he cried eagerly. "Sumfin about tigers—and bumble-bees —and robin-redbreasts, oo knows!"

"Why should you always have live things in stories? said the Professor. "Why don't you have events, or circumstances?"

"Oh, please invent a story like that!" cried Bruno.

The Professor began fluently enough. "Once a coincidence was taking a walk with a little accident, and they met an explanation—a very old explanation—so old that it was quite doubled up, and looked more like a conundrum—" he broke off suddenly.

"Please go on!" both children exclaimed.

The Professor made a candid confession. "It's a very difficult sort to invent, I find. Suppose Bruno tells one first."

Bruno was only too happy to adopt the suggestion.

"Once there were a Pig, and a Accordion, and two jars of Orange-marmalade—"

"The dramatis personae," murmured the Professor. "Well, what then?"

"So, when the Pig played on the Accordion," Bruno went on, "one of the Jars of Orange-marmalade didn't like the tune, and the other Jar of Orange-marmalade did like the tune—I know I shall get confused among those Jars of Orange-marmalade, Sylvie!" he whispered anxiously.

"I will now recite the other Introductory Verses," said the Other Professor.

Little Birds are choking
Baronets with bun,
Taught to fire a gun:
Taught, I say, to splinter
Salmon in the winter—
Merely for the fun.
Little Birds are hiding
Crimes in carpet-bags,
Blessed by happy stags:
Blessed, I say, though beaten—
Since our friends are eaten
When the memory flags.
Little Birds are tasting
Gratitude and gold,
Pale with sudden cold:

> Pale, I say, and wrinkled—
> When the bells have tinkled,
> And the Tale is told.

"The next thing to be done", the Professor cheerfully remarked to the Lord Chancellor, as soon as the applause, caused by the recital of the Pig-Tale, had come to an end, "is to drink the Emperor's health, is it not?"

"Undoubtedly!" the Lord Chancellor replied with much solemnity, as he rose to his feet to give the necessary directions for the ceremony. "Fill your glasses!" he thundered. All did so, instantly. "Drink the Emperor's health!" A general gurgling resounded all through the Hall. "Three cheers for the Emperor!" The faintest possible sound followed this announcement: and the Chancellor, with admirable presence of mind, instantly proclaimed "A speech from the Emperor!"

The Emperor had begun his speech almost before the words were uttered. "However unwilling to be Emperor —since you all wish me to be Emperor—you know how badly the late Warden managed things—with such enthusiasm as you have shown—he persecuted you—he taxed you too heavily—you know who is fittest man to be Emperor—my brother had no sense—"

How long this curious speech might have lasted it is impossible to say, for just at this moment a hurricane shook the palace to its foundations, bursting open the windows, extinguishing some of the lamps, and filling the air with clouds of dust, which took strange shapes in the air, and seemed to form words.

But the storm subsided as suddenly as it had risen— the casements swung into their places again: the dust vanished: all was as it had been a minute ago—with the exception of the Emperor and Empress, over whom had come a wondrous change. The vacant stare, the meaning less smile, had passed away: all could see that these two strange beings had returned to their senses.

The Emperor continued his speech as if there had been no interruption. "And we have behaved—my wife and I—like two arrant Knaves. We deserve no better name. When my brother went away, you lost the best Warden you ever had. And I've been doing my best, wretched hypocrite that I am, to cheat you into making me an Emperor. Me! One that has hardly got the wits to be shoe-black!"

The Lord Chancellor wrung his hands in despair. "He is mad, good people!" he was beginning. But both speeches stopped suddenly—and, in the dead silence that followed, a knocking was heard at the outer door.

"What is it?" was the general cry. People began running in and out. The excitement increased every moment The Lord Chancellor, forgetting all the rules of Court ceremony, ran full speed down the hall, and in a minute returned, pale and gasping for breath.

THE BEGGAR'S RETURN

"Your Imperial Highnesses!" he began. "It's the old Beggar again! Shall we set the dogs at him?"

"Bring him here!" said the Emperor.

The Chancellor could scarcely believe his ears. "Here your Imperial Highness? Did I rightly understand—"

Bring him here!" the Emperor thundered once more. The Chancellor tottered down the hall—and in another minute the crowd divided, and the poor old Beggar was seen entering the Banqueting-Hall.

He was indeed a pitiable object: the rags, that hung about him, were all splashed with mud: his white hair and his long beard were tossed about in wild disorder. Yet he walked upright, with a stately tread, as if used to command: and—strangest sight of all—Sylvie and Bruno came with him, clinging to his hands, and gazing at him with looks of silent love.

Men looked eagerly to see how the Emperor would receive the bold intruder. Would he hurl him from the steps of the dais? But no. To their utter astonishment the Emperor knelt as the beggar approached, and with bowed head murmured "Forgive us!"

"Forgive us!" the Empress, kneeling at her husband's side, meekly repeated.

The Outcast smiled. "Rise up!" he said. "I forgive you!" And men saw with wonder that a change had passed over the old beggar, even as he spoke. What had seemed, but now, to be vile rags and splashes of mud, were seen to be in truth kingly trappings, broidered with gold, and sparkling with gems. All knew him now, and bent low before the Elder Brother, the true Warden.

"Brother mine, and Sister mine!" the Warden began, in a clear voice that was heard all through that vast hall. "I come not to disturb you. Rule on, as Emperor, and rule wisely. For I am chosen King of Elfland. To-morrow I return there, taking nought from thence, save only— save only—" his voice trembled, and with a look of ineffable tenderness, he laid his hands in silence on the heads of the two little ones who clung around him.

But he recovered himself in a moment, and beckoned to the Emperor to resume his place at the table. The company seated themselves again—room being found for the Elfin-King between his two children—and the Lord Chancellor rose once more, to propose the next toast.

"The next toast—the hero of the day—why, he isn't here!" he broke off in wild confusion.

Good gracious! Everybody had forgotten Prince Uggug!

"He was told of the Banquet, of course?" said the Emperor.

"Undoubtedly!" replied the Chancellor. "That would be the duty of the Gold Stick in Waiting."

"Let the Gold Stick come forwards!" the Emperor gravely said.

The Gold Stick came forwards. "I attended on His Imperial Fatness," was the statement made by the trembling official. "I told him of the Lecture and the Banquet—."

"What followed!" said the Emperor: for the unhappy man seemed almost too frightened to go on.

"His Imperial Fatness was graciously pleased to be sulky. His Imperial Fatness was graciously pleased to box my ears. His Imperial Fatness was graciously pleased to say 'I don't care!'"

"'Don't-care' came to a bad end," Sylvie whispered to Bruno. "I'm not sure, but I believe he was hanged."

The Professor overheard her. "That result", he blandly remarked, was merely a case of mistaken identity."

Both children looked puzzled.

"Permit me to explain. 'Don't-care' and 'Care' were twin-brothers. 'Care', you know, killed the Cat. And they caught Don't-care' by mistake, and hanged him instead. And so 'Care' is alive still. But he's very unhappy without his brother. That's why they say 'Begone, dull Care!'"

"Thank you!" Sylvie said, heartily. "It's very extremely interesting. Why, it seems to explain everything!"

"Well, not quite everything," the Professor modestly rejoined. "There are two or three scientific difficulties—"

What was your general impression as to His Imperial Fatness?" the Emperor asked the Gold Stick.

"My impression was that His Imperial Fatness was getting more—"

"More what?"

All listened breathlessly for the next word.

"More PRICKLY!"

"He must be sent for at once!" the Emperor exclaimed. And the Gold Stick went off like a shot. The Elfin-King sadly shook his head. "No use, no use!" he murmured to himself. "Loveless, loveless!"

Pale, trembling, speechless, the Gold Stick came slowly back again.

"Well?" said the Emperor. "Why does not the Prince appear?"

"One can easily guess," said the Professor. "His Imperial Fatness is, without doubt, a little preoccupied."

Bruno turned a look of solemn enquiry on his old friend. "What do that word mean?"

But the Professor took no notice of the question. He was eagerly listening to the Gold Stick's reply.

"Please your Highness! His Imperial Fatness is—" Not a word more could he utter.

The Empress rose in an agony of alarm. "Let us go to him!" she cried. And there was a general rush for the door.

Bruno slipped off his chair in a moment. "May we go too?" he eagerly asked. But the King did not hear the question, as the Professor was speaking to him. "Preoccupied, your Majesty!" he was saying. "That is what he is, no doubt!"

"May we go and see him?" Bruno repeated. The King nodded assent, and the children ran off. In a minute or two they returned, slowly and gravely. "Well?" said the King. "What's the matter with the Prince?"

"He's—what you said," Bruno replied looking at the Professor. "That hard word." And he looked to Sylvie for assistance.

"Porcupine," said Sylvie.

"No, no!" the Professor corrected her. Pre-occupied, you mean."

"No, it's porcupine," persisted Sylvie. "Not that other word at all. And please will you come? The house is all in an uproar." ("And oo'd better bring an uproar-glass wiz oo!" added Bruno.)

We got up in great haste, and followed the children upstairs. No one took the least notice of me, but I wasn't at all surprised at this, as I had long realized that I was quite invisible to them all—even to Sylvie and Bruno.

All along the gallery, that led to the Prince's apartment, an excited crowd was surging to and fro, and the Babel of voices was deafening: against the door of the room three strong men were leaning, vainly trying to shut it—for some great animal inside was constantly bursting it half open, and we had a glimpse, before the men could push it back again, of the head of a furious wild beast, with great fiery eyes and gnashing teeth. Its voice was a sort of mixture—there was the roaring of a lion, and the bellowing of a bull, and now and then a scream like a gigantic parrot. "There is no judging by the voice!" the Professor cried in great excitement. "What is it?" he shouted to the men at the door. And a general chorus of voices answered him "Porcupine! Prince Uggug has turned into a Porcupine!"

"A new Specimen!" exclaimed the delighted Professor. "Pray let me go in. It should be labeled at once!"

But the strong men only pushed him back. "Label it, indeed! Do you want to be eaten up?" they cried.

"Never mind about Specimens, Professor!" said the Emperor, pushing his way through the crowd. "Tell us how to keep him safe!"

"A large cage!" the Professor promptly replied. "Bring a large cage," he said to the people generally, "with strong bars of steel, and a portcullis made to go up and down like a mouse-trap! Does anyone happen to have such a thing about him?"

It didn't sound a likely sort of thing for anyone to have about him; however, they brought him one directly: curiously enough, there happened to be one standing in the gallery.

"Put it facing the opening of the door, and draw up the portcullis!" This was done in a moment.

"Blankets now—" cried the Professor. "This is a most interesting Experiment!"

There happened to be a pile of blankets close by: and the Professor had hardly said the word, when they were all unfolded and held up like curtains all around. The Professor rapidly arranged them in two rows, so as to make a dark passage, leading straight from the door to the mouth of the cage.

"Now fling the door open!" This did not need to be done: the three men had only to leap out of the way, and the fearful monster flung the door open for itself, and, with a yell like the whistle of a steam-engine, rushed into the cage.

"Down with the portcullis!" No sooner said than done: and all breathed freely once more, on seeing the Porcupine safely caged.

The Professor rubbed his hands in childish delight. "The Experiment has succeeded!" he proclaimed. "All that is needed now is to feed it three times a day, on chopped carrots and—"

"Never mind about its food, just now!" the Emperor interrupted. "Let us return to the Banquet. Brother, will you lead the way?" And the old man, attended by his children, headed the procession down stairs. "See the fate of a loveless life!" he said to Bruno, as they returned to their places. To which Bruno made reply, "I always loved Sylvie, so I'll never get prickly like that!"

"He is prickly, certainly," said the Professor, who had caught the last words, "but we must remember that, however porcupiny, he is royal still! After this feast is over, I'm going to take a little present to Prince Uggug— just to soothe him, you know: it isn't pleasant living in a cage."

"What'll you give him for a birthday-present?" Bruno enquired.

"A small saucer of chopped carrots," replied the Professor. "In giving birthday-presents, my motto is—cheapness! I should think I save forty pounds a year by giving —oh, what a twinge of pain!"

"What is it?" said Sylvie anxiously.

"My old enemy!" groaned the Professor. "Lumbago— rheumatism— that sort of thing. I think I'll go and lie down a bit." And he hobbled out of the Saloon, watched by the pitying eyes of the two children.

"He'll be better soon!" the Elfin-King said cheerily "Brother!" turning to the Emperor, "I have some business to arrange with you to-night. The Empress will take care of the children." And the two Brothers went away together, arm-in-arm.

The Empress found the children rather sad company. They could talk of nothing but "the dear Professor", and "what a pity he's so ill", till at last she made the welcome proposal "Let's go and see him!"

The children eagerly grasped the hands she offered them: and we went off to the Professor's study, and found him lying on the sofa, covered up with blankets, and reading a little manuscript-book. "Notes on Vol. Three!" he murmured, looking up at us. And there, on a tab near him, lay the book he was seeking when first I saw him.

"And how are you now, Professor?" the Empress asked bending over the invalid.

The Professor looked up, and smiled feebly. "As devoted to your Imperial Highness as ever!" he said in a weak voice. "All of me, that is not Lumbago, is Loyalty!"

"A sweet sentiment!" the Empress exclaimed with tears in her eyes. "You seldom hear anything so beautiful as that even in a Valentine!"

"We must take you to stay at the seaside," Sylvie said tenderly. "It'll do you ever so much good! And the Sea's so grand!"

"But a Mountain's grander!" said Bruno.

"What is there grand about the Sea?" said the Professor. "Why, you could put it all into a teacup!"

"Some of it," Sylvie corrected him.

"Well, you'd only want a certain number of teacups to hold it all. And then where's the grandeur? Then as to a Mountain—why, you could carry it all away in a wheelbarrow, in a certain number of years!"

"It wouldn't look grand—the bits of it in the wheelbarrow," Sylvie candidly admitted.

"But when oo put it together again—" Bruno began.

"When you're older," said the Professor, "you'll know that you ca'n't put Mountains together again so easily! One lives and one learns, you know!"

"But it needn't be the same one, need it?" said Bruno "Wo'n't it do, if I live, and if Sylvie learns?"

"I ca'n't learn without living!" said Sylvie.

"But I can live without learning!" Bruno retorted. "Oo just try me!"

"What I meant, was—" the Professor began, looking much puzzled, "—was—that you don't know everything, you know."

"But I do know everything I know!" persisted the little fellow. "I know ever so many things! Everything, 'cept the things I don't know. And Sylvie knows all the rest."

The Professor sighed, and gave it up. "Do you know what a Boojum is?"

"I know!" cried Bruno. "It's the thing what wrenches people out of their boots!"

"He means 'bootjack'," Sylvie explained in a whisper.

"You ca'n't wrench people out of boots," the Professor mildly observed. Bruno laughed saucily. "Oo can, though! Unless they're welly tight in."

"Once upon a time there was a Boojum—" the Professor began, but stopped suddenly. "I forget the rest of the Fable," he said. "And there was a lesson to be learned from it. I'm afraid I forget that too."

"I'll tell oo a Fable!" Bruno began in a great hurry. "Once there were a Locust, and a Magpie, and a Engine-driver. And the Lesson is, to learn to get up early—"

"It isn't a bit interesting!" Sylvie said contemptuously. "You shouldn't put the Lesson so soon."

"When did you invent that Fable?" said the Professor. "Last week?"

"No!" said Bruno. "A deal shorter ago than that, Guess again!"

"I ca'n't guess," said the Professor. "How long ago?"

"Why, it isn't invented yet!" Bruno exclaimed triumphantly. "But I have invented a lovely one! Shall I say it?"

"If you've finished inventing it," said Sylvie. "And let the Lesson be 'to try again'!"

"No," said Bruno with great decision. "The Lesson are 'not to try again'!" "Once there were a lovely china man, what stood on the chimbley-piece. And he stood, and he stood. And one day he tumbled off, and he didn't hurt his self one bit. Only he would try again. And the next time he tumbleded off, he hurted his self welly much, and breaked off ever so much varnish."

"But how did he come back on the chimney-piece after his first tumble?" said the Empress. (It was the first sensible question she had asked in all her life.)

"I put him there!" cried Bruno.

"Then I'm afraid you know something about his tumbling," said the Professor. "Perhaps you pushed him?"

To which Bruno replied, very seriously, "Didn't pushed him much—he were a lovely china man," he added hastily, evidently very anxious to change the subject.

"Come, my children!" said the Elfin-King, who had just entered the room. "We must have a little chat together, before you go to bed." And he was leading them away, but at the door they let go his hands, and ran back again to wish the Professor good night.

"Good night, Professor, good night!" And Bruno solemnly shook hands with the old man, who gazed at him with a loving smile, while Sylvie bent down to press her sweet lips upon his forehead.

"Good night, little ones!" said the Professor. "You may leave me now—to ruminate. I'm as jolly as the day is long, except when it's necessary to ruminate on some very difficult subject. All of me," he murmured sleepily as we left the room, "all of me, that isn't Bonhommie, is Rumination!"

"What did he say, Bruno?" Sylvie enquired, as soon as we were safely out of hearing.

"I think he said 'All of me that isn't Bone-disease is Rheumatism.' Whatever are that knocking, Sylvie?"

Sylvie stopped, and listened anxiously. It sounded like some one kicking at a door, "I hope it isn't that Porcupine breaking loose!" she exclaimed.

"Let's go on!" Bruno said hastily. "There's nuffin to wait for, oo know!"

LIFE OUT OF DEATH

The sound of kicking, or knocking, grew louder every moment: and at last a door opened somewhere near us. "Did you say 'come in!' Sir?" my landlady asked timidly.

"Oh yes, come in!" I replied. "What's the matter?"

"A note has just been left for you, Sir, by the baker's boy. He said he was passing the Hall, and they asked him to come round and leave it here."

The note contained five words only. "Please come at once. Muriel."

A sudden terror seemed to chill my very heart. "The Earl is ill!" I said to myself. "Dying, perhaps!" And I hastily prepared to leave the house.

"No bad news, Sir, I hope?" my landlady said, as she saw me out. "The boy said as some one had arrived unexpectedly—"

"I hope that is it!" I said. But my feelings were those of fear rather than of hope: though, on entering the house, I was somewhat reassured by finding luggage lying in the entrance, bearing the initials "E. L."

"It's only Eric Lindon after all!" I thought, half relieved and half annoyed. "Surely she need not have sent for me for that!"

Lady Muriel met me in the passage. Her eyes were gleaming—but it was the excitement of joy, rather than of grief. "I have a surprise for you!" she whispered.

"You mean that Eric Lindon is here?" I said, vainly trying to disguise the involuntary bitterness of my tone. "'The funeral baked meats did coldly furnish forth the marriage-tables,'" I could not help repeating to myself. How cruelly I was misjudging her!

"No, no!" she eagerly replied. "At least—Eric is here. But—" her voice quivered, "but there is another!"

No need for further question. I eagerly followed her in. There on the bed, he lay—pale and worn—the mere shadow of his old self—my old friend come back again from the dead!

"Arthur!" I exclaimed. I could not say another word.

"Yes, back again, old boy!" he murmured, smiling as I grasped his hand. "He", indicating Eric, who stood near, "saved my life—He brought me back. Next to God, we must thank him, Muriel, my wife!"

Silently I shook hands with Eric, and with the Earl: and with one consent we moved into the shaded side of the room, where we could talk without disturbing the invalid, who lay, silent and happy, holding his wife's hand in his, and watching her with eyes that shone with the deep steady light of Love.

"He has been delirious till to-day," Eric explained in a low voice: and even to-day he has been wandering more than once. But the sight of her has been new life to him." And then he went on to tell us, in would-be careless tones —I knew how he hated any display of feeling—how he had insisted on going back to the plague-stricken town, to bring away a man whom the doctor had abandoned as dying, but who might, he fancied, recover if brought to the hospital: how he had seen nothing in the wasted features to remind him of Arthur, and only recognized him when he visited the hospital a month after: how the doctor had forbidden him to announce the discovery, saying that any shock to the over-taxed brain might kill him at once: how he had stayed on at the hospital, and nursed the sick man by night and day—all this with the studied indifference of one who is relating the commonplace acts of some chance acquaintance!

"And this was his rival!" I thought. "The man who had won from him the heart of the woman he loved!"

"The sun is setting," said Lady Muriel, rising and leading the way to the open window. "Just look at the western sky! What lovely crimson tints! We shall have a glorious day to-morrow—" We had followed her across the room, and were standing in a little group, talking in low tones in the gathering gloom, when we were startled by the voice of the sick man, murmuring words too indistinct for the ear to catch.

"He is wandering again," Lady Muriel whispered, and returned to the bedside. We drew a little nearer also: but no, this had none of the incoherence of delirium. "What reward shall I give unto the Lord", the tremulous lips were saying, "for all the benefits that He hath done unto me? I will receive the cup of salvation, and call—and call—" but here the poor weakened memory failed, and the feeble voice died into silence.

His wife knelt down at the bedside, raised one of his arms, and drew it across her own, fondly kissing the thin white hand that lay so listlessly in her loving grasp. It seemed to me a good opportunity for stealing away without making her go through any form of parting: so, nodding to the Earl and Eric, I silently left the room. Eric followed me down the stairs, and out into the night.

"Is it Life or Death?" I asked him, as soon as we were far enough from the house for me to speak in ordinary tones.

"It is Life!" he replied with eager emphasis. "The doctors are quite agreed as to that. All he needs now, they say, is rest, and perfect quiet, and good nursing. He's quite sure to get rest and quiet, here: and, as for the nursing, why, I think it's just possible—" (he tried hard to make his trembling voice assume a playful tone) "he may even get fairly well nursed, in his present quarters!"

"I'm sure of it!" I said. "Thank you so much for coming out to tell me!" And, thinking he had now said all he had come to say, I held out my hand to bid him good night. He grasped it warmly, and added, turning his face away as he spoke, "By the way, there is one other thing I wanted to say, I thought you'd like to know that—that I'm not—not in the mind I was in when last we met. It isn't—that I can accept Christian belief—at least, not yet. But all this came about so strangely. And she had prayed, you know. And I had prayed. And—and" his voice broke, and I could only just catch the concluding words, "there is a God that answers prayer! I know it for certain now." He wrung my hand once more, and left me suddenly. Never before had I seen him so deeply moved.

So, in the gathering twilight, I paced slowly homewards, in a tumultuous whirl of happy thoughts: my heart seemed full, and running over, with joy and thankfulness: all that I had so fervently longed for, and prayed for, seemed now to have come to pass. And, though I reproached myself, bitterly, for the unworthy suspicion I had for one moment harboured against the true-hearted Lady Muriel, I took comfort in knowing it had been but! a passing thought.

Not Bruno himself could have mounted the stairs with so buoyant a step, as I felt my way up in the dark, not pausing to strike a light in the entry, as I knew I had left the lamp burning in my sitting-room.

But it was no common lamplight into which I now stepped, with a strange, new, dreamy sensation of some subtle witchery that had come over the place. Light, richer and more golden than any lamp could give, flooded the room, streaming in from a window I had somehow never noticed before, and lighting up a group of three shadowy figures, that grew momently more distinct—a grave old man in royal robes, leaning back in an easy chair, and two children, a girl and a boy, standing at his side.

"Have you the Jewel still, my child?" the old man was saying.

"Oh, yes!" Sylvie exclaimed with unusual eagerness.

"Do you think I'd ever lose it or forget it?" She undid the ribbon round her neck, as she spoke, and laid the Jewel in her father's hand.

Bruno looked at it admiringly. "What a lovely brightness!" he said. "It's just like a little red star! May I take it in my hand?"

Sylvie nodded: and Bruno carried it off to the window, and held it aloft against the sky, whose deepening blue was already spangled with stars. Soon he came running back in some excitement. "Sylvie! Look here!" he cried. "I can see right through it when I hold it up to the sky. And it isn't red a bit: it's, oh such a lovely blue! And the words are all different! Do look at it!"

Sylvie was quite excited, too, by this time; and the two children eagerly held up the Jewel to the light, and spelled out the legend between them, "ALL WILL LOVE SYLVIE."

"Why, this is the other Jewel!" cried Bruno. "Don't you remember, Sylvie? The one you didn't choose!"

Sylvie took it from him, with a puzzled look, and held it, now up to the light, now down. "It's blue, one way," she said softly to herself, "and it's red the other way! Why, I thought there were two of them—Father!" she suddenly exclaimed, laying the Jewel once more in his hand, "I do believe it was the same Jewel all the time!"

"Then you choosed it from itself," Bruno thoughtfully remarked. "Father, could Sylvie choose a thing from itself?"

"Yes, my own one," the old man replied to Sylvie, not noticing Bruno's embarrassing question, "it was the same Jewel—but you chose quite right." And he fastened the ribbon round her neck again.

"SYLVIE WILL LOVE ALL—ALL WILL LOVE SYLVIE."

Bruno murmured, raising himself on tiptoe to kiss the "little red star". "And, when you look at it, it's red and fierce like the sun—and, when you look through it, it's gentle and blue like the sky!"

"God's own sky," Sylvie said, dreamily.

"God's own sky," the little fellow repeated, as they stood, lovingly clinging together, and looking out into the night. "But oh, Sylvie, what makes the sky such a darling blue?"

Sylvie's sweet lips shaped themselves to reply, but her voice sounded faint and very far away. The vision was fast slipping from my eager gaze: but it seemed to me, in that last bewildering moment, that not Sylvie but an angel was looking out through those trustful brown eyes, and that not Sylvie's but an angel's voice was whispering

"IT IS LOVE."